About the Author

Jack Thompson was born a long time ago in northern England. After spells as a teacher, bus conductor, industrial spy and pianist in workers' clubs, he joined the BBC in 1967 and eventually landed the job of foreign correspondent for the World Service. He reported from Asia, the Middle East, the Soviet Union, eastern and central Europe and South Africa. Since retiring in 2002, he has devoted himself to writing. In 2006 he won the Scottish Association of Writers Pitlochry Award for Crime-writing with his thriller *A Wicked Device*. He lives in London with his wife and a golden retriever.

For Kathryn and her limitless patience

Jack Thompson

SPAIN, GUARD MY BONES

AUSTIN MACAULEY
PUBLISHERS LTD.

A CIP catalogue record for this title is available from the British Library.

ISBN 978-1-78693-590-8 (Paperback)
ISBN 978-1-78693-591-5 (E-Book)
www.austinmacauley.com

First Published (2017)
Austin Macauley Publishers Ltd.
25 Canada Square
Canary Wharf
London
E14 5LQ

Part 1

Chapter 1

The night air was warm and heavy with smells of the farm. Rosemary, thyme, tarragon and dung. Juan José tossed and turned, but his thoughts had chased away the sleep that usually weighed his eyelids down as his head touched the pillow. He threw back the single sheet and rose quietly. He had to take care not to disturb his parents and sisters. His father had a temper. All hell would break loose if he was woken in the early hours.

Juan José pulled on a t-shirt and shorts and fumbled for sandals. Gripping them in his right hand, he crept along the corridor to the main door and slipped the latch. It creaked and he held his breath. No one moved except Orlando the Labrador who stretched and yawned. Juan José knew the dog would want to go with him. With a finger to his lips, he beckoned Orlando who, being a ten-year-old, understood that he must not whine or mewl and must certainly resist the temptation to bark.

In the yard Juan José wriggled toes into sandals. Boy and dog slunk away from the farmhouse, through a gap in the stone wall and out on to the rutted road that led to the village. Juan José looked up at the crescent moon silvering the sky but not bright enough to obscure the constellations. He picked out his favourites. Great Bear, Small Bear, The Twins and the group he had learned to call Cassiopeia. He had the benefit of a young teacher at the local school whose enthusiasm for astronomy had planted a seed in Juan José's mind, so that even his bluff and no-nonsense father was persuaded to buy him an illustrated book explaining the stars. It also offered answers to questions about the universe, which the local priest, Father Trujillo, regarded as undermining what was left of the Church's authority over the minds of children.

On nights like this, Juan José simply wanted to walk and gaze upwards. And Orlando wanted to walk with him, sniffing the dry roadside grasses and the detritus left by animals and humans in the fields. After half an hour they would both be tired. Then they would have the adventure of sneaking back into the house with the rest of the sleeping family none the wiser.

But this time Juan José took a different route. Not the straightforward stroll to the edge of the village where *La Bruja* (The Hag), otherwise known as *Señora* Celestina, lived in a one-room house of crumbling stone, a building that had survived weather, civil war, depression, dictatorship and the chaos of recent times and still defied the municipality which wanted to sweep it away and widen the road. Later, when the sun was up, Juan José would call on the *Señora* and share his secrets in exchange for some orange juice from the cold store at the back of her house. For the real beauty of *La Bruja* lay in her patience with children and her good humour.

They turned right on to a path of dusty earth, taking them into the middle of a field cleared of a worked-out maize crop. It was difficult walking. Sandals were not the best footwear for coping with small stones and dry soil. The boy stumbled and slipped and at one point fell to his knees. The dog wasn't fazed by the rough ground, looked in pity at Juan José and waited for him to get going again.

They pushed on further into the field. For Juan José's latest secret was at the very top where the open ground gave way to an orchard of trees, orange, lemon and olive, thriving among the long grass and low slung tomato and zucchini plants.

Orlando had not been this way before. Juan José noticed his excitement.

"Stay!" he told the dog and again held his finger to his lips. The animal responded with some panting, anxious to know what they were supposed to be looking for.

"There! There it is. Just past the long grass, Orlando."

The dog looked at him as if to ask the obvious question.

"The cemetery?"

They plunged into some thick scrub and emerged to face a whitewashed wall. Juan José knew a spot to his left where this had crumbled, leaving a hole just wide enough for a small human being. On hands and knees, he squirmed through the gap. The dog followed, eager and nimble. Moonlight picked out the rampart of niches where some of the dead awaited their turns to be buried. It flashed on the crosses marking the graves of those whose families had retrieved their coffins and paid for a final resting place.

But Juan José knew that these monuments were not all that marked this site of death and decay. He switched to his left along a narrow path at the edge of the graveyard. And kicked soil away with his sandal.

"See, Orlando. Do you see them?"

The dog sniffed and pawed at a patch of ground that dipped down from the path, a depression revealing the parched bones of a human hand, barely covered by the ochre-red earth.

"My secret, Orlando. My secret."

A cloud shadow slid across the dome of a skull. Juan José stooped and peered and saw the diagonal fracture. Orlando was digging furiously at a jawbone of broken teeth.

"No, dog! No!"

The animal looked up and whimpered.

"Leave it!"

Juan José turned on his heel and they both scampered back to the cover of the fruit trees. He crouched for breath and the dog sniffed at his bare leg and laid its head on his thigh.

"It is a terrible secret, Orlando. We must tell *La Bruja*."

Later, when the sun was high, Juan José and Celestina stumbled through the same field and the grove of trees and entered the cemetery. Orlando bounded ahead, knowing exactly where they were going.

The boy pointed to the ground. The woman bent to look.

"Madre de Dios!" She held a hand to her mouth. "I should not have said that," she whispered almost to herself. But her breathing had suddenly quickened. She bent again and stared at the bones.

"How long have you known?" she asked.

"Since last week. I came here for the first time on the Tuesday after the weekend before last. I don't know what brought me here. I don't know why I came this way. Perhaps the spirits lured me."

"Don't talk nonsense, Juan José. There are no spirits to lure you. Only bodies, or what's left of them. The wind and rain have washed away the topsoil and the sun has done the rest."

"Look," he said. "Look there, in that ditch. More of them. Some of them are so tiny."

"They are the bones of children." *La Bruja* paused. "Or dwarves."

They picked their way carefully along the worn path. After twenty metres or so, she said she had seen enough.

At three o'clock in the afternoon, the mayor, two police officers, one a woman, and another from the *Guardia Civil* were conferring at the site of the mass grave. They were trying to question Juan José, his father and mother, and *La Bruja*. But animated chatter and heated argument among twenty or so residents who'd followed the official party made it impossible to continue this on-the-spot enquiry.

"Back to the *ayuntamiento*," shouted the mayor. "To the town hall."

"The fascists did this," growled one old man. "It's obvious."

"They were Reds," barked another. "They deserved it."

There were more exchanges and the two nearly came to blows.

"Never mind who did it," said one of the police officers. "All of you, back home."

He took Juan José by the hand. The female officer put an arm round Celestina's shaking shoulders.

"She's one of them," a woman cried out. "She's a Red. Should have been dealt with a long time ago."

La Bruja looked up. The insult had composed her. She glared at her accuser. Some of the crowd ambled back to the village. But others defied the police and stayed to wander up and down beside the open grave, still arguing and eyeing the bones and skulls and the bits of rotten clothing exposed by this early investigation.

Juan José's secret was no longer his own. The whole of the village knew it now. And soon the whole of Spain would know.

Chapter 2

The king had abdicated. Juan Carlos was weary and ill. Yet he had done Spain some service. He had nursed its transition from the dictatorship of Francisco Franco to democracy and parliamentary government. On the one hand, he had resisted pressures from devotees of discredited fascism in the military and the Church, and, on the other, had all but silenced the clamour from those yearning for the restoration of the old Republic. In 1981, five years or more after Franco's death, he had set his face against an attempt by army officers to put the clock back and stage a coup. Since then, the soldiers had behaved themselves. And with the help of governments of both left and right, he had more or less seen off the threat from ETA, the violent wing of the Basque separatist movement.

But, like all of us, Juan Carlos was a flawed human being. Outwardly a devout Roman Catholic, he should have been aware, deep down in his soul, that he was prone to original sin. This had not stopped him from enjoying a procession of lovers. He faced two paternity suits. He once embarked on a luxurious elephant hunt in Africa with what the papers called 'a woman companion'. The publicity did the royal family no good at all. One of his daughters was involved in a money-laundering scandal. She had been hauled into court to explain what she knew about the dubious financial conduct of her husband. The details were boring, but they were still a striking display of the naked greed of the privileged in Spain and their misuse of other people's cash.

While the rumours circulated, the people of Spain concerned themselves with more important things. How to get a job, pay the rent or find money for the mortgage; and put food on the table. Some had killed themselves out of despair. Others believed their country was falling apart. Catalonia, that relatively prosperous and rather self-satisfied region in the north east, might break away. This mattered more than the king's peccadilloes or the sad determination of his queen, Sofia, to stick it out as his devoted consort for the sake of the Bourbon dynasty. Spain might become a truncated version of itself. Who else would shake off rule from Madrid? The Basques? Andalucía? Galicia, where Franco came from?

Challenging what they call *la casta*, or the forty-year political stitch-up between conservatives and socialists, were two new parties. One was called *Podemos*, meaning 'We Can'. It had done well at elections. It was full of bright, young people, protesting against corruption in high places and determined to improve the quality of life for the poor and the unemployed. Its rival was *Ciudadanos* or 'Citizens', similarly protesting against financial skulduggery but rather more keen on promoting business and commerce. Its members wore sharp suits and ties. *Podemos* supporters tended towards open-neck shirts, t-shirts and jeans.

****

I already knew some of this as I flew into Seville. Landing there was easy. Immigration waved me through. My bags came on to the carousel in double quick time. Customs didn't want to know. I picked up a dog-eared ticket from Hertz, found the silver Polo, loaded the boot, checked for scuffs and dents and the location of the fuel cap and turned the ignition. I did a careful circuit following the *Salida* signs, reached the barrier and inserted the ticket. Nothing.

"Why do I always have trouble in airport car parks?"

Because you're Charlie Barrow and bad luck stalks you like the plague.

The driver of the car behind sounded his horn. Again and again. There wasn't much space for me to pull over, but I managed it. He sneered. I was obviously a foreigner, too stupid to make a simple device work properly. Stabbing his ticket into the machine, he watched the barrier rise and shrugged. I could have killed him.

"If I drive close in behind and zip out before the thing comes down again…"

Don't be daft. Think of the damage and the hassle.

I heaved myself out of the seat and walked fifty metres to the booth. Two very bored souls in soiled uniforms took no notice until I banged on their flimsy door.

"Que?"

"La barrera automatica. No funciona con este ticket."

One of them held out his hand. After a protracted inspection, which involved rubbing the thing between grubby fingers, he said I'd have to go back to the Hertz office and get a replacement.

I displayed hurt and resignation in equal proportions. I thought they might work in Spain. Especially Seville. But his mangled face, with its badly trimmed moustache, stayed stern and unyielding.

Don't argue. You've got all the time in the world.

Fortune came to my aid. The second potbelly snatched the ticket from his colleague and spat his impatience. With an exorbitant flourish, he opened a draw and produced another ticket, pristine and stiff. He grinned, offered it and held my gaze.

"Soborno no necessario! No bribe. No tip. You go."

He winked and roared with laughter. His friend didn't join in. Instead he gave me a rich litany of abuse and looked me up and down.

"Nunca olvido una cara," he drawled. "I never forget a face."

I retreated with a submissive smile. It seemed the wisest thing to do.

****

It took next to no time to do the twenty kilometres to the *parador*, the state-run hotel, at Carmona. No need to go into Seville. Turn out of the airport and take the *autopista* for Córdoba. Carmona was off to the right, the whole town set, it seemed, on a hill until you passed an industrial estate and dropped down the Calle Sevilla to the Moorish gateway of the same name.

It was early afternoon, siesta time. The shops were shut and there was next to no traffic. I had room to park outside a bank and take advantage of a cash point. A few old boys sat in the autumn sunshine, making brandies and *solos* last a lifetime, but most of the noise I heard came from a bar across the road – shouts and guffaws and some sort of commentary on television.

I drove on, through the gateway into old Carmona, up narrow streets lined with small shops and neat townhouses. Then the road took me by surprise. It widened until I was passing through another Arab portal into a courtyard of setts and arches. Before me, the old Alcazar, converted now into one of the most magnificent hotels in Spain.

I parked among half a dozen other vehicles. Mid-week in October, even in Andalucía, there would be few visitors. Perhaps more would come out from Seville at the weekend. I humped my bag into Reception. It was all peace and quiet. The clerk took my details and said Bernardo, who had silently materialised out of some alcove, would escort me to my room.

Bernardo was seventy if he was a day but insisted on carrying the bag. I followed along a corridor, an enclosed cloister revealing a courtyard in which Scheherazade might well be serenading King Shahryar as soon as dusk took over. We descended a flight of stone stairs and turned a corner.

Bernardo had meanwhile regaled me in heavily accented English. I got a potted version of his history, how he'd worked at a hotel in Bayswater, missed London and found Spain rather boring. He was still chatting away when he inserted the key card into the slot outside my door. Thinking back to the hassle at the car park, I sighed happily as the lock clicked open. The room was almost pitch black until Bernardo applied the key card again and a soft bedside lamp gave him enough light to place the bag carefully on to the special shelf which good hotels have for these things. He explained the electronics, thanked me profusely for the twenty-euro tip and left.

Once upon a time, it might have been a monk's cell. Not large at all but now thoughtfully furnished. The air-con buzzed discreetly. But I wanted sunshine and a breeze. I swept aside the curtains, unfastened the windows and the heavy wooden shutters, pushed and gasped with delight. Before me lay the whole of

Andalucía, a patterned carpet of green and brown, mile upon mile of open country stretching into a blue haze, hardly a house or a farm to be seen. There wasn't a cloud in the sky. A distant road curled southwards and a car crept on its lonely journey to Marchena. If I had had the eyesight of Superman, I would have picked out the Sierra de Ronda and the coast at Marbella.

I looked down. The *parador's* garden fell steeply to the hotel pool, sending back a scent of flowers and plants whose names were a mystery to me. A few brave souls were swimming up and down. Not that they needed to be too hardy. The air was warm, and even at the top of the escarpment on which the Arabs had built this fortress, the breeze that blew into my room was soft and kind.

After all, I was here for relaxation. The Berlin I left behind had cowered in rain blown well-nigh horizontal by a wind sweeping down from the Baltic. And Dagmar wanted me out. It had been a long relationship with even a measure of love. But it was over. She was a cop, working disgraceful hours, and I was the wayward journalist, chasing stories that took me all over Central Europe for days on end. We were spending less and less time together. There should have been a lot to talk about. But we didn't have the energy or the patience to be interested in one another's world. I offered to go. She kissed me and whispered, "Yes, Charlie. It's time."

We made love. I showered and packed. She brewed coffee and smiled. We never said, "Good-bye".

I still had my apartment in a small town on the coast of Portugal. It was full of my books and my piano. Friends had used it from time to time. My good neighbour, Jorge, kept an eye on the place and Maria cleaned it once a week. It was the nearest I had to home. But I didn't want to go there straightaway. I didn't want to hide. And I'd always fancied staying in a grand hotel surrounded by elegance and good taste. This one fitted the bill. The glimpse I'd had of the courtyard suggested it would certainly live up to the publicity material put out by the ministry of tourism.

This was my first foray into Andalucía. I intended to explore, to see the wonders of southern Spain, the Giralda in Seville, the mezquita in Córdoba and the Alhambra in Granada. I would watch and listen to genuine *flamenco* in smoke-filled clubs and taste the food and the wine. And I wanted conversation, even in my halting Spanish, perhaps with a patient young student, or a seasoned professional taking a quick lunch in a tapas bar, or, with more luck than I deserved, a beautiful woman in her late thirties stealing a glass of something under a pavement awning. No work. No stories. No politics. No newspapers, radio or television. No mobile. No laptop.

I hope you have the strength of mind to stick to that.

Chapter 3

Driving up to the *parador*, I'd spotted a restaurant with a terrace looking out over the same rolling landscape I could see from my window. I unpacked, sluiced my face and walked out to the car park and through the Arab portal. The bar was about a hundred yards further on.

I sat at a table on the terrace, eyes closed but lifted towards a weakening winter sun, expecting a waiter to take my order. But no one came. I got up, peered through the glass of the main door and pushed. The dimness of the restaurant unnerved me, but when my eyes grew used to it, I realised it was a converted barn or workshop with a high ceiling of rough, old beams and walls of dark stone untouched by paint or whitewash. To the left an enormous fireplace gaped like the mouth of a mysterious cave. I could hear subdued activity at the back of a high counter equipped with the usual beer taps and a row of bottles. I sat down, again in the hope that I'd be noticed.

"You will wait forever, *Señor*." The voice came out of a dark corner. I could see nobody. Then, like the Cheshire Cat, a thin face emerged, grinning at me over the table top.

I muttered a confused *'Buenas dias'* and the face laughed, mocking me but not without traces of good will.

"Fear not. I am rather small. And rather deformed. I come as a bit of a surprise on first acquaintance."

The dwarf laughed again, swivelled to his right and shouted. "Espiridion! A *Cruz Campo* for my new friend here. Service for pity's sake!" He turned back. "Join me. Please. I have good English and I like to practise it in conversation."

"How do you know I'm English?" I asked.

"Haircut. The way you wear your clothes. And a certain amount of mild unease around the eyes. Typical. Very typical."

"I'm sorry to be so obvious," I said as I moved to his table.

"No need to be sorry. The English are almost my favourite people even if they do want to hang on to Gibraltar."

"Oh, please. Don't let's start on that."

He laughed yet again and extended a hand which I shook after stretching across the table.

"Conversing with dwarves requires a few physical recalculations."

I didn't know how to respond. He put me at my ease.

"Carlito. Carlito Jimenez. Three-foot-six but fully functional. Nice to meet you."

"Charlie," I replied. "Charlie Barrow. Five-foot-eight and similarly functional unless I drink too much red wine at dinner."

"So, we have the same name. Which means we really can be friends."

We lapsed into silence. Espiridion had supplied a beer which I was tempted to gulp down in one. But I drank it gently. The light was fading. Espiridion had switched on the restaurant's discreet wall lamps and was now doing the rounds with a box of matches for the candles on the tables.

Carlito was the spitting image of a famous British dwarf actor I'd seen on television. He anticipated my curiosity.

"Warwick Davis," he said. "I could be his twin, couldn't I?"

"I'm sorry. I don't mean to stare but, yes, you are very like him."

"He's been in the Harry Potter films and in *Lord of the Rings*. People are always coming up to me and saying, 'I've seen you on TV.'"

"I'm not surprised."

"But I am Spanish. Truly Spanish. I am in the tradition of Velazquez's *The Dwarf Don Sebastian de Morra.*"

"A wonderful painting," I said somewhat lamely, relying on a distant memory of a reproduction in a coffee table book.

"Isn't it? A dwarf as a *Don*. Now there's a thing."

"Are you telling me you are a descendant?"

"That too would be something. But no. Sebastian suffered from *achondroplasia*, which is the condition most dwarves have to put up with. I have SED – wait for it – *spondyloepiphyseal dysplasia congenital* – what a mouthful! It's to do with faulty bone growth. A bit like having had arthritis from birth."

"I don't want to patronise you, but you're very brave to talk about it. Almost as if it wasn't there."

"Oh, don't get me wrong. I'm in a lot of pain most of the time. The tablets help, of course, and the physiotherapy. But I could do without it, believe me."

He smiled and heaved a deep sigh.

"Are you from Carmona? Do you live here?"

"No to both questions. I'm here to meet someone."

"Are you staying at the *parador*?"

"Good Lord, yet again no. I can't afford that. Are you?"

He saw me hesitate and chuckled. "No need to be ashamed if you are."

"I'm indulging in a spot of thorough relaxation," I said. "Just for once, no half measures."

29

"I'll let you into a secret. The food here's much better than the menu up the road. Do you fancy having dinner a little later?"

"What a good idea. But I must go back and sort a few things out."

"Very well. See you at nine o'clock. Don't forget we dine late in Spain."

"I think I can last out till then."

****

So, my wish to meet someone willing to talk to me was fulfilled. I returned to the hotel, sorted my clothes and other oddments, showered and decided to while away the time in the bar. The décor was more than acceptable, seasoned wood, exotic ornaments, subtle copies of expensive art, and armchairs and sofas from which it must surely have been difficult to lift a tired or drunken body.

And there were the papers, Spanish and international, laid out on an elegant coffee table.

Leave them be.

Even with my primitive Spanish, I spotted a headline that aroused my immediate interest.

"Andalucía reactiva una fosa parada por falta de dinero." The families of 200 people killed by Franco's

fascists in the Civil War wanted to exhume their bodies, but there hadn't been the money for this. Now the provincial government was putting up the cash to excavate an area where seventeen bodies had already been discovered.

"A touchy subject," said a deep voice to my right, in exquisite English.

"Is it?" I asked again like the innocent abroad. "My knowledge of the Civil War is a little rusty. Indeed, my knowledge of Spain altogether leaves a lot to be desired. My apologies."

"Not at all." He was in his forties, clothed in the manner of Jermyn Street, with a full head of smooth, glossy hair and a lived-in face. "We Spanish must not expect every stranger to be acquainted with our domestic quarrels." He smiled, leaned forward and extended a hand.

"Jaime Martínez Ortiz."

I shook it. "Charlie Barrow."

"A pleasure, Charlie Barrow." He sipped at a glass of white wine, turned and snapped his fingers. The barman clearly knew him. "Fausto. Another Barbadillo, and for you?"

"I'll try the same." I hoped it was a compliment.

"The inevitable question. What brings you here?"

"Nothing but rest and recreation. A desire to do very little, although I would like to see some of the sights."

"This is one of them," he answered. "This *parador* is becoming a must for all visitors to southern Spain."

"It's very fine. It must have an Arab ancestry."

"Now that is very politically correct. I note you don't use the word 'Moorish'."

"I was told by a friend in Berlin who speaks fluent Spanish that it's almost a term of abuse."

"Your friend is right. It was used by the advancing Catholic monarchs when they reconquered Spain in the fifteenth century. The dictionaries sometimes translate 'Moor' as *Morisco*, but that word denotes a Muslim obliged to convert to Christianity. Not really a term of abuse whereas 'Moor' or *Moro* is a little like 'wog' or 'nigger'. Sad really, because it's quite an evocative word."

"Like Othello, the Moor of Venice."

"Now there's a story with a hidden agenda. I wonder what Shakespeare really had in mind when he made an Arab the hero of one of his greatest plays?"

"A pity the English are often so ignorant of their literature and its meaning."

"Dear me. No need to be so gloomy. You could apply the same argument to the Spanish and Cervantes."

He gave me time to taste my wine.

"And the hotel?" I asked.

"It was the *Alcazar de Arriba*. Built by the Arabs to keep a wary eye on the plains of *al Andalus*, as they called it. Lavishly altered by Pedro in the fourteenth century. He lived up to his title of The Cruel by using it to incarcerate his father's mistress."

"Not a nice man?"

"No, but he made the place comfortable enough for Ferdinand and Isabella to select it as one of their favourite residences. Unfortunately it was badly damaged by an earthquake in 1504. Left to go to rack and ruin for centuries until some genius of a bureaucrat – now there's a rarity in Spain – until he got the idea of turning it into this exquisite watering-hole."

Jaime Martínez Ortiz smiled behind his eyes.

"I almost don't need to buy a guidebook after that."

"Oh, there are a thousand beautiful things to see in Andalucía. A good guidebook would more than pay for itself. Had I time, I would escort you to some of them myself. But…"

A mobile was buzzing. I suddenly remembered my own, still stuffed inside my suitcase.

"Excuse me," he said. "I must take this." He rose and moved into a corner of the bar. Turning his back to me, he answered his caller in subdued tones. The conversation lasted no more than twenty seconds. All I heard and understood were the words, "I'll meet you in Castillo tomorrow evening."

The caller clearly wanted to continue. Ortiz was annoyed. He signed off with a burst of irritation. I knew enough to recognise his words as Arabic.

"Work?" I asked, fishing a little.

"I am a lawyer."

I hadn't expected such a quick and open response. He grinned.

"And you?" he asked quickly.

"A member of the much-despised trade of journalism."

"I'm afraid it shows. Have another drink."

We drifted into a silence until Fausto brought more wine. Jaime Martínez Ortiz put his head back and closed his eyes. I picked up the paper again and tried to read the exhumation story. I worked it out that the village where the graves had been unearthed was divided. The children and grandchildren of the victims of Franco's executioners were up against those who fervently wanted to forget the past, obliterate it and live as if the war had never happened. They longed for the certainties of the *Caudillo's* years in power, in place of the democratic chaos that had made them pariahs in the sight of their neighbours. One local businessman, calling for sleeping dogs to stay that way, was quoted as referring to Civil War Republicans as such and worse. The paper said he'd denied there were any bodies buried in the fields alongside any of the roads leading in and out of his village.

But those who wanted the mass graves uncovered had the local Socialist mayor on their side. In any case, the evidence had already been unearthed.

Ortiz's eyes stayed closed. I decided not to disturb him and sidled out to my dinner with Carlito.

Chapter 4

He was already *in situ* eyeing a glass of something white as he slowly twirled it before the light from a candle.

"I was afraid you might not show up."

"Why so?"

"Well, apart from the obvious attractions of the *parador*, I thought you might have been repelled by my appearance."

I was about to protest, but he held up his hand.

"It happens. People in my condition have to be prepared for it."

I didn't know what to say. I sat down at the table, rested my hands on either side of the place setting, took a deep breath and stared at Carlito.

He smiled. "Take a look at the menu – or let me choose for you. Do you trust me?"

"Since I don't think I shall be able to understand it, I'll leave myself in your hands."

"First lesson of Spanish menus, Charlie. *Cerdo* is pork, *cordero* is lamb and *conejo* is rabbit. The three 'C's'. Foreigners get them mixed up."

"And what about chicken, fish and beef?"

"*Pollo, pescado* and *carne de vaca*. In that order. *Cerveza* is beer. And *vino* is either *blanco, tinto* or *rosado*. And that's enough to be going on with, don't you think?"

"I am blinking already."

I let him order for me, having specified that I fancied the taste of lamb and would welcome a glass of red.

Espiridion was on duty again. He seemed to know exactly when to approach our table and stand with pad and pen poised at the ready. He took the order and winked at Carlito who returned the wink with a nod of his head.

"So, have you decided what you are going to do with your holiday?"

I hesitated to admit to Carlito that I had already succumbed to the temptation to read a local newspaper and that a mild and early interest in one particular story was growing into something my journalist's instinct was telling me to follow up. I should have been talking about exploring Seville or Córdoba, swimming none too energetically in the hotel pool, lazing about and acquiring a tan, drinking my fill of the local wine – and all that.

"What's all this fuss about mass graves and the Civil War?" I asked in as offhand a manner as I could manage.

"It's more than a fuss. It's a scandal. Ever since the first mass grave was found a few years ago, relatives of the victims have been demanding a proper burial for their bones. Some want to go further than that. They want compensation from the government. Money, Charlie. And in times like these, who can blame them?"

"But who are these victims? And who shovelled their bodies into mass graves?"

"To begin with," said Carlito, "it looked as if the bones, the skulls with bullet holes in them, the bits of cloth and the odd trinket still adorning the neck of a skeleton – it looked as if all of them were the remains of people executed by Franco's soldiers, either during the war or after it. His policy was to liquidate those who'd fought against his rebellion, Marxists, liberals, freemasons. The only prisoners he took ended up in concentration camps where they were tortured or eventually killed. There was no talk of reconciliation, of bringing enemies together in a new, united Spain. Franco wanted revenge. And he took it."

"You say, it looked as if *all these* were the victims of Franco's brutality. Is there any doubt about that?"

"Not much." Carlito sipped his *blanco* and blew his cheeks. Espiridion arrived with the food and a large glass of red for me. We began to eat while the restaurant filled up with chattering couples and one very noisy extended family party.

"It was a very nasty war. No quarter given. The fascists were bastards. Easy to say. But it sums them up. They never stopped being bastards."

"But...?"

"There were bastards on the Republican side too. Once they'd been drawn into war, they adopted the habits of war. They killed and executed – informers, priests, nuns, factory owners, members of the fascist party, the Falange – and each other."

He started to wax lyrical. "Because the weakness of the Republican side was internal conflict. The Republic forgot its democratic origins, forgot that the people had voted it into power. It became the dupe of anarchists and communists, even woolly-minded liberals – they ended up hating one another and slaughtering one another – instead of killing Franco. The Republic fell apart. Once it decided to accept help from the Soviet Union, because the other side had no compunction about taking goodies from Hitler and Mussolini, it became a state spying on itself, trusting no one, not even its own supporters and fighters."

"So they were as bad as one another – Nationalists and Republicans?"

"No, you can't say that." Carlito paused, presumably to collect his thoughts "The weight of evidence is heavily against Franco and those who fought for him and served his purposes," he concluded.

"The Republicans were plain stupid then?"

"This is murky territory, Charlie. It's wise to take it a step at a time."

We ate and drank again. The nearby family party had become less rowdy, settling into more discreet conversation. I waited for Carlito to tell me more.

"Once the war was over in 1939, Franco set about his surviving enemies with a will. His thugs rounded them up and were still executing them as late as the 1950s. But the mass graves they're digging up now contain no evidence of bodies belonging to priests and nuns. The rags belong to what's left of women, children and old men. And the old men weren't wearing cassocks."

"Forgive my blunt English ways, Carlito. How old are you?"

He laughed. "Fifty-six. Born in 1958, well after the war but slap bang in the middle of the Franco era. He lasted until '75."

"So, you grew up under fascism, went to school under fascism, became a teenager under fascism?"

"I grew up in a small village tucked away in the mountains of the Sierra Morena. It was a special village. Almost all the people who live there were dwarves."

He looked at me, almost defiantly.

"The village is still there. We call it *Fortaleza de los Enanos*. Fortress of Dwarves. We run the place ourselves, elect our own council and the small committees that oversee all our activities, including the local co-operative. Given our physical handicaps, we cater for the demands they put on us. We have our own craftsmen, joiners and carpenters and the like who make our tables and chairs. And the beds we sleep on. We grow most of our own food, mainly vegetables and fruit, and tend our own herds, goats and sheep and a few cattle. The land is pretty rough, so we can't grow cereals. We buy in by trading some of the furniture we make. But we bake our own bread. And there's a small slope of a field outside the village which catches the sun. We use it to grow vines and make a palatable red wine from the grapes. We have a hand press, and despite our size, we can cope with it."

"Self-sufficient except for wheat and maize?"

"Brilliantly so. Not luxurious. But comfortable, even in winter when the freezing winds blow down from the peaks. There's plenty of firewood and kindling in the nearby forest. I'll take you there, if you want."

Careful. Don't get too curious. And remember you're here for a holiday.

"But in Franco's time, how did you manage to keep the goblins off your backs? Didn't they want to make sure you were politically reliable?"

"Remember what I told you about dwarves at the royal court, the tradition of treating them as special servants to the rulers of Spain – not as freaks to be pitied and persecuted? Don Sebastian de Morra in Velasquez's painting?"

41

He surveyed his plate of food and smiled to himself. "Franco seems to have seen us in the same mould. He knew of our *Fortaleza*. Of course he did. He even despatched officials to see if we needed anything, as they used to put it so courteously. They were spying on us, keeping him informed. But for the most part, he left us alone. The old rogue's plan was to restore the monarchy – that came later after he'd played king himself for forty-six years. His court had no dwarves, as far as I know. But he must have had this notion that a new court with a new king had to function according to the old traditions."

"It's one hell of a tale, Carlito. Has anyone written it up?"

"Not to my knowledge. There are plenty of books and articles referring to the persecution of Marxists, Jews, freemasons and homosexuals, all of them classed as mentally retarded. But dwarves as a group in the same category? No."

Carlito was now in full flow.

"Franco was a mix of realist, fantasist, brute and hypocrite. 'I ask pardon of all my enemies,' he wrote when he knew he was dying. 'And I pardon with all my heart all those who declared themselves my enemy, *although I did not consider them to be so.*' This after perhaps more than a million Spaniards had been killed because the man took it into his head to lead a rebellion against an elected government."

"Your people wouldn't have been so lucky under Hitler's Nazis."

"That's true. But in Spain, luck didn't really enter into it. Apart from our physical condition, we are just as intelligent as the rest of you – or as foolish or stupid. But most of us were bright enough to see that if we kept out of sight, isolated ourselves in small remote communities, we could take advantage of Franco's apparent belief that we were still special in some way. And survive."

I breathed a deep sigh.

"You think I'm making all this up, don't you?"

"The phrase 'far fetched' has occurred to me."

"I've told you. I'll take you there. I'll take you to my *Fortaleza.*"

It also occurred to me that we had strayed from the original subject.

"We were talking about mass graves…" Before I could say any more, Carlito clicked his fingers and called for more wine. Espiridion was quick to respond. I noticed I was drinking most of what was on offer.

"The *fuss* about mass graves is why I'm here," said Carlito. "Let me update you. October 2007. A very important month in the history of modern Spain. The Law of Historical Memory is passed by parliament in Madrid. Its full title, if somewhat verbose, is the "Law for the recognition and widening of rights and the establishment of measures in favour of those undergoing prosecution and violence during the Civil War and the

43

Dictatorship." He enjoyed my mystified look. "I am a lawyer, Charlie. A human rights lawyer. And the Law of Historical Memory is where I start from. I use a small hotel in Carmona as a base, to work on what may or may not be evidence of the victims' identities. I've been spending hours in the Seville city registry – births, marriages, deaths and so forth – trawling through what's left of documents which ought to help the campaign we call the Association for the Recovery of Historical Memory. ARMH. They pay my wages."

"The people who want the bodies and remains decently buried?"

"Just so. And they also want redress. Not only cash for the victims' descendants. They want the killers named and, if they're still alive, they want them in court and preferably in jail as well. That's the hard bit, because the Amnesty Law, hurriedly adopted in 1977 in a frenzied effort to bury the past, prevents any criminal investigation into absolutely anything that happened in the Franco years. Unless we change that law, we're not going to get very far."

"Have you had any success?"

Carlito wiped his plate with a piece of bread and drank some wine. I saw traces of weariness in the eyes. His shoulders drooped and I was wondering if he'd become bored by our meeting.

"Yes and no," he said. "Many of the documents we need have been destroyed. But, curiously enough, there are files full of certificates and correspondence which you might think Franco's people would have wanted shredded and forgotten."

"I've always been amazed how totalitarian regimes leave permanent records of their bad behaviour. From the Nazis to Pol Pot in Cambodia. They've never been able to resist the temptation to tell those who came after them how nasty they were."

I hesitated before putting my next question.

"But they weren't nasty to your folks in the *Fortaleza*?"

"Oh, they took a few of us away and did their worst with them. Those who'd made no secret of their allegiance to the Republicans. One or two of our people joined what was left of an anti-Franco guerrilla movement." He paused. "They didn't last long. Arrested or shot on sight. My parents kept out of it. I wouldn't be here if they hadn't. You could argue that I'm the child of collaborators. They didn't collaborate. They just kept their mouths shut like millions of Spaniards, and told me to do the same."

"But when Franco died…?"

"I was seventeen in '75. I'd been thinking for myself long before then. I knew the regime had been a curse. But I didn't pass judgement on my mother and father. And I'm not going to start now."

A thought struck me.

"I met another lawyer at the *parador* this afternoon. Very suave and well heeled, he was. Easily bored

45

though. Fell asleep on me after buying me a drink." I'm trying hard to conjure up memories of my earlier encounter. "He gave his name as Jaime Martínez Ortiz."

Carlito's weariness faded. He sat up and leaned towards me.

"You met Jaime Martínez Ortiz?"

"Him and his mobile phone from which he took a mysterious call. In the bar. He filled me in on the origins of the hotel. Very erudite, he was. Very knowledgeable about the history of Spain and the Moors. Saw through me like a laser beam. Identified me straightaway as a hack."

"If I tell you that he's my enemy, would it shock you?"

"Enemy?"

"He's a servant of the government in Madrid. A prominent member of the Popular Party. Spain's conservatives. He's out to destroy any case we can make for the exhumation of Franco's victims."

"And he speaks Arabic. At least he did when he broke off his phone call."

"Thank you for that. I'll press SAVE and hold it in my memory."

"You're welcome."

"He's a dangerous man, Charlie. You might rue the day you met him."

"Then, I'll tell you what we'll do."

He's taken aback by my sudden burst of decisiveness.

"I'll take you up on the invitation to visit your *Fortaleza*. But before that, we go to this town where they're digging up the graves. What's its name...?"

"Castillo," said Carlito. "It's about an hour's drive."

"Can we go in my car?"

"As long as you find two thick cushions for the passenger seat."

Chapter 5

Oh dear! You're not, are you? Tell me you're not going to Castillo.

Oh, but yes. We were heading north on a morning of pale sunshine and cirrus cloud, Carlito letting the breeze from the open window cool his face.

After our meal, I returned to the *parador* knowing I needed a good night's sleep but also hoping to bump into Jaime Martínez Ortiz again. But he wasn't around. Not in the restaurant or the bar or even lounging in the spacious lobby. So where did he go? Had he seen the glint in my eye, that look on the face of a practised hack which gives him away and says 'this guy's smelled a story and I wish he hadn't'?

I got up early and collected as many newspapers as I could lay my hands on – today's, yesterday's and a few from the days before which the hotel's tiny book shop hadn't thrown away. I sifted through them as well as my poor Spanish and a pocket dictionary allowed. But it was obvious. There *was* a story to be sniffed out...

And you are going to poke your nose in, aren't you? Why do I bother to warn you? You're a hopeless case, Charlie Barrow. And I am giving up on this one.

No, you're not. You are going to be there, sitting on my shoulder while I do the thing I was put on Earth to do. I can't help it. And, in any case, it'll make this holiday a lot of fun. Wandering around aimlessly looking at churches and mosques for no real reason is not me, is it?

I told you. I'm giving up.

I drove the Polo across the *Autovia A4* and the lowlands of the Guadalquivir, past prosperous *latifundios,* farms growing sunflowers, oranges, and olives, then over the river to the ugly little town of Llora del Rio. This was all workshops and sleazy cafés, preoccupied with trade and gossip, not a place to spend much time if you're after scenery, sunshine and architectural wonders. A minor road took us north up towards the Sierra Morena, much of which had been turned into a glorious national park. The route wound over rolling hills, grass, some green, some dry, and tall oaks, through more hamlets, starkly white and comatose, until we rounded a bend and dropped straight into Castillo. Suddenly everything and everyone was busy with a square bustling with market stalls and a children's fair ground.

We found a bar with tables outside under a green awning. The temptation to while away the time with glasses of wine and snacks of ham and cheese was too much. I had my fistful of papers and persuaded myself that this was the perfect opportunity to read them and absorb some of the articles in detail.

You're a fraud, Charlie Barrow.

No, I'm not. This is genuine research. In any case, you warned me against plunging into a fresh bout of journalism. So I'm taking my time. I'm soaking up the atmosphere.

You're still a fraud. You want to kid yourself that you're on to a story when in reality, you're not sure. You're fishing, half-hoping the urge to investigate will go away while the sun shines and you watch the world go by.

Petulantly, I shook one of the newspapers into a readable position.

"What's the matter, Charlie?" asked Carlito. He'd been silent for most of the journey.

"I have a voice in my head telling me I shouldn't get involved in any of this. I'm supposed to be on vacation."

"You can always back out. I shan't object. But it's good to have a day off from all the office work. Thank you for the ride. I'll leave you to think about it while I have a pee."

It was the first time I had noticed his mobile, which he furtively swept from the table. I'd fished mine out of the suitcase but didn't intend to use it overmuch. It would stay in my shirt pocket unless and until it was absolutely necessary to use it. A waiter brought me a small carafe of red while I watched the man I took to be the restaurant owner delicately carve some ham off the bone and some thin slices from a large block of *manchego*. He handed it over with a smile and a flourish. And left me to read.

'The remains of another 31 victims of the Civil War have been found in a makeshift grave in Castillo, a village in Seville province. These are in addition to remains already exhumed by officials of the Association for the Recovery of Historical Memory. This follows the first phase of work undertaken by an organisation of archaeologists and anthropologists aimed at identifying the remains which was completed in July 2011 and brings the total number of corpses unearthed to 80.'

I looked up from the newspaper. Four tables away, Jaime Martínez Ortiz was in deep conversation with a priest. He was clearly an ascetic, gaunt and grey with his long body enveloped in a soutane of high-quality cloth. He was listening intently to Ortiz who had drawn his hands together as if in supplication.

Ortiz looked up and saw me. He waved a little hesitantly. I nodded. He ostentatiously offered his apologies to the priest, rose elegantly from his chair and carefully negotiated a path through a haphazard collection of restaurant furniture. He sat down opposite me. I decided to provoke him.

"And where were you last night?"

"It really isn't any of your business, *Señor* Barrow. But since you ask, I had to meet a colleague at a restaurant down in the town."

"Not the one I went to."

"Carmona has quite a lot of good eateries. But no. You're quite right. You were in the *Molino de la Romera* dining with one Carlito Jimenez."

"How do you know that?"

"Carlito is, to say the least, pretty recognisable. And I have a couple of friends who were also in the *Molino* last night."

"You melted away like a ghost. One minute we were sharing some tasty wine. The next, you were gone."

"And you find that discourteous and unsettling?"

"No, I shall place it in the category of strange things which have happened to me for most of my adult life. I am never surprised."

"Never?"

Watch it. This bloke is not someone to mess with.

He flicked his fingers. The waiter moved alongside. He ordered a beer, and *pinchitos* of ham and cheese. But only for himself.

"And a green salad."

"Ah, the weight-watcher!"

"To strike a balance."

I made a show of returning to my newspaper.

'The prime minister's office says it is reconsidering the possible provision of more funds for the investigation in Castillo. This follows the pattern for similar investigations throughout the country. The Association says additional money would help to further its research into Francoist repression in the region surrounding Castillo, but it is not hopeful that the government will respond positively. It adds that the remains it has unearthed so far are providing hard evidence of what it calls 'violent deaths' in Castillo in 1936. These involved mass improvised burials, frequently one on top of another, the 'distortion' of skeletal remains, including serious wounds inflicted before the killings, the presence of 'projectiles' housed in the backs of several bodies and the discovery of personal effects such as coins, spectacles, cigarette lighters, pencils and the remains of clothing.'

"Nasty," observed Ortiz.

"So, we come to the question that's really bugging me."

"Which is?"

"Who did it?"

He didn't answer. I ploughed on. "Franco's rank-and-file troops and local supporters were given licence to shoot and kill Republicans and Reds, or indeed anybody who resisted the Nationalist advance through Andalucía into central Spain."

"I thought you told me last night that you weren't too hot on recent Spanish history."

"I'm not. But most of this is self-evident."

"And who, you are asking, gave the orders at local level?" It was less a question than an attempt to needle me.

"Well," said a voice from behind me. "We have Franco and his generals at the top and rebel troops at the bottom, a lot of them Arabs and Berbers from North Africa with a blood lust to surpass all blood lusts. But what about those in between?"

Carlito was back.

"Good morning, *Señor* Jimenez." Ortiz stood up and beckoned Carlito to a seat.

"Courteous as ever," said Carlito. "Thank you."

The restaurant and the market fizzed with argument as customers called for food and drink or bargained for what was on offer. But the three of us had been struck dumb. We averted our eyes and found a lot of awkward interest in ham, cheese and carafes of *tinto*.

"Precisely," muttered Jaime Martínez Ortiz eventually. "Who *were* the ones in between? And who else is guilty of murder? Interesting questions. I shall leave you to ponder them, gentlemen." And he slithered away back to his own table where the priest still awaited him.

"He's tailing you, Charlie. The conversation you had with him yesterday and his discovery that you are a man after a story have got him very interested."

"Plus the fact that you and I have struck up a friendship. Incidentally he knows we dined last night."

Carlito looked round. But Ortiz and his friend had left.

"The ones in between," he said again. "That's what *I* am trying to find out, Charlie. That's *my* job."

Today, Carlito looked troubled and angry. And the scowl grew fiercer when I continued the conversation.

"I might make it my job too." I tossed the remark at him to see what the effect would be. He didn't respond. So I told him I'd been reading the local papers again. They were reporting that revenge killings were not the monopoly of the *Franquistas*. As the fascist rebel army had moved up through Andalucía, Republicans in Castillo, supporters of the government in Madrid, formed local committees to commandeer food and other supplies from the richer residents. It would have been a praiseworthy tactic if they hadn't at the same time incarcerated Franco supporters, including local clergy, inside one of the local churches which they then promptly set on fire.

"Are they right, Carlito? Is the local press renowned for its accuracy? Or is someone pushing a line here?"

He didn't dodge the question. "I'm sure it happened," he said. "I'm sure Nationalist supporters were persecuted and killed before Franco's army could save them. I'm sure it was an outrage that was repeated all over Spain as the Civil War raged on."

"That doesn't bother you?"

"I offer you a well-worn cliché, Charlie. War is war. And this one became ever more brutal. I'll say again what I said to you yesterday. The balance of brutality was on Franco's side. As for the Church, it backed him to the hilt. It gloried in the extermination of communists, atheists, freemasons, anybody who failed to sign up to his New Order or disdained to crawl away and keep their mouths shut."

His anger faded.

"And you are also going to ask me if Ortiz's friendly relationship with the local priest in Castillo is a sign of where his sympathies still lie?" The voice trailed away as the jollity of the crowd around us swelled into more lively chatter, the clinking of glasses and calls for more ham and cheese. He smiled.

"The answer's 'Yes'. And I can show you the ruin of the church the Republicans burned down."

"Now that would be interesting."

"If you decide to write the story, Charlie, who would it be for?"

I named my outlets, papers in Britain and Australia, the odd radio station in New Zealand and Canada, even a television channel in Germany.

"Then if you want to see the site of the exhumation here in Castillo, you've got a date this afternoon. We can go up there when the heat subsides."

Before I could respond, I was distracted by the arrival of two men at a table placed under a shaded part of the terrace. Broad-shouldered, shaven headed, sporting light-blue shirts with short sleeves revealing muscled biceps, tattoos, gold chains and Rolexes. Martínez Ortiz had joined them.

"Don't look, Charlie. Concentrate on your wine."

"Who are they, for Christ's sake?"

"Could be *Guardia Civil* off duty or more likely PP heavies."

"And PP heavies are what?"

"Bouncers for the party's meetings. There's one tonight in the town hall, called to protest against what we're doing."

I displayed as much cynicism as I could and Carlito knew what was coming.

"*Guardia Civil* my arse, Carlito! What little history I know tells me that many people in this part of Spain have Moorish ancestry. But that lot look to have slightly more *recent* links to the Arab world. Wouldn't you say so?"

"Your nasty suspicious mind is at work again."

"I'm just curious."

"Save your curiosity for later."

Chapter 6

We needed to stay at least one night in Castillo. I broke a promise to myself and used the mobile to phone the *parador* in Carmona, asking them to keep my room for me. I was quite pleased I could make it work in Spain.

Carlito found us a small hotel, said he had business to attend to and would see me at around four o'clock. I asked no questions and he offered no explanation. I whiled away the time in the shade of the hotel's courtyard, reading more newspapers and pondering on the morning's events, until my eyes closed as the wine, ham and cheese took their expected effect. I managed to retain some self-esteem by waking up with a start at precisely ten to four. I found the nearest toilet and washed my hands and face with cold water. Carlito was in the lobby, standing behind a carved wooden chair.

"Some people have all the luck," he quipped. "They take siestas."

I threw up my hands and smiled. "An old Spanish custom. Guilty, as charged, *Señor*. But fully refreshed."

We drove west out of the town, turned right after about a kilometre and approached the cemetery. The surrounding *sierra* was parched grass, outcrops of white rock, small oaks and pines, and choking dust. We parked the car just off the road and walked through an arched gateway. Carlito moved quickly, his nimbleness a constant surprise.

A tree-lined avenue opened out on to a plot of land lined on one side by a wall of whitewashed brick supporting three storeys of niches. Every one of these was covered by a stone plaque bearing an inscription of a family name and that of the deceased whose corpse occupied the coffin in the niche behind the plaque. A date of birth and a date of death had been added. Some inscriptions bore a verse or dedication from relatives. This was 'internment' not 'burial'.

Carlito explained. "The Spanish are very particular about this sort of thing. Burial may come later, perhaps years later, when the rent paid on the niche runs out. Then the coffin will be moved to a grave opposite the wall and, if the family is rich enough, it'll be marked with a headstone or a memorial."

There were flowers everywhere – roses, geraniums and wilder blooms whose names were a mystery to me. They trailed from vases hanging just above the plaques or grew from pots placed at the foot of the wall.

"All of which is good Catholic practice," said Carlito. "Funerals in Spain follow swiftly on death. In a hot climate, this makes a lot of sense and it's neat and tidy."

"And dignified," I added.

I stood still and listened. The peace and quiet were disturbed only by the murmurings of small groups of mourners, the chatter of birds and a breeze which sent dust and withered leaves pirouetting across the dry ground.

We turned away from the wall and walked a few yards towards a vast pit of red earth. A section of it was covered by an awning of blue and white stripes.

"Down there," said Carlito, nodding towards the far end of the pit.

Groups of young people wearing jeans and t-shirts were busy with small brushes.

I whispered a profanity.

The skeletons lay at all angles. Some of the corpses had fallen forward. Some had lain on their backs. Others had died in the foetal position. Not all were intact. Bones had been scattered haphazardly. One or two skulls stayed isolated as if wrenched from the body to which they originally belonged. A girl teased the earth from underneath a thighbone. She worked with great care and an obvious reverence for the remains she was uncovering. She looked up, saw Carlito and beckoned us to join her.

We trod gingerly. The striped awning kept the sun at bay, but the air down here was stifling.

"Elena. How are you? This is my friend, Charlie Barrow. Charlie? This is Elena Silva."

Elena took off her glove, shook my hand, lifted her spectacles and bent to give Carlito a peck on the cheek.

"Glad of a break, Carlito. But we make progress."

"Given what you have to do, it all looks neat and tidy."

He turned to me. "Charlie has something to tell you."

I decided to come clean there and then. "*Señora,* I am a journalist. I think I want to do a story on all this. Would you see that as an intrusion, or even sacrilege?"

"If Carlito thinks you're a man of integrity, you're more than welcome."

"Are you happy to be quoted?"

"The more publicity we can get for this work, the better." Elena pushed a lock of jet-black hair from her forehead, replaced her glasses and put down the brush she'd been using. I had to stop staring at her. She was beautiful. Olive skin, dark eyes behind her lenses, with everything else most men might desire.

"Now you have ground rules, Charlie. Don't be shy."

We moved to the edge of the pit and sat together. Out of a satchel Carlito brought a bottle of water and plastic beakers. We slaked a little of our thirst.

I learned that Elena Silva was an archaeologist more accustomed to unearthing Roman and Visigoth remains than exhumations. But Carlito and others from the ARMH had persuaded her that they could pay her a decent living wage if she would use her skills to do what she too now considered important work. She was the head of a team of six. She introduced me to her chief assistant, Alex, a lean young man, dark, unshaven and wearing a perpetually anxious expression.

"We think that locating the bodies of Franco's victims and doing our best to give them a decent burial in proper graves are all part of the healing process," he said. "If we can identify the remains, families will know that the people who were massacred here can finally rest in peace."

There was a pause as Elena lifted her head and pushed her shoulders back.

"I declare an interest, Mr Barrow. My own grandparents were killed by the Nationalists. So I am glad to be recruited."

She told me exhumation teams all over Spain had been at work for at least ten years. They'd found hundreds of corpses. Castillo was more recent.

"The remains here were found by a small boy who lived on a nearby farm."

They were using DNA to identify some of them. The victims included the mayor at the time of the shootings, the station master, a local journalist and several prominent trade unionists. Their descendants still lived in Castillo.

"We think at least three hundred bodies are buried here," said Carlito. "Men, women and children of all ages."

"Can I take a closer look?"

"Be our guest."

I peered at one of the skeletons. There was a hole at the back of the skull and the hands were crossed.

Carlito continued his explanation. "Three of the old folk in the village are in their nineties. They say they remember what happened. It was August 1936. Franco's rebels were sweeping through Andalucía. There wasn't much of a fight for Castillo. The fascists brought captured Republicans to the cemetery in trucks. They tied their hands behind their backs, shot them in the neck, dragged the bodies to the rim of the pit, kicked them over the edge and shovelled earth over them. We don't have to dig deep to find them."

Elena pointed to what was left of some leather sandals still strapped to the bones of a pair of feet.

"Can I take photographs?"

They nodded again and left me to get on with it. I used my mobile to amass as many images as I could.

Well, you're in it up to your neck now, aren't you, Charlie? Bang goes your holiday. Where will it all end?

"Can I come, maybe tomorrow, and take notes?"

Again, they agreed. Carlito said that we ought to be getting back into town. "I want to see if I can gate-crash that PP meeting."

I hadn't realised that this was on our agenda. Carlito briefed me as we returned to the hotel. The potential shindig would start at eight in the evening.

"It gives them enough time to attract an audience and stir things up. They hope the whole town will then decamp for the evening meal full of sound and fury, all of them strongly opposed to the work being done by Elena's team."

"So we won't exactly be welcome?"

"No. They'll throw insults at us, but the PP won't want to be held responsible for a punch-up at a public meeting."

"What about the police and the *Guardia Civil*?"

"That will be very interesting."

I was not reassured by Carlito's display of insouciance.

"They'll stay neutral?"

"As I say, it will be very interesting. The local police chief here is a lazy sod, but he isn't a rabid right-winger and he'll have told his men to do their duty."

I had been the victim of violence many times in my varied life, but I wasn't sure I could cope with a situation where I would have to defend Carlito as well.

"Don't worry, Charlie. I know how to take care of myself."

I grimaced. "I'm all agog, Carlito. Simply fascinated by the prospect."

Chapter 7

Carlito told me to take a right turn on the outskirts of Castillo. It was a rough road bounded by the houses of the poor, breeze block huts with roofs of corrugated iron. Children played in the nearby scrub and a few curious grown-ups stuck their faces round makeshift doorways.

Ahead of us a ruin.

"The church you wanted to see. Destroyed by Republicans," said Carlito.

It had been a typical small town place of worship with the ragged remains of a belfry poking up from what was left of brick and stone walls. The church authorities were seemingly in no mood to repair the ruin or even preserve it as a place of pilgrimage. Coarse grass, brambles and creepers had invaded the whole site.

Ortiz and his priest stood in front of what had once been the west door, now a simple dilapidated archway.

"Here you see the other side of the coin," Ortiz called out. "This is Father Trujillo, by the way."

The priest looked at us and kept his hands in the folds of his cassock.

"Jaime tells me you are an English journalist keen to report the exhumations at the cemetery."

I nodded and said nothing.

"Then perhaps you will also send a report to your editors describing this." He waved an arm at the ruined church. "Desecration comes in many forms. As does death. Fifty people were deliberately burned alive in this building."

Carlito stood back, knowing that I would be more than ready to defend myself.

"If, as a priest of the Catholic faith, you were really interested in saving souls," I began, venturing into territory of which I was none too sure, "then you might show as much compassion for the wretches whose bones lie unburied in the cemetery. You pick and choose, Father, for your convenience and that of the politicians you support."

"That is an outrageous statement," said Ortiz.

Father Trujillo took a step towards me. He was composed, without anger or even irritation. "I would have you know that I have spent many hours trying to comfort the families whose parents and grandparents were killed in the Civil War, whether they were supporters of the Republic or welcomed General Franco's Nationalists. Some have accepted my ministry, others have turned me away. I understand why. Many lies have been told about the role of the Church in this country's recent history. They are still being told. I hope, *Señor* Barrow, that you will have enough of a conscience to recognise my point of view and reflect it in your journalism."

I shrugged. "As you will. I acknowledge that what happened here was an atrocity. The same goes for the bodies at the exhumation site."

Trujillo was unprepared for further conversation. He turned on his heel and Ortiz followed, throwing me one last look of undiluted scorn and placing his arm round the priest's bony shoulder.

****

We walked to the *ayuntamiento*, the town hall, a building of no architectural merit, put up perhaps in the nineteenth century. It consisted of two floors of offices and a pleasant courtyard with cloisters fashioned out of simple arches. There was no one around. I'd expected a crowd of citizens eager to have their say on the merits or otherwise of exhumations.

"Why so quiet?" I asked Carlito.

"I admit it's strange," he replied. "Something's wrong."

We found a door marked *Sala de Conferencias* and heard voices. Carlito pushed it open and in we walked. The talking stopped. Half a dozen faces turned to look at us.

"Gentlemen," said Carlito. "We apologise. We thought this was a public meeting."

Six men sat in a semi-circle opposite a seventh who had his back to us. One of the six gathered his wits more quickly than the others.

"It isn't," he said defiantly. "Leave."

But Carlito had recognised the isolated seventh man.

"*Señor Alcalde!* Mr Mayor. Good evening," he declaimed, deliberately and effusively.

With a nod that I should follow him, Carlito walked round the edge of the semi-circle, strode up to the man and held out his hand. The mayor was fortyish and in off-duty mode by the look of it, chino trousers and sports coat, open-neck blue shirt, with jet-black hair brilliantined as straight as he could have got it. He recoiled as Carlito advanced.

"*Señor* Jimenez, this is not a good time."

"Why so?" Carlito asked.

"Because this is a private meeting between the mayor and our delegation. Again, I ask you to leave." This from a portly heavyweight, arm muscles held tight by a striped t-shirt and a face that would have frightened a bull in a ring.

"What delegation is that?" asked Carlito.

"None of your business."

"Mr Mayor?" Carlito raised an eyebrow.

"From the Popular Party, *Señor* Jimenez," answered a second man, more politely than his colleague. "We are here to tell the mayor that we strongly object to the exhumation of skeletons and bones at the municipal cemetery."

"We know you, Jimenez," said another. "We know you work for the organization behind this nonsense."

"That I do," said Carlito. "The Association for the Recovery of Historical Memory, to give it its full and proper title."

"Historical Memory, my arse," spat the heavyweight. "My memory says those who opposed the *Caudillo* deserved all they got. Otherwise Spain would have gone to the dogs."

"It's a point of view," Carlito said sweetly, fixing the man with unblinking eyes. "And, yes, I am a lawyer trying to help that organisation trace the ancestry of Civil War victims so that they can receive what they deserve, a decent internment and burial like all other citizens of Spain." He paused. "And that includes the victims of Republican violence, although I'm bound to say we haven't discovered any in Castillo."

The big man spat again.

"And who is this?" he said scowling in my direction.

By this time, the mayor had recovered his composure and was about to interrupt with some mollifying words. But before he could open his mouth, one of the six who'd so far stayed silent, stood up. I recognised him as the car park attendant at Seville airport who'd told me he never forgot a face.

"You've been told to get out, Dwarf. So, get out."

"Pepe, please..."

"Shut up, you bloody Socialist. How the hell you got elected as mayor of this town, God alone knows."

"But he *was* elected," I said, emphasising the word as much as I could.

My remark produced sudden silence until Mr Car Park Man gathered his wits.

"Yes. I remember you," he said slowly as the light seemed to dawn. "The English idiot who couldn't work the barrier at the airport. So, you speak Spanish?"

"You know I do," I replied. "Not well. But enough to understand that there's a bit of coercion going on here. *Coaccion.* Yes?"

"I should be careful what you say, Englishman. Word has got around that you are a journalist. Keen to report the goings-on at the cemetery. You've already got yourself into bad company with that little shit."

Carlito didn't budge. "And who told you my friend Charlie Barrow was a journalist?" he asked.

"*Our* good friend, Jaime Martínez Ortiz."

"Shut up, Pepe."

But Pepe wasn't for shutting up. He came straight for me. He was about to land one, when memories stirred of some self-defence training the British army had once given me in Northern Ireland.

I side-stepped Pepe and tripped him up, chopping down on the back of his thick neck as he fell. I hadn't done him any harm. He had time to get up and come for me again. But he got the same treatment. And this time stayed where he was, shaking his head and swearing at the world in general. Three of the group were ready to take his place but the one who'd spoken more courteously put his hand up.

"Sit down, you clowns," he hissed.

Carlito and the mayor had moved away from the action into a far corner near the door.

"It really is time to go now, Charlie. I think you've seen all you need to see."

"Yes, please do as Carlito says," pleaded the mayor. He didn't appear to be scared by the group of six but he didn't want his town hall turned into the scene of a brawl.

Pepe had recovered a little. As we turned to leave, he fired one parting shot.

"Fuck off, Dwarf, and take your *ingles* with you. I'll settle with him later."

****

"Now you know what I'm up against." Carlito swirled the beer in his glass and took a gulp, uncharacteristic for one who normally sipped his drinks. "And they were courteous and polite compared to some of their kind, believe it or not."

"I'm glad I was there to help."

"So am I. But I fear Mr Pepe will round up his mates and do you some real mischief if I'm not there to protect you." He laughed at my po-face. "And where did you learn to fight like that, by the way?"

I gave him a short history of my time in Her Majesty's Armed Forces and the spells I'd done in Belfast and Crossmaglen.

"I'm starting to creak at the seams a bit, but I can usually deal with oafs like Pepe."

"So I noticed. But watch your back. There are enough narrow alleys in Castillo to waylay a man, especially at night. Even in Andalucía darkness comes early at this time of the year."

I changed tack.

"Have you got the time to fill me in on the PP?"

Carlito drained his glass and said he had loads of paperwork to get through, but if I bought him another beer, he would give me a quick history lesson.

"My basic questions, Carlito, are, who are they, why are they so opposed to the exhumations and why are they so hostile to your Association?"

"Sit back and listen, Charlie. And don't interrupt."

He wiped his lips with a large red handkerchief and gathered his thoughts.

"The *Partido Popular* is heir to the legacy of Franco's fascism," he began. "No more, no less. It's often described as a conservative party. But it has little in common with your Tories in Britain or the Christian Democrats in Germany. Yes, like them, it is the party of big business, of big money, and in or out of government, it is the party of wheeler-dealing. It's conservative in the sense that it wishes to *conserve* authoritarianism in Spain. The people should do as they're told."

"What does this have to do with the work you're involved in?"

"The PP is made up of people who want to both remember and forget the past. The past was Franco and stability. *That's* worth celebrating. But anything that recalls the brutality of the Civil War, the dictatorship, the oppression and the torture and murder that went with it, should be ignored. Which is why this particular PP government has cut off all funding for my Association. We remind it too much of things it would like to wipe from our memories. So, there's no money for the exhumations unless we raise it ourselves."

I'd started to take notes. Carlito drank more beer and waited for me to stop scribbling.

"But this is a party that willingly took part in what you call *La Transición*," I said. "It signed up to the

Moncloa Pact in 1977. It's committed to political reconciliation."

"I see you've been doing some homework."

I gave him an old-fashioned look and pushed on. "Apart from that crazy coup attempt in 1981, which wasn't its fault, it's accepted the results of elections even when the Socialists have been the winners. It's played the game."

"Of course it has. Because the wiser heads at the top know that if they want Spain to be recognised as an important country, they have to abide by the rules. We must look like a real democracy. Especially now that we're in the E.U. and the euro zone. The same goes for the Socialists."

"Would you have more chance of getting your funds, if they were back in office?"

"We'd have more chance if a movement like *Podemos* wins enough seats to hold the balance of power."

I didn't pursue that one, but I sensed that Carlito had already placed his bets.

"And the jihadists?"

He thought for a moment. "It ought not to surprise me that an opportunist like Ortiz has a Moroccan bodyguard. But I can't believe that even he thinks a deal with a bunch of Muslim fundis is going to pay off."

"What does he want?"

"Power. For himself. He thinks he can be the next leader of the PP. What he ignores is the long memory of many Spaniards. Many of the victims in the mass graves were put to death by Arab and Berber mercenaries. And it was a bunch of jihadists who planted the bombs on our trains in March 2004. Bombs that killed 191 people."

"You're hoping he's made a big mistake?"

"I'm hoping. I always hope, Charlie."

I closed my notebook.

"Now you are fully briefed," he declared.

"Shall we go for a walk?" I asked.

He laughed. "You have a romantic desire to breath in the balmy late night air of a small Spanish town."

"Something like that."

"Not me, Charlie. Back to the paperwork and then bed. And, like I said, watch your back."

Chapter 8

I woke up with a blinding headache and a nose blocked by congealing blood. I wasn't so much on my back as curled up, with pains in my chest and a vicious cramp in my right leg. It was dark but getting lighter.

Someone had thumped me in the small of my back, sliced at my neck, kicked hard behind my knees and left me for dead. But I didn't remember the attack. I had sauntered out of the hotel, breathed in that night air I had so looked forward to, walked a few yards, turned a corner and that had been that.

My eyes slowly opened and my ears took in the birdsong heralding the dawn. I thought I knew where I was. Then I heard footsteps of people in a hurry.

"Christ," said Carlito. "What the hell happened to you?"

I didn't have time to answer. Someone who wasn't Carlito put his arms under my battered body and manoeuvred me into a fireman's lift. I didn't cry out. There was no extra pain. Whoever it was humped me down the alleyway and turned into the street leading back to the hotel.

I heard Carlito say something about an ambulance.

I opened my eyes again. A small crowd had gathered. I heard chatter and even laughter and then a siren. My saviour eased me on to a trolley. I felt the needle plunged into my right buttock. I faded into a half-dream of waving colours and featureless shapes.

****

"Drink this," said Carlito. He lifted up my head and with my eyes closed I slurped at a glass of ice cold water. I blinked and saw four faces staring at me as if I was an exhibit in a natural history museum.

"Well, Charlie. They don't like you, do they? They don't like you being around and shoving your nose into things that don't concern you." Carlito's attempt at mild sarcasm had its effect. I grinned or at least pulled my mouth into what I thought was the right shape.

"I don't recall a thing," I croaked through the gurgling water in my throat. "I was behaving myself. After your magnificent history lesson, I wasn't particularly tired, didn't feel like sleep, so took a stroll to clear my head."

"Only, somebody cleared it for you," said one of the faces at the foot of my bed.

"Who am I talking to?" I asked, turning to Carlito.

"Friends," he replied. "May I introduce Juan Codina, plainclothes policeman, and Pedro Fraguas who is your doctor. Elena you already know."

My fuzzy eyesight had melded the faces into one. I re-focussed so that I saw four again. Only now did I recognise Elena, which was exceedingly stupid of me since the beauty I'd acknowledged at the dig was there before me in all its glory. She smiled and a few of my aches and pains suddenly vanished.

I remembered my manners and nodded as courteously as I could to the whole group. I was embarrassed by becoming aware that under the sheet I was wearing a hospital gown and not much else.

"Pedro says you were lucky. Bruises and cuts by the bucketful but no broken bones."

"Cuts? What cuts? Who cut me?"

Pedro was examining the medical chart attached to a clipboard hanging from the foot of the bed. "Your attacker tried to use a knife on you. He seems to have had a go at your right arm. Thankfully, he left it at that. I suggest you stay there for today."

"And I will square it with the hotel that they don't charge you for a night's lodging."

"You can be boringly practical, Carlito."

"I know, Charlie. It's the lawyer in me."

I was still eyeing Juan and Pedro.

80

Juan was tall and all muscle. He explained that he'd been the one to haul me up and put me in the ambulance. As and when I felt well enough, he'd like a bit more information.

"You've said you can't remember much. But Carlito tells me you went with him to a meeting at the *ayuntamiento* earlier in the evening where you might have made a couple of enemies."

"In a moment," I said and turned pointedly to Pedro.

He gave me a comforting smile. He was in his thirties and, as I was about to learn, much more than a hospital doctor.

"Pedro is also a politician," said Carlito.

"I belong to *Podemos*."

I couldn't stop coughing. Carlito handed me the glass of water. "Look," I said, trying to control myself. "This is all very interesting but my brain..." I lifted my right hand and put a finger to my forehead.

Elena came to my rescue. "We will leave you to rest. Carlito has asked me to come back this afternoon and keep you company..."

There were knowing looks all round and Pedro started to laugh.

"I can't think of anything nicer." I sighed.

Carlito moved a footstool closer to the bedside, climbed on it, bent towards me and gave me hug.

"*Un abrazo,* Charlie." He withdrew. He sniffed, turned and waved them all away.

You've joined quite a club there. Maybe you're right. Maybe you are doing what you should do, you interfering old hack. But look behind you next time you go for an evening paseo. *Please!*

Chapter 9

Elena and Juan came back in the late afternoon. I had slept for most of the day but not deeply. The small ward had buzzed quietly in the background with occasional suppressed dialogue between patients and staff. There were five other beds, but I hadn't the energy to lift my head and find out who was occupying them. At midday a young male orderly shook me gently and observed with heavy humour that my teeth seemed to be intact. So, would I like a *bocadillo* with ham and cheese? He even offered a glass of *tinto*.

"Not the very best but quite drinkable."

I accepted, chewed happily, sipped the wine and drifted into sleep again.

I woke when Elena kissed me on the forehead.

"Ola, mi héroe!" she whispered.

She took off her spectacles. I didn't want her to move. I wanted her to stay just there, her face not six inches from mine.

"Juan wants you to talk to him. Are you up to it?"

"Of course." I looked past her and waved a hand at the policeman. Elena stepped back and he took the bedside chair.

"I know you want an account of our little meeting at the town hall," I said. "Has Carlito given his version?"

Juan took a notepad and pen from his shirt pocket.

"He has. I'm not expecting yours to differ very much. But just tell me about this man, Pepe. Do you know his full name?"

"No. But I know he works as a car park attendant – Seville airport. First met him when I landed there two days ago. Turned shirty with me over a ticket. Said he never forgot a face." I gave him the story. "I was a bit surprised when I saw him again. Got a temper on him."

"How so?"

"Came for me – twice. But I still have a little combat training in me from the old days." I paused. "Mind you, it doesn't help a lot if you get ambushed from behind in a dark alleyway."

"Old days?" he asked.

"British army. Northern Ireland."

Juan raised an eyebrow and made an entry in his pad.

"Would you be interested," I offered, "if I told you that friend Pepe referred to one Jaime Martínez Ortiz as 'their good friend'?"

"The lawyer?"

"The same. With whom I have also met and conversed. In the bar at the Carmona *parador* and at that restaurant in the main square here."

"Did this Pepe say what the connection was, other than 'friendship', so to speak?"

"No. But since this bunch openly paraded themselves as members of the PP, I might assume Ortiz also belongs to the party."

"You assume correctly. He's a big name. Has a seat in the Madrid *Cortes.*" Juan paused to think. "But he wasn't there?"

"No."

I thought he was going to pursue a line about a top lawyer not being in the habit of cavorting with the party riff-raff. But he kept his counsel.

"Did Pepe threaten you again?"

"Yes. He said he'd settle with me later."

More scribbling.

"Have you any evidence that he was the one who bounced me?"

"Sadly, no. At least not yet. We've looked at your clothes and found a few hairs and possibly some stuff we could use as DNA. But we need samples from you as well."

"Got a pair of scissors and a swab on you? And please can I have my boxer shorts back?"

"You've still got your sense of humour." He smiled.

"Despite all. I try not to let it escape."

Juan did the necessary, cut a hair or two from what was left on my head and took a swab from inside my cheek.

"I shall leave you in peace," he said, "with this gracious lady." He gave me an old-fashioned look and an equally old-fashioned and very deep bow.

"And whose side is he on?" I asked when Juan had disappeared.

Elena had taken his place at my bedside. She wore her usual jeans and a much-laundered blue bush shirt. Her ebony hair was tied back into a bun on to which sunlight from a nearby window painted an iridescent sheen. She was laughing behind her spectacles and scrutinised me demurely.

"Juan? I would put him on the side of the angels. Not all our policeman are corrupt, especially the young ones."

I tried to concentrate on matters serious.

"Where's Carlito?"

"Who knows? I suspect he's holed up in his makeshift office behind large piles of paper. He's determined to sift out any trace of an identity for all the bones in the cemetery."

"Yes. He's conscientious to a fault."

She turned her head and gave me a disapproving look.

"I'm sorry," I said. "Carlito is amazing..."

"Given his disability, you mean?"

"Well, I don't see that his size has anything to do with it. It doesn't get in the way of what he wants to achieve. And he's certainly very brave. I was witness to that last night when we met the PP heavies. He never flinched. Never gave ground."

"But he was glad you were there to deal with the man called Pepe."

I admitted to that. "I certainly helped."

She laughed out loud this time. And took my hand.

We stared at one another for a long time.

"Elena. You don't want to get involved with an old fart like me."

Finally she said, "Oh, but I do."

She stood up, leaned towards me and kissed me full on the mouth.

"Now what do we do?" I asked stretching out my sore arms to grab her wrists.

"We fall in love. And your love for me will help me with my work. As will your expertise." She frowned. "And my love for you will provide all the background and all the facts for a story that has to get out." She paused for breath. "I'm pretty straightforward, aren't I? Pretty exploitative."

"Exploit away," I whispered in her ear as she bent towards me again.

"If only I could get into that bed," she said, fingering the sleeve of my gown.

"I don't think I'm in a fit state for that sort of thing."

"I can wait."

You've gone and done it again. You are going break her heart. Or she will break yours first.

I became boringly matter-of-fact. Since I had no serious injuries, I told Elena I was determined to discharge myself after one more night of sleep and the kind ministrations of Pedro and the hospital staff. After which, some time tomorrow, and with her permission, I would like to pay another visit to the cemetery, take some pictures and use my eyes a little more intelligently.

"Agreed," she said. "And I must get back there."

We kissed again, longingly and with our eyes open. She slipped away. I didn't exactly hear a chorus of angels, but I lay back in wonder that such a thing had happened.

****

But what story was I following? What was new about it? The exhumations were common knowledge. Even foreign news outlets like the BBC had done reports from Castillo, with pictures of mass graves and mutilated skeletons. There were no more secrets to come out. Just more stories about more incidents during the Civil War. Carlito told me they surfaced every week. Some hack would find yet another old woman in some small village who told him her husband and perhaps her children had been beaten and killed by Franco's troops. Or a newspaper would track down an old boy well into his eighties or nineties, still an avowed Franco supporter, who was doing his best to stay hidden in case he was recognised as a killer or one who had given orders to kill.

Right now I was too tired to think, too weary to mull over how it might develop. The afternoon wore on. I did wonder whether Carlito might return with some news about last night's encounter. Was the police investigation getting anywhere? Had any one picked up the dreadful Pepe? Or was he still making motorists' lives a misery at Seville airport?

But there was no Carlito, or Juan.

Pedro turned up in the early evening to give me the once-over.

"Good progress, Mr Barrow. Everything healing as it should. But you'll need some more painkillers." He didn't linger.

The orderly offered me a paella for an early supper – "Not too big – just enough to fend off starvation!" He had decided I was an appropriate target for his odd sense of humour. It might have been a strategy to stop me feeling sorry for myself. He needn't have bothered. I was happily distracted by thoughts of Elena.

The paella was genuine enough, with lightly cooked rice and full of the right flavours and bits and pieces – seafood, chicken and herbs. I realised I was hungry. Another glass of local *tinto* added to the momentary pleasure.

I had no reading matter but didn't care. My bruises were still sore and shifting around in bed brought back some of the pain. I couldn't have concentrated. When the orderly returned, I said I would like to go to the bathroom. He asked if I could manage on my own since he was busy with the evening meals. I considered the prospect and decided not to be a wimp. I heaved myself gently out of bed. It took me no more than a minute to hobble my way to a wash basin and toilet at the end of a corridor. When I'd finished, I braced myself for the return trip only to find Pepe blocking the doorway, leering like a hyena and holding something which looked very much like a baseball bat.

"I'm settling my account," he said.

I was in no state to fight him but instinct told me to stand my ground. He stepped forward and lifted the bat to shoulder height.

And crumpled gently to the floor. Then I saw Juan lift him up by his armpits only to let him drop again.

"You okay, *Señor* Charlie?" The question came from Pedro, standing behind Juan.

"How the hell did all this happen?" I asked.

They guided me to a small chair.

"Very easy," said Juan. "He's been advertising himself. After talking to you, I went back to the *ayuntamiento* and had a word with the mayor. He confirmed the details of what happened last night and I had a scout round the room where the meeting had been held. Then I went to the alleyway where you were attacked and found one or two more samples of clothing and hair, not to say a little dried blood. I walked back to the main street and into your hotel. And I have to tell you I had a look in your room."

I nodded. "I'm not outraged. You were doing your job. Did you find anything useful?"

"It had been trashed a little. Your books and papers were all over the place. Your clothes had been dragged out of the wardrobe and scattered over the bed."

"My laptop?"

"Still there. Case unopened."

"Lucky me."

"I think they were disturbed and got out fast. When I came down from your room, the guy in reception told me he'd tried to stop two visitors from bulldozing their way upstairs, but they'd pushed him so hard that he fell behind his desk. He'd called the police but no one answered. Later he said your visitors were definitely not Spanish. More like Moroccans or Algerians."

Juan paused and took a deep breath.

"Idiots," he said. "We have an old sergeant at the station who's supposed sit in his booth, deal with callers and take phone messages. But he wanders off for a smoke when he feels like it."

By this time I had lifted myself back into bed. Two young uniforms had pulled Pepe to his feet and handcuffed him. He was bawling like a demented bull. Orderlies rushed in to see what was happening.

"No need to fuss," said Pedro. "All under control. Back to work."

"Take him and put him in a cell," said Juan to the uniforms. "He'll talk to me later if he knows what's good for him."

I looked at Juan. "But how did you know Pepe would wander in here and threaten me again?"

The tale was that Pepe had gone on a bender and was walking about the streets, insulting all and sundry not least me, the workers up at the cemetery and his bête noire, the Socialist mayor. All Juan had to do was follow him.

"He wasn't so drunk that he failed to work out where I was," I muttered ruefully.

"Good thing I was right behind him then." Juan grinned.

"And where, by the way, is Carlito?"

"He left a message with our unlucky receptionist. He's gone down to Carmona to get some important papers. He'll be back this evening."

"How's he travelling?"

"Took the local bus. Carlito is nothing if not intrepid."

Juan gave me a knowing look. "Stay in bed, Charlie. You've still got some recovering to do. We'll put an officer on the front door."

I told him of my plan to stay in hospital for one more night.

Pedro nodded his assent. "That sounds sensible," he said.

"But I'll be around and about tomorrow." I wanted to make a point of that. "We need to talk – you, me, Carlito and Elena. I want to find out why an apparently respectable governing party like the PP employs thugs to stop journalists doing their job. And I also want to know why Ortiz has well-heeled assistants from North Africa to do his dirty work."

"Sleep on it, Charlie. Let's see what friend Pepe has to tell us."

****

This time I cursed the fact that I had no reading matter. I could have asked the orderly to fetch me a Spanish newspaper, but I wasn't in a state to wrestle with a language I had only just begun to understand. I lay back and thought of Elena and wondered why she had admitted to falling for me.

It must be your battered English charm. And you're letting yourself get carried away. I know all the signs.

I conceded I was in love again. My wish to meet a substitute for Dagmar had been granted.

You are suffering from an unsettling combination of hubris and sentimentality and an inability to spot emotional mine fields before they blow up in your face.

Don't be so pompous.

But I admitted that I should have been thinking about other things. I should have been thinking about why I'd been beaten up, about the meeting in the town hall, about Pepe's appearance in the hospital and about the exhumations. But I wasn't in the mood. My limbs still ached and my nose had started to bleed.

Christ, Charlie Barrow, you are in a mess.

I stretched out an arm and rang the bedside bell.

"Ay! Vaya con Dios. Qué desorden!"

94

The orderly found a damp towel, sponged my face and said he would bring me a strong painkiller. I swallowed it down, lay back and tried desperately to utter my thanks. The pills worked fast. The pain ebbed away and I sailed into semi-consciousness. No dreams this time. Just a miasma of floaters and more strange colours at the back of my eyes.

I opened them. The ward lights had been dimmed. It was early evening. A shape appeared in the doorway. I began to toy with notions that it might be one of the ungodly on a mission to finish me off.

"Charlie?"

The shape lost its menace. It was Juan. I relaxed and gave him a lame welcome with my right hand.

"Jesus. I thought you were another Pepe," I croaked. He wasn't smiling.

"Don't worry. He won't be bothering you again."

"I can bank on that, can I?"

"He's dead, Charlie."

There was a long silence. I heard the distant noises of the hospital and the wisp of a gentle guitar from someone's radio. Juan let his news sink in.

"How?"

"We found him sprawled on the floor of his cell with a bullet hole at the back of his left ear and an exit wound on his forehead."

"You went back to question him?" This, on reflection, was not a particularly useful contribution to our conversation but it was all I could think of right now.

"True. A colleague unlocked the cell door. He took one step inside, turned round and nearly fainted. I pushed past him and there was our friend, face down on the tiles."

Juan took the bedside chair and sat close to my left ear.

"Before you ask, we have no idea how it was done. The station is in panic mode and my seniors are the worst of all. We thought the sensational was a thing of the past. Clearly we're wrong. We've screwed up."

"You haven't screwed up. You caught him in the act and handcuffed him. Your lads marched him back to the station and locked him up. You stayed here to question me. Why are you taking the rap?"

"I'm not, Charlie. I've already interrogated those who were on duty and I've gone as far as I dare with accusations of incompetence and appeals to my superiors to calm down."

Another pause while he scratched his chin and I shifted into a more comfortable position.

"I've already been told by the woman who heads the Scene of Crime team that the slug they found in a far corner of the cell was a nine-millimetre bullet from a Sig Sauer combat pistol – standard Police and Civil Guard issue."

"An inside job?"

Juan stayed non-committal.

"So, what do we do now?"

"You, Charlie, do nothing – until tomorrow. But I would like to leave you with a question or two. What did Ortiz tell you when you met him in Carmona?"

"I can answer that now. Not much. He told me he was lawyer. And he caught me reading a piece in a newspaper about the exhumations. Called it 'a touchy subject'. Gave me a short lesson in Spanish history and took a call on his mobile. He turned away from me and all I could pick up was some rapid mumbling. But I did hear him say something like 'see you in Castillo tomorrow night'."

"That's useful."

"And he gave his caller a burst of angry Arabic."

"It gets better."

"But I've already told you – he wasn't at the bust up in the *ayuntamiento* even though Pepe blurted out his name and called him 'a good friend'. Presumably a friend of those opposed to the exhumations?"

"Anything else?"

"Well, when Carlito and I stumbled across him in the restaurant here in town, he made it clear he knew Carlito and I had dined together at another place. He also said it was none of my business asking him who he'd been dining with. And he asked me why I was so interested in knowing more about the Civil War and its legacy. I never gave him an answer because he shoved off to join his Arab friends and the man I now know to be Father Trujillo."

"Describe these Arabs."

"Big tall blokes with fashionable stubble and shaven heads. Smart black chinos, blue short-sleeved shirts. A bit of discreet jewellery. Gold chains and such like."

"That's all?"

"I'm doing my best, Juan." I looked at him apologetically. "It almost proves he's got his eye on me and, given his status and connections, he'll probably find a way of getting me chucked out of Spain if I start asking too many questions. But none of it gets you very far, does it?"

Juan adopted his wise look. "It doesn't tell me much that I don't already know about Ortiz, but it helps to reinforce the impression that he's closer to the opponents of exhumation than I thought he was."

I didn't see that as progress.

He pushed his pad and pen into his shirt pocket and left. I kept my eyes on the ward entrance for a while before my lids drooped for one last time and I subsided into sleep.

Chapter 10

I woke early. The hospital was quiet, but I sensed bustle in the air. A new orderly asked me if I wanted breakfast – rolls, ham, jam and sweet meats, and a pot of coffee. This brought me to my senses. There was work to do. I must get up.

Pedro appeared, scanned my charts and gave me the professional eye.

"Okay. You can go. As long as you take it carefully for a while. I'll probably see you later at your hotel. I have things to pass on to Carlito."

Curious as I was, I decided not to ask the obvious question.

The orderly fetched my clothes. As I dressed, I realised my mobile had been tucked into my trouser-pocket all the time I'd been in hospital. But I didn't have the numbers I wanted – Carlito, Elena, Juan.

"Bugger." As if responding to my curse, it buzzed.

"Carlito!" I shouted. "Where are you? Where've you been? I'm discharged. I'm on my way back to the hotel."

Carlito told me in no uncertain terms to stay where I was. He was coming round with the car. Juan had assigned a junior to drive it to the hospital. I was to sit quietly in the reception area and wait for him.

He sauntered through the front door, sized me up and grinned. I bent down to receive his *abrazo* and realised how strong he was.

"Careful now. I have some tender spots."

"Come on," he said. "Time for that council of war."

He didn't tell me if he knew about Pepe. He wanted to get back to the hotel before catching up on the news.

Deep down, you know who's boss, don't you?

And why do I think it matters?

****

The pains were fading. I could walk surely and steadily, but my face still felt sore. It wasn't the physical infirmities I was worried about. I was trying to dispel fears that I was losing my grip on events. I sat down in one of the lobby armchairs and listened quietly to Carlito telling me how he had filled the twenty-four hours I'd spent in hospital. I made a desperate effort to appear knowing and wise.

"I made discoveries," he said. We had a large pot of coffee in front of us and mountains of paper. "I have

100

managed to match names to some of the bones and corpses. I burned the midnight oil in my Carmona office, but I did it."

If he was suffering from lack of sleep he didn't show it.

"We must now get back up to the cemetery and you will help me put the jigsaw together."

"Fortress of Dwarves?"

"That will have to wait. You see, what's important is the fact that I have been able to do the matching but the paperwork also provides proof of who gave orders to kill individual victims – even who actually pulled a trigger or wielded a spade or an iron bar. The documents give them away."

We swallowed two more cups of coffee.

"I must get some notebooks and my laptop," I said. I carefully climbed the stairs to my room. I didn't notice that the door wasn't locked. The thought of having to use a key had gone out of my head. Someone had tidied my belongings and made the bed. Everything I needed was where it was supposed to be. Juan had been a good boy.

We walked out to the car.

"Can you drive, Charlie? Arse not too sore?"

"Just watch me," I countered.

I suppose you're better off doing this than nursing your wounded pride between cotton sheets.

I took the road to the cemetery, trying to keep within the urban speed limit. I persuaded myself that it gave me time to work out my own plan of action.

****

She stood in the centre of one of the trenches, weeping bitter tears. She clasped her hands over her mouth and let her shoulders shake as if she had no control over what was happening to her. The area had been taped off. Three police officers in uniform and a couple of Civil Guards watched her, with arms folded or hands fingering their guns, nonchalant, without expression, until Carlito and I appeared, walking the path to the exhumation site.

An officer raised his hands to bar our way.

"You cannot enter. This is a crime scene."

"Who are you?" asked Carlito, standing his ground.

"Delgado," he said. "Inspector Delgado. National Police. Who are you, *Señor*?"

Carlito took a deep breath and launched into an explanation of his work with the ARMH. The officer looked doubtful.

"And who is this gentleman?"

Carlito embarked on a verbose description of my part in proceedings, trying hard to inflate my importance.

She had heard the chatter and looked up.

"Let them through, officer. Please."

We ducked under the police tape. Elena stepped towards us and held out her hands, one grasping Carlito's, the other my forearm. She kissed us both and held my gaze with eyes as sad as they could have been.

"Come and look at what they have done," she said.

Delgado had got the message and waved us in.

The trench was a shambles. Bones and skulls lay scattered and smashed with remnants of clothing torn into ever thinner shreds, as if whoever had done this had given way to an all-consuming rage and a desire to vent their wrath upon the dead. Someone had taken a spade or a pick to the red earth, turning it over into random heaps. The carefully laid markers and measurement ropes had been wrenched out of position and ripped to pieces. Painstaking work had been wrecked in a single night.

I turned to Delgado. "Is it a crime scene because of the damage and the vandalism or because these graves have been desecrated?"

"We haven't got as far as formally classifying it," he replied not without some sympathy. "Scene of Crime officers will be up here in the next hour. They'll decide how we proceed after that."

We stood at the edge of the vandalised trench, my arms round the shoulders of Carlito on my left and Elena to my right.

"I wish I knew how to pray," she said, trying hard to compose herself.

"I'm not in a mood to pray," I ventured.

"I can lay good odds on who did this." said Carlito. "Especially after what's been happening to us all in the last forty-eight hours."

Elena fought back her tears and explained. "I got here at first light. As soon as I saw what had happened, I called the police. They were here within ten minutes. And the two from the Civil Guard. It looks as if there's a dispute between them over whose case this is. But they haven't come to blows yet."

We heard shouts and curses. The Civil Guards raised their guns and readied them. The police uniforms ran to where the noise was coming from. A small, angry crowd emerged from the trees, about forty women and men of all ages and one or two children.

"We want to see what they have done," shouted a girl holding the hand of a frightened toddler.

"How the hell did this get out?" I asked one of the uniforms in English. He understood me well enough to shrug his shoulders and mutter, *"Rumores y pueblerino."*

"Rumour runs fast in a place as small as this." Delgado had placed himself in front of his men and raised his hands. The crowd calmed down a little.

"You speak English then?"

"Enough, *Señor.*"

Carlito had caught us up. Delgado asked him to tell the crowd what had happened. "A warning though. Name no names. Just describe it."

"I know what I'm doing, Inspector. I'm a lawyer."

"Exactly," said the policeman.

Carlito asked them if they knew about the work Elena and her team had been doing at the cemetery. They clapped their hands in unison.

"Yes," said one woman. "We know you are trying to find out who killed these poor people in '36. Some of us have watched you. We've watched how you arrange the bones and the other stuff. We watched how you treated them with respect so that they can be given a decent burial when time allows."

"That's good," said Carlito. He then explained who he was, what his work involved and why it mattered. They listened while a breeze fanned a spiral of red dust and a flight of quarrelsome sparrows settled in the trees.

Again they nodded. An old man pushed his way to the front.

"They have violated the place," he shouted. "We want to see."

Carlito asked him how he'd found out what had happened.

"It's all over town. Come on. Let us through."

Some in the crowd cheered him on.

A boy with a dog came forward. "I found them first," he said. An old woman stepped alongside him.

"I am Celestina," she said, "otherwise known to most of these people as *La Bruja*. This is Juan José and this is Orlando." She pointed to the Labrador who squatted patiently next to the boy. "It was about three months ago. They came to me and Juan José told me what they'd discovered during the night."

Elena stepped forward. "That's true," she said. "It was soon after that that we started work here. Once the boy had told the police, the whole town came to look. The press got hold of the story. We had to act quickly – organize the site before it was disturbed again."

"We want to see," grunted the old man.

Delgado looked at Elena and Carlito. Then at me.

"I can't have them wandering all over a crime scene," he said.

There was more shouting and yelling among the trees. Half a dozen men in t-shirts and jeans appeared, one of them waving a hand gun. Yet another pushed past them. He wore a smart suit and designer shades. And with him came his minders.

"Bloody Arabs," someone shouted.

Jaime Martínez Ortiz strode up to Delgado. He pulled a piece of paper from inside his jacket.

"I have here a *mandamiento judicial...*" Then, looking straight at me, he said, "An injunction, in your language, Charlie Barrow. An injunction from a judge ordering all work on this site to stop – and stop right now."

"It has been stopped," I said. "Stopped by a bunch of vandals who've desecrated the place. Do you want to see for yourself, Ortiz?"

He hesitated, looked at Delgado, at the uniforms and the Civil Guards then at Carlito and Elena and the assembled throng. Delgado snatched the paper from him gave it a quick glance and handed it to Carlito. Carlito smiled. He held it out in front of him, peered at it and then very slowly traced the first finger of his right hand over the text.

"Come on," urged Ortiz. "You know what it says. You're as much a lawyer as I am."

"All in good time, *Señor.* Meanwhile, why don't my friends here escort you to the site and let you see for yourself what's been done to it?"

Elena seized Ortiz by the arm. He was off balance and had no choice. She dragged him through the police tapes and forced him to look at the damage.

The minders who'd accompanied him barged their way through the crowd of villagers, but the two Civil Guards blocked them.

"Give me that gun," one of the Guards ordered. The thug waved it in the air. The Guard was too quick for him. Using the butt of his firearm, he knocked the weapon out of the man's hand and in one unbroken move had him in an arm lock. The man yelled in pain.

"Shut up," hissed the Guard.

"Well, well," said Delgado picking up the gun. "A Sig Sauer nine-millimetre."

"Police issue?" I asked.

He nodded. The other Guard had advanced towards the remaining minders who stood their ground, while the villagers shouted more obscenities. The dog Orlando decided the time had come to indulge in some fearsome barking.

Carlito, meanwhile, had joined Elena and Ortiz. Inspector Delgado decided to confide in me.

"The usual bunch of suspects," he said. "Probably from Ceuta or Melilla just across the water. They go around with that toffee-nosed lawyer all the time."

"But what about this one?" I asked. The minder who'd brandished the gun was now in handcuffs. The Civil Guard who'd disarmed him handed him over to a police uniform.

"Keep him in the car," ordered Delgado.

"What I mean is," I ventured, "who sent him and his mates with intent to make mischief? And why was Ortiz with them?"

Elena, Carlito and Ortiz had walked back from the graves.

"Seen enough?" I asked.

Ortiz was silent. His bluster had vanished but not his polish and his pride. He was stunned and confused but adept at hiding it.

"I think," said Carlito carefully, "that *Señor* Martínez Ortiz has seen what he needs to see to conclude that his injunction is a little premature if not irrelevant."

There was another buzz of chatter from the villagers. Out from among them stepped my favourite detective, Juan Codina. He walked straight up to Ortiz.

"Jaime Martínez Ortiz. I have a warrant for your arrest," he said.

Ortiz stared at him. "I don't think I understand you," he said. "Who are you?"

"Detective Juan Codina, Castillo police. You are charged with the murder of Ernesto Baron, otherwise known as Pepe. You will be detained in jail until I am ready to take a formal statement from you answering the charge."

It was briskly done. Ortiz began to say something, but Delgado stepped forward, brandishing a set of cuffs. He seized the lawyer's wrists and had them clipped in double quick time. Again the minders made no move. They tried to outstare the Civil Guards, but the officers were too well trained to be intimidated. And they had weapons.

Delgado handed over his captive. Then Juan Codina marched him off, pushing his way through the crowd which was now as quietly transfixed as the rest of us. The minders made no attempt to interfere. They retreated slowly, step by step. Then took a collective decision to leave, scurrying out of the cemetery back to their vehicles.

Carlito broke the general silence.

"Back to town, Charlie. We have work to do."

I looked at Elena.

"*We* have work to do too," she said. "I must help the others."

Delgado and his men had started to herd the villagers towards the path leading to the exit.

"My colleagues from the *Guardia Civil* will stay to prevent any more intrusions," he said. "My men and I will follow Detective Codina." Turning to Carlito and me, he said, "I think you should follow us."

We were not about to refuse.

Chapter 11

"They're bringing him before the examining magistrate. tomorrow morning," said Carlito. "The *juez de instrucción.*"

We were back at the hotel, sitting at a low table in the lobby, Carlito with a coffee, me with a beer.

"Where is he now?" I asked

"In a police cell. He'll stay there until they take a formal statement from him. This gives him a chance to answer the murder charge. I don't think they'll let him out until after tomorrow's hearing."

"I expect he's got a good lawyer."

"Won't do him much good today. All a lawyer can do now is have a private chat with him." He frowned. "But I expect you're right. He'll have the best the PP can provide. The man will be rushing down from Madrid right now."

He paused.

"Or he might decide to defend himself. God knows, he's got all the qualifications."

"What will happen in court?"

"Oh, Charlie. Don't ask me to second-guess that one."

"But the procedure. Tell me about that."

Carlito sighed. I detected impatience – impatience with me. "There'll be a brief oral examination by the magistrate. The public prosecutor will be there too. They'll look at the evidence provided by young Juan and decide whether Ortiz has a case to answer. If they say 'yes' to that, then they'll decide whether he should be released for the time being – it's call 'provisional liberty' – with or without bail, or they could remand him pending further investigation. If the magistrate and the prosecutor say 'no', he'll be released without further charge. And Juan's going to look silly."

"What do you expect?"

"Don't keep pushing me, Charlie. I don't know. Let's see tomorrow."

Carlito was being his cautious lawyer's self. But he did tell me of cases in Spain where murder suspects had been held without trial for up to two years. And if the magistrate had reason to believe the accused might abscond if released, he could extend the pre-trial detention period by a further two years. In theory, Ortiz could languish in jail for four years before the case went to a criminal court. But that was wishful thinking.

"So, he's in deep?" I said, trying not to show that I was building up my hopes.

"It all depends on Juan Codina, who's not going to tell us much more at this stage. We don't know how watertight his evidence is."

I didn't want to believe that our young detective had made a mistake or done a sloppy job. On the other hand, someone somewhere had slipped up or been paid to turn a blind eye. How else had they got to Pepe and finished him off?

My immediate concern was to fill the hours between the afternoon and the next morning. Carlito looked as if he didn't want to be bothered with me. He was keeping something back, I was sure.

"I'm off to explore," I said.

"Well, don't get bashed over the head again. You've caused enough trouble as it is."

I was about to mouth a clever rejoinder but given his mood, thought better of it. I got up and left.

****

I kept clear of police stations and town halls and official-looking buildings. I found a small *libreria* and bought the newspapers. Then headed for the restaurant where I had run into Ortiz the day before. It was three o'clock or thereabouts. The place was humming. Elena sat at a table in a corner, shaded by one of those vast parasols for which bars and cafés throughout Europe seemed to have developed a fondness.

She waved, beckoned and tried to smile.

"I thought you might come," she said.

"A bit of a long shot," I replied. "How could you know I'd be making for this place?"

"Instinct, I suppose. But you remember – you told me you were here with Carlito on your first day in town and ran into Ortiz."

"Did I? Events have moved rather swiftly of late. My advancing age is taking its toll of my powers of recall."

"Don't be facetious, Charlie. In any case, aren't you glad to see me?

"More than you know."

We ordered food and drink. Elena said she'd left her team to work on clearing up the devastation at the exhumation site.

"I didn't have the guts to go on looking at the damage," she said. "They've been very kind to me, letting me go. They're tougher than me."

"We'll both go back later and I'll impart some moral courage."

"You're being facetious again."

"No. Just trying to relieve your heartache. In any case, I want to spend more time with you up there, prising more detail out of you – I'm not quite sure what sort of detail, but I suspect you know more about the individual corpses and bones than you've passed on so far. And if I can get some names out of you, I'll make my own enquiries about the surviving families of the victims. And all that sort of thing," I finished airily with a wide grin and an expansive wave of the hands.

She laughed. We ate and drank and sniffed the smells of the restaurant, cheeses, herbs, meats and a whiff of cooking from the distant kitchen.

Elena leaned back, took off her glasses, closed her eyes and let the sun do more work on her tawny skin and ebony hair. While she relaxed, I stole a look at a newspaper. And there it was – the first report of the arrest of a rather influential lawyer attached to the *Partido Popular*, in a small town in Andalucía, charged with the inexplicable murder of a man locked in a police cell after beating up a foreign visitor, said to be a British tourist officially registered as a resident at the *parador* in Carmona.

At least they hadn't fingered me as a journalist. But it was nimbly done. And once Ortiz was in court, the pace would quicken. In which case I had better move a little more briskly myself – email my desks in the UK and Australia and sell them the story.

"Charlie," she murmured. "Let's go."

"Where to?"

"Just pay the bill and follow me."

I threw up my hands again. Instead of waiting for the waiter, I walked into the bar and slapped some notes on the counter. "Okay?" I asked.

"Okay, *Señor*. Pretty lady?" He didn't snigger, just eyed me sympathetically.

Outside, Elena took my arm and led me a few yards from the restaurant into a narrow street of small houses with blindingly white walls and balconies festooned with blood red geraniums. We came to a small green door and sidled into a shady passage, out into a small courtyard with the obligatory fountain splashing merrily away. Climbing a spiral ironwork stairway, we came to another green door through which we slipped and fell into one another's arms.

We stayed absolutely still for a couple of minutes. Then Elena slipped from my grasp, walked across the room and opened one of the large windows. A light breeze fluttered the flimsy cotton curtain. We heard the distant noises of the town and a smattering of an animated conversation between two women in the street below.

Elena looked straight at me, peeled off her t-shirt and bra and waited for me to make the next move. When men undress, they seem incapable of doing it elegantly or efficiently. I fumbled at buttons and belt and, Goddam it, socks. Elena took charge. Suddenly we were both naked and breathing deeply.

To say that the next hour of my life was pure paradise would be a callous understatement. Making

116

love to this woman, stroking her olive skin with its slight sheen of sweat, tasting her lips, holding one soft hand and touching softer breasts, I could hardly believe that one of my missions to Spain had been accomplished. I had stumbled on absolute splendour. This was not just sex and lust. This was romance and adulation all rolled into one vast emotion.

"Why me?" I muttered at last.

"You asked me that before in the hospital."

"So?"

"Why do you need an answer? It's happened."

I could not think of a suitable reaction. She lay to the right of me, stretching to her full length. I ran my fingers into a dimple in one of her thighs. She sighed and began playing with me again, bringing me to another climax. I stayed quiet and let it happen. We must have made love three or four times in no more than half an hour.

"I didn't know I was still capable of that," I said.

"Has it been a long time since you had sex?"

"Not that long." I told her about Dagmar in Berlin and the manner of our parting.

"That's sad," she said.

"Yes and no. We were getting nowhere."

"Are we getting anywhere?

"Elena! We shall have to wait and see, shan't we?"

She sighed and moved a little. Then turned towards me again.

"I have not had sex in months," she said.

"Well, you certainly haven't forgotten very much in that time."

"I love your cheek, Charlie. I love your wicked smile. I love your English scepticism."

"Do you love my English paunch?"

"There you are, you see. You love bursting all the balloons, don't you?"

I fondled her again.

"Stop!" she said.

Now you've gone and done it. Obviously you've committed a sexual solecism. All your visions of contentment are about to evaporate.

"What have I done?" I spluttered. "What's wrong?"

"Nothing's wrong." She giggled. "I just want to see this paunch of yours."

I was told to get off the bed and stand up. She eyed me up and down. And laughed again.

"That's no paunch, Charlie Barrow. That is, if anything, the slow start of middle age spread."

She knelt on the mattress and held out her arms.

"Come here." I felt her embrace again. She pushed me back and patted my stomach. And kissed it.

If ever I felt waves of relief engulfing me, I felt them now.

"Why are you crying?"

"Am I?" I answered. "Isn't it obvious, why? I have never felt like this in my whole life, Elena."

She dragged me back on to the bed. We made love yet again.

"Neither have I," she said.

"Neither have you what?"

"You've just said that you have never felt like this in your whole life. So, I'm telling you – neither have I."

"Sex made me forget."

"Oh, we mustn't let it do that again, Charlie."

She rose from the bed and tiptoed into her small kitchen. I heard the tinkling of glass and the gurgle of poured liquid. She walked back holding two *copas* of white wine.

"To us, Charlie."

I said nothing, simply raised my own glass in return.

"We know next to nothing about one another," she said. "We must talk."

"Well, you know that I'm a journalist, who's supposed to be on holiday, supposed to be getting away from it all. I'm nearly fifty. I was born in the north of England. I was sent away to school. I hated it but learned enough French and German to get me a place at university. I decided to join the army so they took me into Intelligence and taught me Russian and Hungarian. I served in Northern Ireland. Not a pleasant experience. When I got out, I bamboozled a couple of London newspaper editors into taking me on. I learned on the job and lingered on their news desks until boredom turned me into a freelance and I went abroad – all over the place – south east Asia, the Middle East, communist Europe."

I stopped. Then said, "Sorry about my Spanish. It's just getting going."

She smiled. We were still naked. I couldn't avert my eyes. She stepped towards me.

"I'll tell you about myself later," she said. "And your Spanish is getting better and better. Almost as good as your lovemaking."

Chapter 12

We went back to the exhumation site. Buoyed by what we had done, we grinned like baboons in a zoo and violated all road safety regulations. We held hands, avoided trite conversation and let the wind waft through the Polo's open windows. Elena drove with her slim fingers on the wheel, faster than I'd expected. I laughed out loud, just once. She continued smiling silently behind her sunglasses, occasionally tossing a knowing glance towards me.

Her team had done a magnificent job. The site had been put back into something like good order.

"In so far as we could," said Alex, Elena's chief assistant. He looked exhausted, his denim shirt smeared with sweat and dust. It wasn't that hot now, in the late afternoon, but there had been precious little cloud to hide a persistent sun. "Marrying the bones to the right skulls again and sorting out the bits of clothing – it's well-nigh impossible, Elena. We will have to do it piece by piece and we will have to make educated guesses about matching them to one another."

"But you've made a good start."

He gave a resigned smile. "We need more DNA tests. It'll take time."

"That's a handsome young man," I said to her later.

"That handsome young man is gay, Charlie. I love and respect him dearly but not quite in the same way as I love and respect you. He's a well-qualified anthropologist and a very hard worker. And he needs all the encouragement I can give him right now."

"I haven't done *anything* to earn your respect," I said.

She ignored this. "Come and look at the bones more closely." She took me by the hand and almost dragged me into the pit of russet earth.

"Kneel down. Look really close."

I bent my head as near to one of the skulls as I thought decent. Elena had donned some surgical gloves and slowly rotated the skull. I saw two holes, one in the forehead, the second in the nape of the neck.

"The bullet was fired from behind and went right through the head so that the victim would fall forward into the grave."

I was used to seeing dead bodies and the consequences of violence. But I almost retched as I took this in.

"Look again."

I scanned the ground and saw a row of shell casings neatly arranged by one of Alex's team.

"Now look at the rest of the skeleton."

"Male or female?"

"Female. Young. Might have been pregnant."

From the way the bones of the arms had been laid out it seemed clear that the victim's hands had been tied behind her back.

This time I had had the foresight to bring a camera. Elena left me to shoot as many pictures as I could manage. She strode back to the shade of the blue and white awning and fell deep into conversation with Alex and the other workers. I pulled out a notebook and started to write key words and phrases to be used in later copy – femur, tibia, fibula, clavicle, scapula, cranium, mandible – and so it went on. Knowing how pernickety the editors at my outlets were, I had to make sure I got all this stuff right.

"You work the old-fashioned way?"

I was so preoccupied I hadn't noticed that she'd returned and was watching me scribbling and sucking the end of my pen.

"This is the way I *know* how to work. A camera is a sufficient enough hindrance. I can do without tape recorders, mobiles, MP3s and all that."

"What do you want to do now?"

"A very leading question, *Señora.*"

But Elena had decided. For the time being there was no more to see here. We bade goodbye to Alex and his colleagues and drove back into town.

"Instead of making love, Charlie Barrow, I want to do something else with you."

Don't be disappointed. Over-gilding the lily of this affair will be unwise. Patience. Not a quality you are especially gifted with.

"Such as?"

She drove on in silence and I didn't interrupt. We parked outside a different restaurant just off the main square. She took me by the hand again. We entered a room where the air was cool and the light refreshingly dimmer than in the sun-baked street outside. There was music. I had been in Spain less than a week but might have expected to encounter the sound of a guitar well before now.

"Listen to him," said Elena.

"Where is he?" I couldn't see the source of the music.

"The other side of that pillar." She nodded in the direction of a dark corner where a small figure caressed the six strings of his instrument. The sequence of notes was soft and smooth, yet sharp enough to cut through the general murmur of conversation.

I focussed my eyes on the dark corner.

"Christ! It's Carlito."

When the opportunity presented itself, I got pleasure from playing a kind of lazy jazz on a piano. I'd picked it up as a teenager just before I left school. After a hefty and indigestible dose of instruction in the classics, I knew I would never play Mozart, Beethoven and Bach with any skill. But I did learn my chords and became hooked on Oscar Peterson, Teddy Wilson, Art Tatum, André Previn and many others. For a time, between jobs in the Intelligence Corps and newspapers, I made a shilling or two playing in bars and hotel lounges up and down the motorways of England. I found I could improvise my own tunes and even sold a couple of songs to a man who performed regularly at Ronnie Scott's in London.

But I had never known the guitar except as an instrument that went with rock and heavy metal. And I didn't like rock and heavy metal.

"This is what he does when you don't know where he is."

Carlito was using no amplification, no plectrum, nothing but his long fingers and nails and the thumb of his right hand. Elena put a finger to her lips. I listened and watched him pluck and stroke the strings, sometimes so violently that I expected them to snap. His left hand moved up and down the finger board, often at high speed, but static at other moments as if his life depended on clinging to a single chord. He stared almost ferociously, now at his instrument, now at the wooden beams above him, then at his sunburned hands.

Elena led me to a table well to the rear of the restaurant.

"Don't wave, Charlie. Don't distract him. He will join us when he's finished."

I didn't need to be told. I slowly moved a chair and sat down, very carefully indeed.

Carlito played on. He had exchanged his lawyer's suit for a loose, white shirt and a pair of red trousers. I wanted to ask Elena many questions. Where, how, when had Carlito found the time and the opportunity to study and practise his instrument? Later she told me that Carlito's music was a kind of *flamenco*. Not the sort to inspire dancers dressed in traditional costume to stamp their feet and snap their fingers or grasp the air with outlandish movements of the hand. This was music designed to be listened to, absorbed and mulled over. The sensations it might arouse were to be savoured like fine wine.

"But listen hard. And you will hear the dance within," she said.

A waiter had responded to a sign from Elena, bringing us a carafe and the usual *tapas*. He placed them in front of us so deftly that I hardly noticed. When the music came to an end, there was sudden, wild applause from the clientele. Decorum was discarded. People rose from their chairs and continued clapping and shouting for more. Holding the neck of his guitar in his left hand, Carlito raised his right in a gesture of thanks. The applause turned to laughter as Carlito made a solemn promise to do more after a little refreshment.

He put his guitar safely into a case and handed the whole thing over to a delighted head waiter. He wove his way to our table, shaking many hands en route. Heads turned towards us. Who were we to be so fortunate as to have this man for a friend?

"I made Elena promise not to tell you about this until you actually heard me," he said. "Now you know that..."

"...You are not just a lawyer with a mission?"

"I object to your use of the word 'just'. But to all intents and purposes you are right, Charlie Barrow."

"So tell me the history."

"All in good time. I need a drink."

Elena poured some *tinto* and he sat back and smiled at us.

"When I first met you," I said, "you seemed a prime example of a realist, a man without sentimentality, someone a million miles from art and music and all the sloppy stuff of life."

"Well, now you know better." He grinned at Elena. "Charlie has a lovable naivety that's easy to exploit," he said. "I convinced him I was such a cynic..."

"I didn't say you were a cynic. You wouldn't be doing your painstaking work with the Association if you were. But I didn't expect you to be a consummate artist as well."

"This conversation is getting nowhere," scolded Elena.

We were subdued by this and took a moment or two to drink some wine and eat the food.

Carlito said he'd taken to the guitar in his youth. Given his disabilities, he'd had problems with the size of a standard instrument but was determined to get instruction and training from the best teachers in Spain. He sought out one José Luis Morón, not an Andalucian but a native of Barcelona, now in his fifties, who'd exploited *flamenco* to provide a mixture of styles that suited Carlito's tastes. Morón had been so intrigued by Carlito's enthusiasm that he sent him to the village of Algodonales, not far from Cádiz, where two rival guitar makers had their workshops. Using all his cheeky charm and most of his savings, Carlito persuaded one of them to fashion him an instrument that would fit his size, smaller than normal models but with a tone sonorous enough to satisfy *aficionados* and audiences in busy restaurants.

"Morón spent three years putting me through a rigorous regime of practice and yet more practice. He introduced me to the simpler mainstream repertoire, until I was able to move on, improvising my own material from *flamenco* and any other source that took my fancy."

"Like him, I suppose?"

"I wish it were as good," said Carlito.

"But how did you find the time to fit the guitar into a busy schedule as a lawyer? And one with a specific agenda?"

"That's life, Charlie. I could ask you the same question about your piano and your jazz and your journalism."

He drained his glass and made off back to the platform in the dark corner. I watched him lovingly extract the guitar from its case, sit on the stool provided and retune. He was lit by a single spot just bright enough to pick out his withered face and his long, thin hands.

After a sweet and almost muted introduction, he launched himself into a frenzy of scales and *rasgueado*, striking the nails and knuckles of the right hand across all six strings, a typical *flamenco* sequence of rapid chords, loud, unrestrained and passionate. Then he was into an energetic twelve-beat rhythm and the customers were clapping and tapping their feet but not so loud as to drown him.

We heard two shots. Carlito stopped playing. The clientele froze. One slug shattered the spotlight; a second smashed a ceiling lamp. Carlito dropped to the floor, doing his utmost to protect his guitar. Glass from the lamp spattered a group of diners, drew blood from terrified faces, smeared white shirts and blouses with red polka dots and raised screams from all quarters.

In the confusion, I didn't notice the arrival of Detective Juan Codina until Elena snatched at my arm.

"What the hell...?"

I kicked at a chair and made for Carlito. He was still taking cover and trying to shield his instrument.

"I'm okay," he said. "Charlie, keep your head down. There may be more. Look after Elena."

"How about the guitar?"

"Also okay. I think. If it's taken a few scars from broken glass, they're scars of honour."

I scuttled back to what was left of our table. Elena was calmly setting chairs, plates and glasses aright.

Codina was helping her. He beckoned us to go outside. This was almost an order.

"Is that wise?" I asked.

"He's made his point," said Codina. "He won't be back."

"Who?"

"The gunman. He was paid to issue a warning."

We rose as discreetly as we could and followed him into the street.

"Martínez Ortiz," he said abruptly.

"What about him?"

"He's escaped. Sprung from jail by a slick lawyer from Madrid bearing gifts, several thousand euros by the look of it."

"Fuck!"

Elena eyed him quizzically. "And you had no power to stop him?"

"You know I haven't. I'm a simple, provincial cop. The lawyer burst into the station with a team of heavies in suits, walked into the chief's office, and within five minutes, they were off in a big, black Mercedes."

"And they left behind a man with a shooter to make sure?"

"They left behind two of their Moroccan friends who knew exactly who you were and where you could be found."

"You are sure they were trying to kill Carlito?"

"Him and you – and possibly Elena."

Codina was angry and bewildered but well trained enough to keep it all in check.

"If only I had the men..."

"What about the boys who were up at the cemetery earlier in the day?"

"You'd only laugh if I said 'off duty'."

"What does the chief say?"

"He doesn't. He's scarpered as well. Gone home. Leaving orders not to bother him."

"I'm going to bother him," I said. "Where does he live?"

It might have been the effect of Carlito's music plus a little wine. I was spoiling for another fight with

131

authority. Corrupt bastards. Takers of bribes. It stuck out a mile.

"Hold on," said Elena. "I love you, Charlie Barrow..."

Juan raised his eyebrows.

"...and you have all the right instincts. But your Spanish is atrocious. Even if you got to see the police chief, he'd bamboozle you with self-righteous indignation and rapid-fire accusations which you wouldn't understand."

"I'd understand them if you came with me."

"No, Charlie. Not a good idea. The police chief knows me already and while he is not a rabid right winger, he is not a fan of what we're doing at the mass grave. I'd be a red rag to a bull."

"She's right, Charlie. The chief is not fond of those he calls subversives. The dear old mayor, the *alcalde*, has a hell of a job keeping him in check."

"I was told he was something of a liberal."

"In Spain, all labels are relative, Charlie. Especially political labels."

Carlito arrived carrying his guitar case.

"I hope that's bullet-proof." I did not mean it as a joke.

Chapter 13

I didn't wait for more explanations. I was going to Madrid.

"I'll find the bastards," I said.

I surrendered to Elena when she said she was going with me. And Carlito was as wise as ever, insisting that he had to stay behind and continue the Association's work in Andalucía.

"I shall be bored to death in that office wading through more paper," he said.

"No you won't," I replied. "You will respond to adrenalin and start to match names to names and names to corpses. You'll do the work more quickly if we're out of your hair."

"Am I allowed to go on playing?"

Juan Codina said the restaurant owner would be only too glad to have the place returning to normal. Carlito and his guitar would be the guarantee of that.

"I'm sorry, Juan." I was trying to reassure him. "I have to do this myself and with Elena. We'll stay in touch."

"Fear not." He smiled. "I've got plenty of things to clear up here." He rose to his full height. "I'll beard that chief of mine in his den if it's the last thing I do as a policeman."

He looked at me severely. "Remember, though. This is a police matter. I can't stop you being a journalist. But cross the line in Madrid and you might find life rather awkward."

"What did you discover that pointed you in the direction of Ortiz?"

"You're very clever, Charlie. I thought you might forget to ask me why I'd arrested him."

"Why would you want to keep it to yourself?"

"I wanted to spring a surprise at tomorrow's hearing in front of the magistrate."

"Go on."

"When we found Pepe's body in his cell, we looked around for any evidence that would lead us to a suspect. Obviously. We couldn't find any to start with. No old fashioned fingerprints on the corpse or his clothes. We are trying DNA from his shirt and jeans but nothing so far. We sent the body to the morgue and sat at our desks drinking coffee and chewing our nails."

"But...?"

"I decided to take another look. The cell was dark. There's a window high up on the outer wall, but not much light gets through. And there's a ceiling lamp with a low-wattage bulb."

Juan was teasing me with details. So I kept my mouth shut and waited. We played a game of 'who blinks first?' He did.

"Despite the gloom, I saw something glinting in a corner. I picked it up. It was a pen, an expensive one with a gold clip. Ortiz's name was embossed on the shaft."

"Hallelujah!"

"It's not conclusive proof that he ever entered the cell, let alone that he murdered Pepe. But it's a start. Or it would have been if he'd stayed where he was supposed to."

Elena asked him if he was going to disclose this to the magistrate and the prosecutor.

"I'll have to. They'll probably pour cold water on it as evidence. But if forensics or the pathologist find something, I may have what I need to convince the court."

"Does your chief know?"

"Since he's gone into purdah, I haven't had a chance to tell him anything. I want to see his face when I do. The magistrate might just haul him back to work and give him a good dressing down for trying to wash his hands of the whole thing."

We said our farewells. Carlito repeated Juan's warnings about the wicked city we were driving to.

"I won't ask you what you think you're going to do when you get there. In fact I'm not so sure I want to know."

"We haven't got a clue right now."

"That doesn't give me a lot of comfort and joy," he said.

Elena embraced him "I'll look after Charlie, I promise."

"I'm sure you will. I hope he looks after you."

I gave him a look of dignified reproof and a quick hug. Then walked away.

****

It's 140 kilometres from Castillo to Córdoba and another 400 from there to Madrid. Which is why we set off early. It may have been winter, but this was an Andalusian winter and the sun was working quite hard. We braced ourselves for a sticky journey.

The Polo wasn't too uncomfortable. It was kind to my old injuries and it was certainly robust enough to swallow miles of motorway more quickly than I'd expected. I drove the first leg to Córdoba while Elena did her best to alleviate the tedium with occasional commentaries on the landscape and the places we had to negotiate. I was a good boy, sensitive enough to appreciate her efforts, admire the beauty of the *sierra*, respect the literary associations of La Mancha and marvel at the splendour of the river Guadiana.

But my mind was firmly fixed on that fountain pen.

I should have suspected but hadn't realised that Elena was well up to date with communications. She was working hard at her Smartphone.

"What are you doing with that thing?"

"You said you wanted to go straight to the PP's headquarters. It's in Calle de Genova. So I'm booking us into a hotel in the same neighbourhood."

"Not too expensive, I hope."

"We can afford it."

"You can do it on that contraption?"

"This and a thousand other things you'll be needing."

I could manage a simple mobile. I could even send and receive messages. And there was one occasion when I stuffed an earpiece into my orifice and listened to a radio station. But those were my limits.

Elena knew what I was thinking and laughed.

"I'll bring you up to date with a new phone and all its bits and pieces when we get to Madrid."

"Who's buying?"

"You are."

"You really will have to teach me how to use it."

She'd finished doing the business and switched on the car radio. We heard a rapid-fire newscast.

"You have to listen to the rhythm of the language," she said. "I'll translate when he's finished."

"Then can I have some music?"

I drove on until somewhere outside a place called Valdepeñas. We stopped to buy petrol and grabbed a couple of *bocadillos* and some bottles of water.

I took note of a big black Peugeot which had pulled in at a nearby pump. Whoever was driving it realised I was staring hard at his car, changed his mind about filling up and shot off with a squeal of tyres.

"A man in a hurry," said Elena. "Should we be keeping a lookout for him?"

"He may pull off the road and tuck himself in behind us again. So the answer to your question is 'Yes'. I'm sure some goblin or other has their eye on us."

Elena took the wheel.

I didn't know what to expect from Madrid. I still knew London well enough although I hadn't been there for some time. And I certainly knew old haunts like Berlin, Budapest and Lisbon (See *A Wicked Device* and *Breaking the Cross*) from past assignments and adventures. But this, the capital of Spain, was a riddle. At first sight it was like all European cities, with a suburban sprawl of high-rises, mini-markets, cafés, bars and thousands of parked cars.

"It gets better," said Elena as she manoeuvred the Polo down urban freeways and the narrower streets leading to the centre.

"I hope so."

"I've lived here. So I know. You'll enjoy the architecture."

"I'm not here to enjoy the architecture."

She sniffed her disapproval and didn't smile.

I had a sudden, depressing thought. How strange, when a man of my age falls in love with a much younger woman and starts to ruminate on her past. How many men had she known? What had she been doing before I met her? Why is she so cold towards me right now? Or is it my imagination?

Stop ruminating. Just be happy with what you've got. She told you she loves you. Isn't that enough?

"Calle de Genova," she announced.

"Better than I expected." It contained blocks of five or six storeys in what the estate agents would doubtlessly have called tasteful styles, a mix of twentieth-century European, with all the usual curlicues and gargoyles, and the starker and more functional modern. Some clearly housed pretty expensive apartments; others were hotels, including the modest but comfortable hostelry into which Elena had booked us.

"Let's dump our bags and see if we can find the *Partido Popular*'s HQ," I said, still full of purpose to get at the missing Ortiz as quickly as possible.

"You won't have to look far," said Elena. "The PP building is at the end of the street."

I detected that she was not willing to accompany me on a precipitate mission to root out our quarry.

"Look," she said. "I will go and check us in. You do what you have to."

She was right. I took a short walk and found the PP ensconced in a no-nonsense five-floor edifice at the end of Calle de Genova. It was taped off and guarded by local police. I learned later that there'd been a protest by an irate small businessman who'd rammed his car into the front door of the building. His demonstration against intolerable taxes had ended with a few panes of smashed glass, but by now all had been repaired. And there was no attempt by the uniforms to stop me walking through the front door.

"I am looking for Deputy Jaime Martínez Ortiz."

The spruce young lady at Reception tapped into the computer in front of her and took stock of its offerings.

"I'm sorry, *Señor*." She looked at me apologetically. "He is not here."

"Do you know where I might find him?"

She asked me for credentials. Then much to my surprise, she answered, "I can give you phone numbers and an email address. Perhaps they will help."

I delicately accepted the piece of paper she handed over and left. There was a bar just across the street. Even though the sky had clouded over and threatened rain, I sat at an outside table, ordered a large beer and scrutinised the information I'd been given. What to do? Plunge in with a phone call and hope for the best?

I looked up and Elena had arrived.

"Well?" she asked.

"Not that well." I drank my beer. "But I have some nuggets I can use."

"Come on, Charlie. Relax. We have a nice room and a decent bar on the ground floor. You can take it from there."

I almost resented her lack of concern. I felt suddenly weary and I wasn't desperate to abandon my beer.

"Are you hungry?" she asked.

"I suppose I am."

She let me finish the beer and took me by the hand.

See? I told you to stop ruminating.

It was a short stroll to Plaza de Alonso Martínez, a bustling square of people and pigeons, as typical of central Madrid as you could get. She led me to a place which turned out to serve some rather tempting cuisine.

We ate almost in silence. Too early for most Spaniards. But we were tired. There were a few words about the aim of our visit and how it related to her work, to the Association for the Recovery of Historical Memory, and to dear old Carlito stuck down there in Andalucía.

"I'm for bed," I said.

"And so am I," she whispered.

We ambled back to the hotel, took the lift, undressed and fell under the duvet. After a purposeless bout of fumbling, I was fast asleep.

Chapter 14

When I awoke, I was lying on my back and someone was shining a torch in my eyes. I tried to sit up but I'd been handcuffed. My mouth was taped. I grunted out a protest.

"Don't move, Mr Barrow. It won't do you any good."

I understood the Spanish all too clearly.

The torch was switched off and an overhead light turned on.

The speaker standing at the foot of the bed was the double of Danny DeVito, almost as round as he was tall at about one-metre-fifty. He wore thick glasses and a crumpled suit. The voice was deep and low, a smoker's, and strangely without menace. But I could see the barrel of a gun stuffed into his trouser belt.

I tried to say, "Where's Elena?"

'Danny' understood well enough. "Was that the whore you'd been shagging when we found you?"

My grunting became more vehement. He saw the look in my eyes and was suddenly forthcoming.

"It seems we were lax. We obviously let her escape."

He beckoned to a tall and younger man wearing a much sharper suit and a vacant expression which I guessed belied his avowed intent to do me harm.

"I have been sitting here for about three hours, I suppose," 'Danny' explained. "I was told to. By my bosses. They were the people who handcuffed you and taped your mouth."

And I had never felt a thing while they were doing it. So the questions were obvious. Who had drugged me into a deep sleep and how the hell had Elena avoided the same fate?

'Danny' decided that keeping the tape on was a waste of time. His companion strode towards the bed and, careless of my comfort, ripped it off in one swift movement.

"Thanks, pal. You're a real nursemaid, aren't you?" Before I could say any more, he clipped me hard across the left cheek.

I had guessed correctly.

"Don't provoke him, Mr Barrow. It's not a pleasant sight if Aldo's given a free rein."

He passed me a glass of water. I drank the lot in one go and raised my hands almost in supplication.

"The cuffs stay on."

"How generous of you."

Aldo moved a step closer, but 'Danny' waved him back.

I was working out how to manipulate the conversation. A strange notion came out of the blue.

"Are you by any chance acquainted with the novels of Manuel Vázquez Montalbán?" I asked.

He looked at me as if he thought he'd confronted a raving lunatic.

"I don't read books," he said hesitantly.

"Pity. Because in his *Murder in the Central Committee* he has a chapter in which, our hero, private eye Cavalho, faces a situation rather like this one."

I paused. His eyebrows were knitting together in one enormous frown. I ploughed on.

"Well, you see, he too wakes up to find himself in bed, not with the lady he originally thought he was going to make love to, but with a terrified teenager screaming that he'd tried to rape her. Then in surge people like you and Aldo here, and accuse him of trying to ravish their under-age sister. They do all kinds of nasty things which leave him in acute pain."

I stopped. 'Danny' was even more confused and Aldo's face was not so much vacant now as devoid of any understanding of why he was where he was.

"Now, if you are going to do similar things to me, would you please get on with it and then leave me to die?"

'Danny' scratched his bald patch and thought of something to say.

"You won't die." He coughed, almost politely. "We think you're too valuable."

"'We'? Whose 'we'?"

'Danny' was working out how much more to tell me. He'd slipped up and he knew it. He took a deep breath.

"The Party," he spluttered.

"Which fucking party?"

Aldo made another move. 'Danny' held up his hand again.

"The *Partido Popular*."

He winced as he said it. Why he thought I hadn't worked it out already was difficult to fathom.

"So, you're telling me the party that forms the government of this country uses methods like yours to threaten people like me. Simple question – why?"

'Danny' stayed mum. I realised he hadn't been told as much as he ought to have been. He didn't know the answers. Just keep me trussed up for further questioning. Those were his orders. It was all he had to do. And apart from Aldo's little spasm of violence, it was the way things were going to stay. I was to be bored into submission which was when the 'bosses' would come for me.

'Danny' was downcast. But he didn't have time to wallow in his ignorance and despair. The door burst open and three young men in t-shirts and jeans fell on Aldo, twisted one of his arms up his back, which caused him to utter some very fruity examples of Spanish profanity, and marched him away. The other three seized 'Danny' and shoved him into an armchair. One of them frisked him, found a set of keys and carefully unlocked my handcuffs.

"Well now, that does feel better," I said rather lamely. "Thank you."

"*Señor* Barrow?"

"That's me."

"You are not to worry any more."

"I stopped worrying about two minutes ago. But I am a little bewildered. Who are you?"

Elena entered.

"They are friends from *Podemos*, Charlie. Raul, Nico, and Pedro." She nodded towards them in turn. And then I started to get the full story.

"You recall the black Peugeot at the filling station outside Valdepeñas?"

Yes, we had been followed all the way from Castillo. And I had made matters worse by clumsily walking into PP headquarters and leaving obvious traces of our whereabouts. We had been sold a bottle of *tinto* at our restaurant in Alonso Martínez into which a waiter had been paid off to pour a little extra something, thus bringing me sweet and lasting slumber.

"But I didn't drink a whole bottle of wine. I had two glasses at most."

"Two glasses did for you."

"And you?"

"I drank water."

"No, you didn't. You took a sip of wine. I saw you."

"No, I didn't."

Before this mystifying and aimless exchange could go any further, one of the crew from *Podemos* pulled 'Danny' to his feet and was about to frogmarch him out of the room.

"Wait," I called. "He gave me one or two bits of information. He was sitting here for about three hours before you lot arrived. And he's taken his orders from PP officials."

"Raul and his friends will get more out of him, Charlie. Leave it to them," said Elena somewhat haughtily.

I looked at her hard.

"I hope they don't get too rough with him. He made me, let's say, uncomfortable, but it wasn't much more than that. Aldo might have wanted to put his boot on my balls and pull my nails out but he didn't get the chance."

She knew I was wittering on like this because what I really wanted was answers to some awkward questions.

"Let's order some coffee and a little breakfast," she said.

"Let's stop dodging the questions," I replied, as disapproving as I could be.

It was Raul's turn to say something.

"I think Mr Barrow wants to know why you weren't here when the villains showed up."

"I know he does." She was annoyed. "I'm about to tell him."

· I gave her time. Still naked and with a jaw smarting from Aldo's attempt to keep me quiet, I grabbed a shirt, boxers and trousers and ambled to the bathroom. I shut myself away and spent a good twenty-five minutes shaving, showering and doing whatever else was necessary. Then I put on the clothes I'd picked up and went back into the bedroom.

The *Podemos* crew had left. Elena was sipping coffee and reading a newspaper. She didn't look up. I found socks and shoes and completed the process of getting dressed. I saw there was a second cup and helped myself. There was also a croissant on a plate, a pat of butter and a small jar of jam. I demolished them and longed for eggs and bacon. I didn't speak.

"I suppose you want to know why I wasn't lying at your side when you woke up, cuffed and gagged."

"It might help to alleviate my growing suspicion that you are not quite what you seem."

"Not just an archaeologist supervising the operation in Castillo, you mean?"

"Along those lines, yes."

"Did you believe me when I said I had fallen in love with you?"

"I did. And I hope it's still true. Because..."

You're afraid to say it, aren't you? This is the point at which you think I might have been right. You took the plunge a little early, perhaps. You are in love but now you're not sure you want to shout it from the rooftops.

"I didn't fall asleep like you." Elena had left her chair and knelt in front of me holding the one hand that wasn't brandishing a buttered croissant. "I lay beside you for about half an hour. Wide awake. Thinking. Thinking too much perhaps."

"About us?"

"Not just us. Perhaps more about how we were going to get help to find Ortiz. I didn't want to disturb you, so I retrieved jeans and shirt and sandals and quietly let myself out of here. I made for the coffee shop, found a quiet corner and called the *Podemos* office. I had some luck. They got Raul to come to the phone. I've known him for a long time."

I smiled. "An old boyfriend?"

150

"Sort of. Nothing passionate. But we've been loyal to one another. I knew he would help. Or at least I knew he would give good advice."

I finished my croissant, wiped my hands and gazed at her. She rose on to her knees, stretched her neck and gently kissed me. I relaxed and waited. But she had more to say.

"I told him as much as I dared over an open phone. He more or less ordered me to stay where I was. He would be with me in fifteen minutes."

In the meantime, she had seen a group of young, nattily dressed Arab males, plus 'Danny' and Aldo, pass through the hotel lobby and head for the elevators.

"I didn't dare follow, but I knew where they were going."

Raul had arrived late. Frantic to explain why we were in Madrid and to tell him what she'd just seen, Elena admitted that she'd succumbed to his common sense. He dismissed her fears that I was about to be killed or tortured. It wasn't their way. They simply wanted to put on a show – put the frighteners on me.

"Well, they certainly did that," I said. Given what had happened to me, I wasn't sure I admired Raul's *sang froid.*

"But he was right, wasn't he?"

By now word had got out that some crazy British journalist was after a PP big wig who'd escaped from police custody in Andalucía. It was in the papers; on the news. And I had been quietly drinking doctored *tinto* and sleeping it off, totally unaware that half of Madrid was buzzing with the story.

Raul had called up his mates from *Podemos* and decided to play a waiting game. After several cups of coffee, they told Elena to sit tight. They'd squared the staff at reception who in any case were clued up about what was happening, and finally headed for our room. The rest I knew.

"Well, they took their time," I said "I might have been more seriously roughed up or even killed. But then I could, I suppose, be judged as simply expendable."

Soft-soaping me wasn't going to work, Elena. You'd better know that.

"But, put out the flags. Here I am in one piece. Isn't that nice for everybody?"

Elena eyed me defiantly.

"What now?" I asked.

"If you'll stop feeling sorry for yourself, I will show you the delights of the metro and take you to the most exciting place in Madrid."

Chapter 15

We were in Lavapiés, where a good Catholic housewife might once have washed the feet of her fellow worshippers before walking into church for Mass. Centuries ago this was the Jewish quarter, but the Jews were bundled out of Spain by Ferdinand and Isabella in 1492. Now it was home to a motley array of humankind, native Madrileños, Asians and Africans, Chinese, Indian, Bangladeshi, Algerian, Moroccan and Senegalese, and the food they ate and sold you with delightful relish. A place of steep, narrow streets and four- or five-storey tenements, not so long ago Madrid's squatters' paradise – *los okupaciones*. Today the balconies with their iron grills and the walls of pastel pinks and blues contained small but attractive apartments.

Calle de Zurita was just wide enough for a single line of traffic and highly prized parking spaces. We climbed from Plaza Lavapiés and found number 21 on the right hand side with the *Podemos* logo, unashamedly proclaiming itself to the neighbourhood, attached to a smart glazed double door. This was party headquarters.

We didn't really need to present ourselves to Reception. Elena was clearly well known. The girl behind the desk embraced her and smiled warmly at me. They exchanged the usual pleasantries.

"Raul knows you're here," she said and, as if on cue, he appeared. He gave Elena a light kiss and shook my hand.

"How are you feeling, Mr Barrow?" he asked in English.

I shrugged and said I was none the worse for wear.

"I like that expression," he said.

"*Desmejorado,*" quipped Elena. "One for your Spanish vocabulary, Charlie."

This was all very delightful and amusing, but it wasn't getting us anywhere. Raul saw the look on my face.

"Okay. Down to business," he said. "But not here. Somewhere more convivial."

We walked back into the street and retraced our steps to Lavapiés metro.

"I think we'll take a cab," said Raul. "Your face is becoming too well known, Mr Barrow."

Ten minutes later we were sitting at a table in *Ocho y Medio*, a combined bookshop and restaurant in Calle Martin de los Heros close to some of Madrid's landmarks like the monument to Cervantes. The decor was all pictures and posters to do with film. Directors and actors from various parts of the world looked down on us as if we needed reminding of their power to persuade.

"Hungry?" asked Elena.

The dishes on offer also had a cinematic theme. I chose an omelette that had some connection with Almodóvar. And a glass of wine from a bottle which had seen happier times.

Elena was working hard to keep me calm and patient. But Raul was aware of my body language.

I got a quick surprise.

"We think we know where he is," he said.

"Ortiz?" Elena's face shone with relief.

Raul told us of an old warehouse in the suburban wastelands of Castellana Norte. His boys had discovered that the businessman who owned the place leased it to people who wanted to store hardware and publicity material – hoardings, screens, loudspeakers – all the paraphernalia needed for rallies and big meetings. It also housed a fleet of vehicles, trucks, vans, minibuses and a collection of smart cars.

"We think the PP makes use of it especially when there's an election due."

He produced a road map of the area around the capital and put his thumb on the spot where the factory was located.

"Are you telling me our friend is inside this place?"

"A contact told us of a small apartment at the back of the building."

"You're guessing then?"

Raul said the place wasn't guarded. "Nobody stops you from walking through the main entrance."

"How do you know all this?"

Raul smiled the smile of the conspirator.

"Some people think *Podemos* and people like me are walking examples of naivety, Mr Barrow."

"You have your little ways of finding things out then?"

"As I said, we have our contacts."

I toyed with my omelette. We fell silent.

I changed the subject. "What about your boys and fat little 'Danny'?"

"What about them?"

"You told me you'd sorted him out. And Aldo. I'm asking again. What does 'sorted out' mean?"

Raul looked me straight in the eye. "We questioned them. That's all. Aldo needed restraining for a while, but since he was as thick as a brick, he couldn't tell us anything useful. We let him go without a mark on him."

He smiled again.

"And 'Danny'?"

'Danny' had squealed a bit. Enough to suggest that someone he referred to as 'a party VIP' had been taken to the warehouse. He hadn't known his name, but he'd given a good description.

"And you're convinced it was Ortiz?"

"Now you're persuaded that we don't go around torturing our opponents, perhaps we can eat and drink."

The café was busy and noisy. There was some sort of background music I didn't like. I thought of Carlito and his guitar. I said I'd like something with meat in it. And a better glass of wine.

Elena scowled.

"I'm doing my job, Elena."

"So I see," she replied.

"We'll take a look at this place later on," I said.

Raul didn't argue. He wanted to let me think I was in charge.

****

We drove out to the northern fringes of Madrid and skidded to a halt in a flurry of dust. The lay-by was just opposite the warehouse. It had started to rain. This time there was definitely no easy access. The gates were shut and a squad of police and *Guardia Civil* had taken up positions just outside the chain-link fencing. They were using special gear and expending a lot of energy trying to smash the locks. The job didn't take long. We watched as four of their colleagues rushed into the warehouse compound, brandishing semi automatics, and found cover behind stunted trees and withered bushes.

We approached the officer in charge. He wasn't pleased to see us. The rain dripped off his cap and ran down the plastic poncho he wore over his uniform.

"Who the hell are you?"

We explained as succinctly as we could.

"Then, keep back, for God's sake. There are villains with guns in that building."

"But what the hell's going on?" I asked.

"I've told you. Stay back."

We retreated to the car, but I wasn't satisfied.

"I'm not taking 'No' for an answer," I said. I walked up to the officer again followed by Elena who knew I needed her skills as an interpreter.

"I told you to stay back," he said.

"There's a man in there who's wanted by your colleagues down in Andalucía," I announced. "And I need to speak to him." It was a lame try, but to my surprise, he weakened.

"Why do you need to speak to him?"

Elena laid it out again.

"Not good enough," he replied. "Before you get anywhere near this Martínez Ortiz person, I have to rescue a hostage. And my boys might have to use those guns to get him out of there."

"A hostage?"

"My senior officer. My boss. Lieutenant Felipe Suarez Vicente. Who was either brave enough or foolhardy enough to walk in there in the hope of persuading those tossers to part with their guns."

"Who are they, for Christ's sake?"

"Gentlemen from across the water in Morocco, or perhaps Algeria. Or maybe Libya. Or even, maybe, Syria. I wish I knew exactly but I don't. Just let's call them Arabs."

"What guns have they got?"

"Kalashnikovs."

"Send me in," I said. "I'll take his place."

"Whose?"

"Your boss, of course."

"You *are* mad, aren't you?" He gave me a look, a mixture of pity and scorn, which I tried to counter with pigheaded defiance. Elena had walked away. I couldn't tell whether she'd lost patience with me or the GC. Perhaps she just wanted to get out of the rain.

When the shots rang out, a bullet came towards me in what later memory insisted was slow motion. It smashed into my right shoulder, spun me round and floored me. The pain was hideous but short-lived. I didn't remember anything else.

Chapter 16

Are you hearing me, Charlie Barrow? You have done a very foolish thing. No, you are not dead although you bloody well deserve to be. You got in the way and fucked up a well-planned police operation.

Thanks for your sympathy. It's just what I need right now.

Even when you're semi-conscious and in need of considerable care from some very skilled people, you resort to unwarranted sarcasm. It smacks of an ungenerous nature. But why should we be surprised? You are a remarkably unfair and selfish person.

I am not unfair and no more selfish than anyone else. I was doing my job, hunting down a man who is a murder suspect and has jumped bail with the assistance of some influential bastards in the governing party. If that's not a story a good journalist should be pursuing, I don't know what is.

Let me remind you. You came to Spain for a break, a holiday, for God's sake. But you're so obsessed with what you do and what you are, you'll justify any action to accommodate that obsession. Christ, Charlie, you need a break. You're losing your grip. You can't see the difference between doing the job properly and professionally and doing it at the expense of others.

It isn't at the expense of others, arsehole.

It's at the expense of a team of doctors and nurses who are even now trying to make you whole again; it's at the expense of Elena who should be back in Castillo exhuming those graves instead of sitting by your hospital bed again; it's at the expense of the guys in Podemos who were trying to help you, one of whom also stopped a bullet, in his case, a bullet to the right thigh; it's at the expense of those cops who put themselves in the line of fire and, so far as I could tell, mercifully dodged all the shit the bastards in the warehouse threw at them.

Did they get Ortiz?

I don't know, Charlie. I was whisked away in the ambulance, buzzing around in your thick head.

****

It was dark when I came round. I wanted a drink. Someone guessed correctly and placed a glass to my lips.

"Charlie."

It was male voice. I suppose I'd hoped it would be Elena. Where was she now? Why wasn't she here? My

162

voice had suggested she would be. But even my voice could get things wrong.

"Who's this?" I whispered.

"Carlito, Charlie."

Hold on. Carlito was meant to be wading through paper back in Castillo or Carmona. But I was too tired to ask the obvious questions.

I heard Carlito leave his chair and mutter something, perhaps into a mobile. After a couple minutes he sat down again and switched on a dim bedside light. I had thought of a question.

"How long have I been here?"

"Three days. You're staying here for at least another week."

"I can't spare the time."

"Listen, *Señor*. Your shoulder's buggered. They've put it back together as best they can. But you won't be doing any right arm bowling for a while."

"You don't know anything about cricket."

"I'm full of surprises, Charlie."

"Indeed you are. Why are you in Madrid, for a start?"

"Elena phoned me soon after the shooting. I got here as fast as I could."

He gave me an account of events after I hit the ground.

"According to her, the *Guardia Civil* opened up on the warehouse. Then the boys in special gear tried to storm the place. The villains responded with some high-quality firepower. There was one hell of a battle. It lasted an hour. They brought in another specialist team from the army. They threw all kinds of stuff into the building. When they finally got inside, they found five bodies riddled with bullets and shrapnel."

"Did they get Ortiz?"

"Ortiz wasn't there. At least they didn't find him. And they didn't get their hostage back – the lieutenant or whatever he was – he was found in a storeroom, with his throat cut."

"Are you telling me we went through all that for nothing?" I croaked.

I tried to sit up and winced. Carlito raised his eyebrows and gave me a long, hard look mingling pity and admonition. It said I had to accept that I was a prisoner of my wounded shoulder, that I'd failed in my mission to track down Ortiz and that, when I'd recovered, I'd have to head back to Carmona and call off the search, enjoy a few days by the pool, sidle off to my apartment in Portugal and play my piano.

Except that the whole of Spain knew all about me. Television, radio, the papers and social media had put out graphic accounts of the siege, the shooting and the slaughter of a senior GC officer. All that plus the deaths of the goons who'd holed up in the warehouse for a reason no one could work out right now. If Ortiz wasn't there, if they weren't protecting him, why go to all that trouble to confront the forces of law and order?

"We were screwed," I said. "They pulled a fast one."

"Someone did," said Carlito. "Someone in the PP cheated his contact inside *Podemos* into telling his people what he thought was the truth. Or he went along with the deception. I'd put money on the latter. It smells."

"I don't think I've ever heard you sound so cynical."

"This is Spain, Charlie. Politics here are as dirty as anywhere in the world. *Podemos* say they want to bring it to an end, but its leaders must know that even now, even though they've only been in existence for five minutes, they're going to be tainted by placemen and spies put there by *la casta*, the very establishment they want to get rid of. Raul and his mates have a snake in the grass – *un judas* who's playing games."

"I still want to know why a bunch of well-armed Arab gunmen chose to fight it out like this. We know Ortiz has Arab friends. But this is ridiculous. They didn't do an Atocha. They didn't kill crowds of people or create havoc in the centre of Madrid. They murdered a police officer and then decided to die. What was the point?"

"They saw you, though, pinpointed you and tried to kill you. Explain that one."

The drugs they'd pumped into me to take away the pain from my shoulder were making me drowsy again. I couldn't concentrate on what Carlito was saying.

"The plan is," he said, "you stay where you are for the time being. I'll bring you stuff to read, and a radio to improve your Spanish. You'll get a visit from the police or the *Guardia* tomorrow. I'll be here. As will your doctors. If you don't feel up to it, you can put them off. But you'll have to talk to them at some point."

He took my hand. "I've known you for about a week, Charlie – a week in which some nasty people have tried to kill you – twice, for God's sake. I really would like you to stay alive."

He didn't let go. I squeezed his fingers and tried to smile. At last he relaxed.

"Where's Elena?"

He hesitated. "I wish I knew the answer to that," he said. "If I find her, I'll tell her to come and see you."

I wanted to ask him, why wouldn't he know her whereabouts? How long was he staying in Madrid? *Why* hadn't she come to see me? And would I see the *Podemos* guys again?

He didn't give me time to speak.

****

I stayed in that bed for ever. I neither spoke, nor thought, nor dreamed. I sank into an oblivion I never believed it was possible to enter. I knew Carlito came every day and held my hand. But no one else. Not even the guys from the *Guardia Civil*. No Elena. No Raul. Later I would ask what it was they were giving me. They were to tell me it wasn't the drugs. It wasn't strong painkillers. It wasn't even the anaesthetic. They said I just sort of switched off. Which, added the doctors, had been a good thing while they wheeled me back and forth for surgery. I never knew they'd done anything to me. Of course that made no sense at all, as I later realised when I was putting my brain into gear again. But God damn it! I don't remember feeling the need for a piss or a shit. I didn't eat. Carlito told me he made me drink large glasses of water.

And you were supposed to be on holiday. Remember?

I was never on holiday. It was an illusion, a bout of self-deception.

Then the music came out of nowhere. Or so I believed until I opened my eyes and in the dim light of the hospital cubicle saw Carlito again. Carlito and guitar. He was playing a softly, slow, sweet tremolo in a minor key.

He stopped. "Close them. Just listen," he said.

Later I would recognise the piece as something to do with memories of the Alhambra, a classic of Spanish guitar literature. I would play a version of it on my piano, but it never sounded as good as the real thing. Half-way through, Carlito did the heart-rending shift from minor to major, from melancholy to optimism, angst to consolation. I resisted tears but allowed myself a smile, holding on to it until he plucked the final chord.

"You can open them again," he said.

I blinked. I hadn't dreamed it. There he was, sitting with his long hands resting on strings and fingerboard, nestling the guitar as if it were a small child.

"A tonic and a half," I said. "Thank you."

We held a long silence. The machinery they'd attached me to murmured and beeped discreetly. My head ached. It must have been time for some more medication because my shoulder was making its presence felt again.

Carlito laid his instrument to one side and stared at me rather as a doctor might look at a patient who was about to get some bad news.

"The music was meant to bring you some relief," he said. "Because you are going to need it."

His gaze was an open book. Easy to read and almost threatening.

"Elena?"

"Elena is dead, Charlie."

I lay very still. "How?"

"You don't want to hear this but you must."

168

She'd been found in our hotel room. Strangled, or rather garrotted, a thick, rough rope round her neck, biting deep into the flesh and spilling a lot of blood. She'd failed to display the 'Don't Disturb' sign. Four mornings ago, household staff had assumed they could go in to clean the bathroom and tidy the bed. They found her lying on her back outside the duvet, naked. She'd been beaten, legs badly bruised and face as well. She may well have been raped.

I managed not to throw up, intent on keeping traces of vomit at the back of my throat. Carlito had yet another glass of water ready. I gulped and gulped again and again.

"Now you know why I couldn't tell you. I couldn't tell you why she hadn't come to see you – why she was never coming. I'm sorry, Charlie. I'm really sorry."

I took in mouthfuls of air, held them in my lungs, and felt my heart slowly subside.

"What had she been doing all this time?" I whispered.

"I don't know. She never got in touch. I tried very hard to reach her, but she was never at the hotel when I phoned and her mobile was switched off all the time. I gave up and concentrated on you. All I can tell you is that she did enough to attract some unwanted attention. And I don't know who from."

"What about a funeral?"

"It's already happened, Charlie. We do these things rather quickly in Spain. It's the Law. The guys from *Podemos* helped me to arrange it. You were in no fit state to leave the hospital. So I didn't tell you."

I didn't protest.

"But young as she was, Elena had the good sense to make a will. She wanted a cremation, which is not the usual way we despatch the dead but she obviously insisted. She also decreed that her ashes be scattered at the site of the graves in Castillo. I have the urn and we will do it when the time comes."

I heard him sigh deeply. "I wish I knew more. That's my failure."

I couldn't think of a reassuring answer. I sensed he was watching me perfervidly but keeping absolutely still. After an age of more silence, I heard him rise from the chair. His sleeve caught the strings of the guitar. The muffled chord faded. I opened my eyes again. He wasn't there.

I called out. But the cubicle was empty. There was nothing to do and nowhere to go. Except, "*like someone dead permitted to exist*", back to my own black hole.

****

But the black hole wasn't black at all. I saw multi-coloured shapes, swirling like kites in a children's playground. Yet everything intangible and without definition. Grey clouds moved swiftly against an azure sky. I was standing on a high ridge of pasture, looking down on to a picture-postcard village, pretty red-brick houses with thatched roofs, a church with a clock tower circled by all the trees of the English countryside, oaks, horse chestnut, hazel and beech. I looked up and saw a flock of small birds dancing in the clear air.

But I heard nothing, no birdsong, no church bells, no breeze, no bleating of sheep or lowing of cattle. Except for Elena's voice, hectoring, harsh and unforgiving. I anticipated her accusation.

"I did not lead you to your death," I said. "You abandoned me. I never knew what you were doing or where you were. I thought we had a pact to work together and love one another."

"You were a fool, Charlie Barrow."

"Why? Because I fell for you without knowing who you really were, without solving your mystery and deciphering your body language?"

"You should have asked more questions."

"I asked and you never answered. So I ask you now. Why did you come to Madrid with me? What was your 'agenda', as the jargon of the day has it?"

"Too late, Charlie. Too late to tell you the truth about myself."

"Too damn right."

I realised I was simulating the act of begging, hands held together and outstretched. I felt ashamed.

She had vanished. Silently and swiftly.

The vision of the placid English village faded. The weird shapes and the whirling colours returned. Now I was shielding my face against fierce wind and penetrating rain that battered everything in its path, trees, rocks and the coarse grass with its creeping roots. I was trapped in a dark gorge. I could not move ahead. I was being driven from the rough track into a cave, its walls covered in slime and lichen. I stumbled towards a slab of grey stone, sat down and watched twitches of lightning.

But I still heard nothing at all.

And felt totally unafraid. I laughed at it all, defied its silence, jumped to my feet and knew that if this was the end of everything, I would welcome its emptiness and solitude.

I shouted obscenities until I knew my lungs were bursting and my voice was dead. But now I heard the noises, wind, thunder and lashing rain, passing through a crescendo to an overwhelming climax.

Everything stopped, as if a cinema projectionist had thrown all his switches and screen had gone completely blank. No shapes. No colours. No visions. No sounds. Nothing. Nothing at all.

Chapter 17

And then I woke one morning with a clear head and no pain. And a phone buzzed. They had given me back my mobile.

"Well," said a dark voice full of the remnants of tobacco and alcohol. "You've got yourself into one hell of a mess – *Señor* Barrow!"

It was Fred. Dear Fred. News editor on the paper in London for which I had worked in various capacities over the years. He knew my numbers and, having diligently read the wires and webs and watched TV newscasts from innumerable networks, understood yet again that I was in the midst of a damned good story – that I might even be the story.

"Okay. You know the rules, Charlie."

"Yes, Fred. The mantra is as always, facts and more facts."

"You have learned well, dear boy. I don't say you can't file on events that have overtaken you personally. But I suspect you want to tell me more." A gentle pause. "How are you by the way?"

"Kind of you to ask. Mending, as they say."

It didn't take long for me to explain what I was chasing. Fred knew me well enough not to push his ingrained philosophy of sound journalism down my throat.

"Christ, Charlie. You are a lucky sod. In spite of all that's happened to you, you are a lucky, lucky sod."

"Why so?"

I sensed an acute melancholy at the other end of the line. "At the close of this working day, dear boy, I shall shuffle off to Waterloo station and catch the 2005 to Cobham, my beautiful, boring green suburb. And I shall ponder the question – why did I stick to desk work?"

"Because you're Fred, Fred. That's what you're good at."

"What a kind man you are, Charlie."

"Always willing to oblige."

"Take care, Charlie. And file away – as and when."

"That's it," I shouted. "I'm back in business and I've missed the fucking obvious."

"And what is the obvious?" said a reassuring voice.

Carlito had arrived as dutifully as ever, bringing rolls and croissants to add to a hospital breakfast. Behind him was Raul, wearing a serious face and apparently unwilling to look me in the eye. More of a surprise was the third young man in a smart uniform. *Guardia Civil.*

Two metres tall, he had obviously spent time in the sun and indeed in the gym. He had all the attributes of the outwardly perfect human male, square jaw, broad shoulders and highly intelligent blue eyes.

"Raul, you know," said Carlito. Raul nodded diffidently. "May I also introduce *Teniente Coronel* Carlos Manresa of the *Servicio de Información.*"

"Usually known as the SIGC, *Señor* Barrow. I am pleased to meet you and I hope you are recovering well."

I held out a weak hand and the officer gripped hard but didn't shake it. "Your shoulder will take more time, I think."

There was an awkward pause. I was clearly expected to say something, but it was Manresa who took the lead.

"SIGC means Intelligence," he explained. "That is Intelligence with a capital 'I' even if intelligence in lower case is sometimes lacking in the ranks of the GC."

It was a heavy-handed joke but it broke the ice.

"I am to be questioned at last?"

"*Señor* Barrow, I don't think you know how ill you have been."

"No, he doesn't," chipped in Carlito. I flashed him a hard stare. "He thought he was superman and could shake off the trauma by being crusty and cantankerous."

"Well, to some extent it looks as if he's succeeded," conceded Manresa. "You should know that your shoulder was badly damaged. But it was, thank God, a flesh wound. The bones were chipped but stayed intact. And the surgeons have done a magnificent job filling in the holes."

It was my turn.

"Let me get this straight. You are from the intelligence branch of the *Guardia Civil*?"

He nodded, took a chair and sat down.

"So, how do you fit into an investigation about a missing MP who is wanted as a suspect in a murder case? And what is it you want from me?"

Before, Manresa could get going, Carlito explained that the Ortiz case had been taken out of the hands of the police in Andalucía. Given the shoot-out at the warehouse, the killing of a police officer and all that had had happened to me and the guy from *Podemos...*

"Who thankfully wasn't as badly wounded as you and has given the *Teniente Coronel* some useful information," interrupted Raul with a touch of belligerence.

Carlito continued. The whole thing was now a matter of concern at the highest level.

"The highest level – meaning what exactly? Who, at the highest level?"

"The government," said Manresa. "*Señor* Jimenez would have told you much of this earlier if you had been in a condition to absorb and understand it."

"Well, I'm absorbing and understanding with a vengeance right now. So, please continue."

"You are a big story, Charlie Barrow."

I noted the change to familiarity.

"You may have uncovered the extent of some nasty skulduggery by groups of influential and powerful people aiming to undermine other groups who oppose them."

"These being people either inside the governing party or in some way connected to it who are getting worried about the rising popularity of our friends in *Podemos*?" My intervention caused Raul to relax a little."

"I have to choose my words carefully," said Manresa. "But, yes, you are essentially on the right lines. Except that the opposition Socialist Party is also the target of protests against the establishment." He folded his arms and ran his eyes over me. "Up to now, the politics of Spain, since what we call the *indignados* protests of 2011 against corruption, have been relatively civilised, without violence if not without rancour."

Raul was going to intervene, but Manresa held up his hand.

"Raul is going to tell me that my account misses out the rise of *Podemos*. It would be hard to ignore *Podemos* given their success at elections. And it would be hard to ignore rulings by the courts that the PP has been running well-stocked slush funds even if the prime minister denies it."

"And now we have a bunch of Moroccan or Algerian gunmen armed with AK47s. So where is this taking us?" I asked abruptly.

"You came to Spain for a holiday, Charlie Barrow. But you are a journalist and you got curious very quickly. You met Ortiz. You met Carlito here. You quickly learned about the exhumation of corpses in Castillo and you witnessed at first hand Ortiz's crude attempt to put a stop to it. Do I need to go on? You know yourself what's happened to you since. You arrived in Madrid and undertook a freelance search for a man charged with a murder in strange circumstances apparently inside a police cell in Castillo. You established a friendship with the woman in charge of the exhumations."

Carlito coughed and avoided my gaze.

"She came with you to Madrid and helped you by roping in Raul and his people from *Podemos*. You were shot in broad daylight. She has been killed. The story's all over the media..." He was being very matter of fact.

"And you still haven't found Ortiz who caused all this mayhem."

He raised his hands almost apologetically. "That, *Señor* Barrow, amounts to an admission by you that we in SIGC do have a legitimate interest in the case."

Carlito laughed. Raul followed suit.

178

"Very clever," I said. "Masterly. You must be another lawyer."

"By training."

"What do you want me to do? I asked.

"First of all, you can explain what you meant by what you shouted out when we first arrived."

"I meant what I said. I have missed the obvious. In looking for Ortiz, I should have looked up his address in Madrid and bearded him in his own den."

"We've done that a long time ago. He's not there. Never has been. You would have wasted your time."

"So he's still at large?"

"So it seems."

"At the grave risk of boring the pants of everybody, including myself, I ask again. Please tell me why the goons at the warehouse were so keen to hold one of your men hostage, cut his throat and use automatic weapons against us, so keen in fact that they even tried to kill two of us, if they hadn't got something or someone important to defend. If Ortiz wasn't with them, why go to all that trouble, indulge in a fruitless gun battle and die for their pains? My educated guess is that they were under orders to keep your people busy until their mates could spirit Ortiz out of the back door, so to speak, and whizz him off to another hiding place."

"If of course it was Ortiz they were protecting. It also assumes that they consider him very important. Why? We simply don't know. Not yet at any rate."

I shook my head in furious disbelief. What was this man trying to tell me? But he quickly shifted to a different tack.

"You have an obligation to help us by facing the news media," he said.

"I have what?"

"I am requesting that you appear at a news conference at *Guardia Civil* headquarters, say, in two days from now."

I managed to throw out my left arm and waved it vigorously to show Manresa I was far from happy about any of this. It was Raul who intervened.

"He's right, Charlie. You are up to your neck in this story and you owe the hacks some good copy – from the horse's mouth. You owe it to us too, *Podemos,* who put themselves on the line for you."

"Oh, I see. You'd like a bit of favourable publicity. Politicians riding off the backs of others as usual."

"That's an unworthy remark," said Raul.

Carlito stepped towards my bed. "You owe it to Elena, Charlie."

I bowed my head.

But I hadn't revealed what my "obvious" factor was. I hadn't mentioned the point they were all missing. They wanted a meeting with the assembled media pack. They would get one. On my terms.

****

So what is it that's so obvious?

It's a coup, or at least an attempted coup.

What coup? Nothing's happened.

Martínez Ortiz is planning a coup.

How do you know?

Instinct.

Am I allowed to laugh?

If you want to.

But you have no evidence.

I have circumstantial evidence.

On the basis of the shoot-out at the warehouse? You must be kidding.

It's a good start. Plus Elena's death and the buggering about I've been subjected to.

To stage a coup, Ortiz would need the army and the Guardia. These days, the army does as it's told. And if you want proof that the GC is on the side of the angels, the boys who ended the siege and a man like Manresa ought to be good enough for you. February '81 and that silly ass, Tejero, won't happen again.

I'm not expecting it to be like that. Think about it. Ortiz is an ultra-right wing member of the governing party. He is the child of Francoists. There are others like him. They want to see the restoration of what they believe were the certainties of dictatorship. Authoritarian government. A strong Church and a strong monarch. They want an end to organisations like Carlito's and projects like Elena's. And they are not choosy about who they team up with to achieve their aims.

And how are they going to stage their coup?

They'll form their own army, their own militias. Just like Jobbik in Hungary. Remember what we saw there? Remember Mihaly Kozma? Remember Peter Kovacs who lost his life bringing those bastards to heel? Spain has the same. And we have to stop them.

We?

Carlito, Raul, Manresa, *Podemos*, the boys and girls carrying on Elena's work in places like Castillo.

I think you're letting your imagination run wild again.

Listen. There are plenty of guns knocking around. All over Europe, North Africa and the Middle East. All for sale at the right price. Loads of them are smuggled in from South America and the Balkans. And Ortiz and his mates have money. Money to buy the drugs which get swapped for weapons. Money to pay Arab gunmen. What price a juicy alliance between the likes of Ortiz and a group of mad jihadists?

I'm afraid I think I know what this is leading up to.

Then you'll have to stay afraid.

You're seeking revenge for Elena.

Actually I'm not.

Chapter 18

It was a Friday, mild but cloudy, threatening rain. Carlito was as busy as ever. He had rightly judged that once discharged from the hospital, I should move into a different hotel and it should be one close to the *Podemos* main office. He had seen to it that my clothes and belongings were collected by some nice people from the party. He stood on a chair and helped me into a clean white shirt. The shoulder ached like fury and my stiff right arm would stay that way for many weeks. But I could move it and even grip small objects – cups and glasses, books and newspapers. And I'd bought newspapers as if my life depended on them. My Spanish was now good enough to understand most of what was in them. I read and read and read again. I watched TV news and listened to radio bulletins. When the news conference started, I would be as prepared as I could be.

Inside the headquarters of the *Guardia Civil*, Manresa had laid on a large windowless room, almost a lecture theatre, for an event I was now only too keen to attend. It was only when I saw the crowd of reporters and TV crews gathered in front of me that I finally understood the waves I'd been creating. There were six chairs at the front of the platform. I sat between Carlito and Raul. And there were several surprise visitors. To my left at the far end sat a very composed eleven-year-old boy and an old, dignified woman – Juan José and *La Bruja*, *Señora* Celestina. And right at the end, Juan Codina, the detective who'd tried to nail Martínez Ortiz for the murder of big Pepe in a police cell in Castillo. Squeezed in behind us sat Juan José's mother and father, three of Raul's mates from *Podemos* and three *Guardia* officers.

Manresa stayed in the background, assigning Carlito to chair the proceedings. I saw him standing at the rear of the room, arms folded, next to a smart grey suit from the interior ministry, or so I assumed. They looked on with poker faces, unsmiling, keeping the journalists at arm's length.

Carlito picked up a gavel, banged it hard six times and the hubbub subsided. He told the journalists they would hear from every one of us in turn, starting with Juan José followed by Celestina and Juan the detective. I would then make my contribution and Raul and Carlito would speak if they felt something had been left unsaid which should have been said. There was some muttering at this.

"We want to hear from Barrow," one old hack shouted in English. "And we want to hear from him now."

For all his small size, Carlito affected a presidential air which wasn't going to brook objections to his running order.

The hack shrugged and his colleagues tittered at the put-down.

Juan José explained how he and Celestina and the dog, Orlando, had come across the mass grave in Castillo. He showed no sign of nerves. His voice was clear and he even raised a laugh with his rather poetic description of the night-time visit to the cemetery. *La Bruja* confirmed the story, adding that she now scolded herself for failing to realise the graves had been there for most of her lifetime.

"How old are you, *Señora*?"

"Eighty," she replied, proudly throwing back her head. She said that as a child, she had survived the last months of the Civil War and Franco's dictatorship. She'd been bullied and harassed by the *Guardia Civil* and local officials.

"But I was too ugly to rape," she said.

There was a collective gasp and the room became oppressively still. "To my shame, I never suspected the place contained a gruesome secret."

A young reporter broke the spell. "Did you ever hear shooting?" she asked. "Did you see soldiers marching civilians to the graveyard?"

"I heard some shooting, but I was too young, too innocent, to understand what was going on. I thought they were still fighting those the grown-ups called 'Reds' or Republicans." She lowered her gaze. "I should have known better."

There came a brief burst of applause from some of the hacks. Carlito let it die down and indicated it was Juan Codina's turn to speak.

"I got involved in all this when *Señor* Barrow was assaulted in the street outside his hotel in Castillo." He gave a swift rundown of all the events leading up to Pepe's death and his own efforts to detain Jaime Martínez Ortiz on a charge of murder. He also fired a discreet salvo or two at his own superiors suggesting that they might have been more concerned than they had been at the lawyer's escape from the local jail and his flight to Madrid in a large black Mercedes accompanied by some smartly dressed North Africans wearing designer shades.

"What conclusions do you draw from that?" asked a reporter.

"It's not my business to draw conclusions," he replied.

"But you are hinting that someone with power and influence sprang the man from his cell and your local bosses turned a blind eye."

Juan smiled and touched his lips and kept them shut. Carlito judged the moment.

"Mr Charlie Barrow will speak next. In English."

The journalists coughed, shuffled their backsides and flicked the pages of their notebooks. Cameramen adjusted their lenses, radio reporters tapped their microphones and photographers rearranged themselves as they tested their sight lines.

I did my best to keep it short and succinct but there was a lot to tell. My first job was to explain Elena's role in the search for Ortiz, how she'd been so angered by his attempts to stop the work on the exhumations in Castillo and by the desecration of the mass grave that she'd decided to throw in her lot with me. I kept clear of our relationship but wondered how long I'd be allowed to remain silent on the subject. I didn't dwell on my brief detention in the hotel room by people I now knew had connections with the governing party but made it clear that someone "at the top" was after my blood.

I fixed my gaze on the nearest television camera. "They've already shed Elena Silva's," I said. Another oppressive silence took hold of the room.

"I have two stories to tell my editor," I went on. "One, the story of the mass graves and the work my good friend Carlito Jimenez and his Association are doing to identify the corpses and the other remains and ensure they finally get a decent burial. Add to that the attitude of certain people in authority who've been trying to block him."

"And the second?" someone shouted.

"The second story concerns a rich and influential member of your governing party who's been at the heart of attempts to sabotage the exhumations and is now on the run after being held on suspicion of murder. The irony is that his victim..."

"Always assuming he's found guilty," came a sharp intervention from one of the hacks.

"Agreed," I said trying to summon up an impenetrable smile.

"And the irony?"

"...is that the man he is accused of murdering was one of his own, so to speak. A big man with a foul temper who beat me up in the street, tried to do it again in the hospital at Castillo, and made no effort to hide his contempt for Carlito's work and *my* efforts to cover all this for a British newspaper."

"So, why accuse a man like Ortiz of killing him?" asked the same reporter.

Juan Codina interrupted to say he'd collected the evidence to justify an arrest. He didn't go into details.

"So," I countered quickly, "why skip bail and stay out of sight?"

Carlito broke in to say that I should be allowed to tell the rest of my tale.

This gave me a chance to thank the people at *Podemos*, but before I could continue, the same reporter was back on the offensive.

"*Podemos* apparently told you that Ortiz was holed up in the warehouse. I should like to hear from their representative how they got that information." He gave me a long, hostile, look. "And was it true?"

Raul made as if to speak but Carlito held up a hand.

"He'll tell you all in good time, *Señor.*"

The man started to protest but those around him told him to keep quiet. Carlito bent towards me. "He's from a pro-government paper, Charlie. He has an agenda," he whispered.

I ploughed on. But I didn't have to go into detail about the shoot-out and the wound to my shoulder. They'd known all about that for some time, which was why my mug was all over their front pages and their television screens.

Then I took my chance.

"If I suggest to you that someone somewhere in government or the governing party, or the army, or perhaps the security services, is planning something rather disloyal..." I lingered over the word. "...would any of you be surprised?"

The hacks were in sudden disarray. Some were shouting at one another, some were shouting at me. TV cameras and the photographers were focussing on us like hyenas after their prey. I marvelled at young Juan José who seemed to be enjoying it all. But Celestina clasped her bony hands together in an obvious effort to stop them shaking. At last a general fatigue restored some order but not before there were several shouts of, "Explain! Explain!"

I brandished a newspaper.

"While some kind person was massaging my shoulder yesterday, I read a report..."

Don't try to play with them, Charlie Barrow. It'll rebound on you.

"It said a man had been arrested in Galicia and charged with possessing a rather large collection of weapons. They included 120 firearms of one sort or another and nearly two hundred thousand cartridges and bullets. The paper said it was probably the largest haul of unauthorised arms found in Spain since the end of the Civil War. It was discovered in A Coruña by the *Guardia Civil*, as part of their campaign to snuff out attempts by Islamic fundamentalists or jihadists to obtain weapons and explosives from traffickers based in Spain. The GC said the man arrested had bought them online as scrapped items and restored them to full working order. They included thirty assault rifles, eighteen submachine guns, pistols, carbines and revolvers. And finally the paper quoted a man from the interior ministry as saying that as none of the weapons was officially registered, they could have been sold on to terrorists. The GC is trying to trace their origin to find out if any of them have been used in unsolved crimes. But the curious thing is that this haul of weapons was accompanied by some documents. And whose name is on those documents?"

I slapped the newspaper down in front of me.

"Jaime Martínez Ortiz," I declaimed. "Cited as the customer taking official delivery of the arms."

"You'd better be sure that what you've just said stands up in a court of law," shouted the hostile hack. "In any case, we all know there are loads of arms knocking about in Spain. Why wouldn't there be? Have you ever heard of ETA? Has nobody told you about 11-M?"

"I know all about 11-M," I lied, although I knew enough to fend him off. "Atocha train station, 11th March 2004, three days before a general election. All put down to a possible Al Qaeda cell from Morocco."

The hack scowled at me. "Unless we get a look at those so-called documents with *Señor* Ortiz's name on them, I, for one, don't believe you."

"You wouldn't, knowing who you work for," said another reporter to a gentle wave of embarrassed laughter.

"Okay. Okay. Okay!" I threw my hands up and called for calm. "You all should be aware that this haul contained rifles bearing labels like Mauser, H & K, Sako and Sauer. Makes issued to the police and the *Guardia.* So I ask myself – where did those come from? I also know enough about arms trafficking to tell you that anyone having anything to do with this little heist is in with some of the oldest criminal groups in Spain, or their successors. They operate mainly in Andalucía, along the Costa del Sol. But they have branches in Galicia, the Basque country, Valencia and Catalonia. They're made up of all sorts of villains, Spanish, Arab, Colombian, Russian. They're also involved in drugs, property and tourism. A bunch of Russians has even tried to buy one of your banks. They make lots of money and buy lots of arms."

Fifty or so faces were staring hard at me, apparently drinking in every word I spoke.

"In the old Yugoslavia, a Kalashnikov with four hundred rounds can be bought for about four hundred euros. Those in the know scoop them up in large numbers. Most of them end up in Belgium. If you want to buy one from a man lurking around the Gare du Midi in Brussels, it'll cost you a thousand to two thousand euros. Some of these weapons find their way into France and Spain. You might care to ask yourselves, what are the arms for and who's going to use them?"

I took a little water from the carafe in front of me.

"You have just referred me to 11-M," I said staring at the reporter who'd raised the subject. "Let me refer *you* to a man called Hassan el-Haski sentenced by a Spanish judge to fourteen years for belonging to the group that carried out the 11-M bombings. He was later extradited to Morocco to stand trial for taking part in the Casablanca bombings in 2003. Then he shows up in Brussels, in the suburb of Molenbeek, well known for being a place where would-be jihadists can find a safe house. Belgium, my friends. Nice little country, but keep your eyes focussed on it. Because that's where the trouble either starts or the trails lead back to."

"You seem remarkably well informed," one reporter declared. "And you are suggesting...?"

"I'm suggesting that, after what I've been through in the last few weeks, after the brutality of Elena Silva's murder, and the curious behaviour of Jaime Martínez Ortiz, after everything I've told you today and all the other stuff you know, I can legitimately reach the conclusion that someone in your beautiful country is taking advantage of these networks and plotting a coup."

There was more kerfuffle and general clamour. I watched Carlito whose face gave nothing away. Did he approve of what I was doing? Or would he give me a good bollocking when it was all over?

Again I held up my hands for a little less noise.

"I've seen all this before. I saw it in Hungary after the collapse of communism. I reported on it. They thought they'd got democracy and freedom. Instead they got plots and private armies. And an intolerant right-wing government. Those who had been in control in the bad old days wanted to keep control. They simply changed the labels. Like Putin's Russia. The only novelty was a chance for a very few to make loads of money. It's happening in Spain. Look at your so-called conservatives, the children of Franco's timeservers. Even your socialists are tainted. Money. Greed. Corruption. Why do you think you've got people like Raul here trying to change things? They might just put the mockers on people like Martínez Ortiz. Let's hope your army and the *Guardia Civil* behave themselves this time. Let's hope there are no more Tejeros around – no more little jaunts like February 1981."

Manresa and his ministerial colleague stepped out of the shadows and left the hall. Few of the hacks noticed. Carlito and I exchanged anxious glances. But it was Raul who took over.

"*Señor* Barrow is right..."

Before he could go any further, the hack with the agenda shouted, "I want an answer to my question. How did *Podemos* know, or how did you suspect, that Martínez Ortiz was hiding in the warehouse?"

Raul squared his shoulders and leaned forward. "I know your paper. I know the line it takes against us. You think we're amateurs, don't you? You think that because we've only just arrived on the scene, we're incompetent, disorganised, inefficient and all the other insults you can throw at us. We knew about Ortiz because, like every other political party, we have a network of contacts."

"You mean informers, spies?"

"You can call them what you want. We have members and supporters who supply information." He stressed the word as if to educate the journalist into its meaning. "And I'm not going to apologise for telling you that we have friends in other parties ready to tip us off. We all do it. It stinks. But given the dirty tricks our opponents are ready to play, we have to watch our backs. And those friends help us to do that."

I was wondering whether Raul's indignation had carried him too far. What he'd said would make good copy and there were bound to be clips on TV news. But he hadn't finished.

"What we didn't know was that there were armed men inside the warehouse ready to shoot it out with the *Guardia* and the police. So, like Charlie Barrow, I ask you – who were they protecting? Who were they fighting for? Who paid them?"

This time the enemy rose from his seat and wouldn't give way.

Carlito indicated that he should be given the roving mike.

He took it and licked his lips. "You do realise, *Señores,* that in precisely thirty-seven days from now, this country will hold an election. What you have said today cannot but have an impact on voters' intentions. Do you not think that your performances have been scandalous and irresponsible in the extreme – an attempt by *Podemos* to manipulate a gullible British journalist into spreading alarmist stories and destabilise the whole electoral process?"

As he sat down, he treated his fellow reporters to a look combining scorn and self-righteousness in equal amounts. The rest of the room mumbled and fidgeted, totally uncertain as to what to do next.

Manresa had returned and walked on to the platform.

"That's it," he announced. "The news conference is over. Thank you, ladies and gentlemen."

He turned to Carlito. "I want you all in the green room at the back. Now!"

Chapter 19

"Quite a performance, Charlie Barrow."

Manresa had us sitting in a semi-circle. He surveyed everyone in turn. Juan José's parents had been waiting for us. They looked bemused.

"Juan José did an excellent job. You should be proud of him. *Señora* Celestina too."

"I was scared to death," she said, still wringing her hands but managing at last to control her shaking body.

"I wasn't," the boy said, cockily. His father moved as if to admonish him but Manresa raised his hand.

"That was obvious." Manresa smiled. He was anxious not to patronise. "I want to thank you both and Juan Codina for coming all this way, backing up *Señor* Barrow's story."

There was an awkward pause.

"So you're not reading the riot act?" I asked.

"No. Why should I? You all did exactly what I wanted you to do. Raul as well. Thanks are due all round."

"We could accuse you of using us," I said.

"I did use you. But what happened out there redounded well for us. I'm not apologising. We all gain credit."

"You are a very clever policeman, *Teniente Coronel.*"

He didn't move a muscle.

"Do I get the impression that Carlito here was in on your scheme to give us our heads especially when that obnoxious gentleman 'with the agenda' did his best to provoke us?"

Carlito looked at me as if he thought I was a complete fool. "I plead guilty, but it was for the best," he countered. "After tonight's TV news and tomorrow morning's papers, we'll have a country fully alert to possible, even probable, *tejemanejes* – skulduggery again, Charlie." Then as a deliberate afterthought. "Sorry to sound so morally superior."

Manresa intervened. "Juan Codina will take our visitors back to Castillo this afternoon on the AVE. Keep in touch with one another."

The boy's father finally plucked up the courage to speak. "You must understand, *Señor*, that our family doesn't often have close dealings with the likes of you. We steer clear of authority. But we hope we have done our duty by letting our son come to Madrid. I just hope that between us we haven't disturbed a wasp's nest – that we won't live to regret all this."

"That's partly what it's been about, *Señor*. Your son's tale needed telling and it will help us to make Spain a better place. I know that sounds pompous, but I can assure you that when all the gentlemen in this room have finished the tasks they've set for themselves, you and your family will be left in peace. We also hope to recompense you with a sum of money for your pains."

I looked at the father's expression. He wasn't convinced. For all Manresa's kindness, he would have to do as he was told. He and his wife, and *La Bruja*, got up to leave and said their farewells with admirable dignity. Juan José shook Manresa's hand and saluted. The policeman laughed his thanks and nodded towards Juan Codina.

"I know you'll look after them, officer. You'll go to the station in an unmarked car with two of my men. They'll see you on board the train. You'll go first class. And I'll keep you posted. Please do the same for me. When you reach Castillo, act normally."

Juan Codina said he had already made arrangements for them to be met and escorted back to their homes. It would be dark and he doubted anyone would notice their arrival.

"Well, you have enemies there. So stay alert."

They shook hands. "We may still get your man," said Manresa. "And you'll have him in court in Andalucía."

He swung round to face me and Carlito. "Now it's your turn. But first I have some business with my friend from the ministry." He left the room.

"What's all that about?" I asked.

Raul and his colleagues from *Podemos* had slipped quietly away.

"They know the ropes," said Carlito. "After the fracas you caused, there'll be reporters and crews hanging around. TV will want to interview you. Raul will try to fend them off. Manresa will calculate that you've said enough for now. He'll have to face his bosses and possibly some prominent politicians – in and out of government."

I certainly didn't want to face the cameras again, not in what the trade calls 'a one-to-one'. I was exhausted and punch-drunk and my shoulder was protesting again. Manresa returned.

"Okay," he said. "This is what we do. It has been agreed by my bosses," he said and smiled almost perversely, "that you two spend the rest of the day and tonight as guests of the *Guardia*. You are obviously not under arrest or in detention, but this is for your own protection. We have some very relaxing rooms in this building."

"You mean cells," I said.

"No, Charlie Barrow. I do not mean cells. You'll be very comfortable and you'll be well fed and watered."

"My gear? And Carlito's"?

"It will be picked up and brought to you. This is not a five-star hotel, but it is pretty civilised for a public building."

I was reminding myself of other places where I'd been in a similar predicament, in Berlin and Budapest, seeking refuge when life got too hot.

"All I ask in addition," said Manresa, "is that you stay in your quarters. Do not wander around the building. And for God's sake, don't go outside, not even to the car pound. In any case, it's raining hard."

I wasn't about to argue. Carlito pointed out that we would need to spend time watching the newscasts and assessing the impact of what I'd done. We'd also need to plan for the immediate future. Back to Castillo? Or keep our heads down somewhere else?

"Can I file a story to London?"

"I don't want you using your mobile. It can obviously be traced. You can try the secure line from your room. But, yes. Go ahead and make as much fuss as you can. Especially in that prestigious newspaper you work for."

"What do I do if they phone me – if anyone phones?"

"I doubt a signal will penetrate these walls, Charlie. But if they do get through, just cut them off. The phone should tell you where the missed call came from."

"And if someone messages me?"

"Note it and delete it. Don't answer it with the mobile."

Which was a great relief. It meant I would have time to collect my thoughts and write something.

"My laptop?"

"It's on its way."

Carlito too was anxious to have his hard drives back. The intelligence he'd collected on death certificates, the DNA data on some of the Castillo corpses which Elena had given him, and the hard information he'd amassed as opposed to the mere speculative, all of it was a gold mine.

Elena!

I'd been so preoccupied with Manresa and the presser and the subsequent brouhaha that I'd laid her to rest in the far corners of my memory. But if her soul still lived on somewhere out there, I wanted it to know that I was trying to conjure up her presence – the tanned face, the bronzed thighs with the sheen of sweat on them, the ebony hair, the dark eyes, her whole lithe being. Even if she had told me in a bad dream that I might have been completely mistaken about her.

Right now I just didn't care. I needed her. And it wouldn't happen.

"I love you." I mouthed the words, hoping Carlito wouldn't notice.

"You were really in love, weren't you? I'm truly sorry that her death brings you so much pain."

"Don't, Carlito. Please. Don't."

He let it rest and my dream faded. But for once I didn't hold back the tears. Carlito made an excuse to leave me alone.

****

Our billet at *Guardia* headquarters was everything Manresa said it would be. Modern, sparsely furnished but relatively congenial. It consisted of a lounge, two small bedrooms and a shared bathroom. Our bags and belongings had arrived. I took a long, hot shower and donned the cotton robe provided. Then I slept.

I was deep down under when Carlito shook me awake just before nine in the evening.

"Time to watch the box," he said.

I tottered out, bleary eyed, and sank into an armchair. Carlito handed me a strong black coffee. The television was jabbering something I could not understand. Title music faded away and I found myself focussing on a stylised bright blue map of the world rolling across the screen accompanied by what passed for triumphant music. A beautiful female wearing an orange blouse began to regale us with the day's news.

We were the lead story – clips of the news conference with interventions from the hostile reporter, some speculation from so-called experts and the head of the *Guardia Civil* reassuring the people of Spain that they were well protected from threats of terrorism and the remote possibility of a *coup d'état*.

Manresa joined us.

"I note that you kept your face off the screen, colonel," I said as meaningfully as I could manage.

"Just the way I like it. Since I'm inclined to believe what you have been telling me rather than the crap coming from those above me, I try to stay incognito, at least until we find Martínez Ortiz and get him into court."

"What crap is that?"

"Oh, Twitter messages from politicians in and out of government asking me what the hell I'm playing at – and worse. But I do have the support of my immediate superiors, thank God."

I was about to congratulate him on his strategy when the television pulled sharply out of our story to show an anxious anchor announcing 'breaking news'.

Paris had exploded. There'd been shooting inside a hall staging a rock concert; blasts outside a stadium where an international football match was being played; and more shooting at a number of restaurants and bars. The latest count put the death toll at 128 with many more seriously wounded. It was, said the newscast, all the work of suicide bombers or gunmen with Kalashnikovs and clearly prepared to die in shootouts with the police. There was an additional report that one of the attackers had escaped and was now on the run heading for the Belgian border in a Seat saloon.

"We have been knocked off the top," I said. "Dumped unceremoniously into second place."

We stared at the screen and stayed silent, absorbing horror and chaos on the streets of Paris.

"Puts us in the shade," I muttered, which on reflection I deemed an ungenerous comment.

But not completely. The newscast swung between Paris and Madrid, twenty minutes or so of early reports using material from French TV and then back to our news conference and my allegations. It returned to Paris as the TV newsroom received updates on casualties, locations, suspected numbers of terrorists and police action. There were clips from the football match with the clear sound of explosions as the players tried desperately to concentrate on the game.

The studio in Madrid had become full of pundits from newspapers, think tanks and academia, several of whom mulled over the possibility that what had been said at our news conference in Spain might have distinct connections with the sensational news from France.

We watched for a further ten minutes until Carlito grabbed the remote control and turned down the sound. Manresa slumped into an easy chair. He looked exhausted.

"If your friends in the media are now turning their eyes to Paris, it means we can push on to other business almost unseen."

Now we were entering new territory. Manresa seemed to have a strategy. Was it a reflection of his ambition or a genuine attempt to investigate the serious possibility that there were elements in Spain ready to re-impose authoritarian government with the aid of some very dark forces in the Muslim world? I hadn't gone that far at the presser. Or had I? What I *had* postulated was the employment of well-paid gunmen, Arab or otherwise, who might just do a lot of the dirty work for ambitious types like Ortiz. Had I dragged Manresa too far down the path of fantasy? If that's how he felt, I could point to the news from Paris and argue that villains in Spain would gladly exploit the same violent scenario to get at power.

"I don't think we can proceed without exposing ourselves," I said. "There'll be endless media speculation and posses of reporters charged by their editors with picking up from where we left off this morning."

The windowless room was becoming oppressive. I was developing a headache. We had to get out of the place.

Carlito said, "I know what we do now." He personified certainty and conviction. I could tell by the light in his eyes and the jaw he'd thrust out that he had a plan. Manresa seemed not to have heard him. His eyes were closed. I was preoccupied with shifting my aching shoulder, desperately seeking a more comfortable position.

"We go to *Fortaleza de los Enanos*," Carlito declared. "Tonight."

"We do what?" I stammered.

"Where's our hire car, colonel?"

"In the pound here at HQ."

"Can we have it back?"

"You can. But the journalists will recognise it. You'll be pursued."

"Simple. Lend us another one or change the plates. The *Guardia Civil* can do that for us, can't they?"

Manresa was in retreat. He nodded, grinning at Carlito's cheek and ingenuity.

"It's a Polo," observed Carlito. "It's black. There are thousands of them in Spain. It's as good a disguise as any for two men trying to give the press the slip."

"We are going to drive through the night in the pouring rain to a remote part of the *sierra*?" I was contemplating the powers of concentration we would need to negotiate Spanish roads in the dark.

"That we are," said Carlito in triumph. "We wait until two in the morning. My bet is that the hacks will have got fed up with hanging around. They'll have pushed off for a bite to eat."

"I hope you're right."

"In any case, we can't stay here forever."

Manresa said there was an exit into a narrow street which led to the Avenida de los Reyes Católicos. If we waited in the Polo for a full minute, we could drive the car gently and as quietly as possible up to the compound gate until it began to open.

"You keep it nice and slow. And take it easy in the street. Don't draw attention to the vehicle. Then you hit the Avenida and put your foot down. It'll still be busy even at that time of night but it should be pretty clear."

We turned up the TV sound. Coverage had evolved into repetition of pictures from Paris and clips of what the editors considered to be the best quotes from the news conference.

"Your big problem now is to pass the next three to four hours without subsiding into fatigue and cat naps."

"Right now, I shall sleep," said Carlito. "Because later, *I'll* be doing the driving." Pointing at me rather ferociously, he ordered me to wake him at one o'clock. He rose, shook Manresa's hand and made for his small bedroom. "I know the way, Charlie," he called over his shoulder. "Don't worry."

"Determined, isn't he?" quipped Manresa.

"As ever was," I replied. "I am continually assailed by the notion that he's always the one in charge." I paused. "And I'm glad of it."

Part 2

Chapter 1

Later, when I was wrestling with loneliness and depression in my apartment in Portugal, watching the Atlantic break on to the sands and a big red sun drop over the horizon, vivid memories of that journey to the *Fortaleza* swam into my mind's eye.

The plan worked. We packed and inspected the Polo. The *Guardia* mechanics had done us proud. The height of the foot controls had been adjusted to accommodate Carlito and a couple of thick cushions velcroed to the driver's seat. The car had new plates, as asked for, and a full tank. They'd cleverly left it unwashed. We did as Manresa had instructed. We sat still until the security lights in the pound were switched off. The gates leading to Calle Guzman El Bueno tested our patience by opening like withered limbs afflicted with arthritis. Carlito slid the vehicle out into the street. There were two TV cameras positioned opposite the gates, but the crews were prone on the pavement, apparently seeking shelter from the damp night air inside sleeping bags. They never moved. Carlito took advantage of some dim street lighting and covered the first hundred metres or so without revving the engine more than he needed to. We turned the corner.

"I don't really know where I'm going," I muttered.

"Then shut up and go to sleep."

I lay back in the seat. Traces of neon glow drifted across my eyelids. I allowed myself a glimpse of Carlito and saw a face fixed in concentration as he drove us out of the city on to the motorway. He kept the internal temperature at a minimum and the radio off. Wind and tyre noise seduced me into a doze from which I soon sank into deep slumber.

****

I woke with a start. Carlito had pulled up under the phosphorescent lights of a service station.

"I need coffee," he yawned. "And a stretch." He parked the car at the outer edge of the station perimeter. There was one other vehicle at the pumps. "No need for juice yet," he said.

"I'll get the coffees," I said and wandered over to the shop. The customer in front of me was buying *bocadillos* and a bottle of water. He was small and thin and wore worker's overalls. A large TV screen glared at us from the top right hand corner behind the counter. It showed yet more pictures of Paris and general mayhem.

"Kill the bastards," pronounced the vendor.

The little man stared at him and blinked.

"*Que?*"

"Kill them. Shoot them. Hang them. I don't care."

Without another word, the customer handed over a note and waited, nonplussed, for his change. It came with some inaudible grumbling. The little man sidled out, hunching his shoulders, gazing resolutely at the floor. It was my turn. I gave my order. The vendor had calmed down. He concentrated on pulling the levers of his *máquina* which sluiced coffee into two plastic beakers.

I looked up at the TV. There I was in all my glory. The sound was down but my image energetically waved its arms and pointed its finger. The picture cut away to a row of reporters. The vendor wasn't watching. I thanked him, lowered my head and carefully holding the coffees, walked steadily out of the shop towards the Polo.

"You look a little frazzled," observed Carlito.

"I was there. On that TV in his shop. I thank my stars he didn't recognise me."

"Drink your coffee and relax."

We took to the road again. There was a full moon but all I could see was a flat, rolling landscape of endless fields, harvested down to stubble, with a few ungainly trees and the occasional crumbling barn or cottage. This time I didn't sleep. I let the thoughts I knew I had to wrestle with creep into my consciousness to be tossed about until I could get them organised.

Carlito? Who was he? What was he? That he was truly Spanish could not be doubted. He was blessed with that mixture of the romantic and the pragmatic which I was beginning to acknowledge as a basic characteristic of the people. Romantic, because he could play his guitar with a skill and musicality that were perfect examples of Spanishness, of everything *hispanohablante*. Pragmatic, because of his work with the Association for the Recovery of Historical Memory. He had toiled for hours over dusty documents and fading certificates, trying to decipher the details of those killed in Franco's purge of the old Republic and aiming to reveal the identities of the corpses unearthed in places like Castillo.

He had a sharp mind. He was competent, super efficient and kind. He had seen me through two medical emergencies, held my hand, wept for me and devoted himself to my cause. He was brave even if he was 'an abnormally small person', the expression the Oxford English Dictionary selects while acknowledging that there are 'no accepted alternatives in the general language' to 'dwarf'. Carlito, I knew, couldn't give a monkey's for this political correctness. He was not insulted by being called an *enano*. He took pride in it.

But there was something missing. Carlito had secrets. He might tell me what they were in his own good time. I was hoping the journey to his *Fortaleza* would bring some of them out into the open.

Moonlight revealed a change in the landscape. The plains of Castile, sometimes called the black crucible of Spain, were giving way to silhouetted hills and deep, dark valleys, a sombre vista of granite outcrops, scrub and brush. Then the night sky was lost to thunder clouds and shafts of lightning.

Elena! I tried to subdue my anger at the speed with which she had been taken from me by some unknown killers simply because they had linked her with my clumsy attempt to solve the mystery of Martínez Ortiz. I accused myself of indecent haste in harbouring doubts as to her real purpose and her strange reluctance to mingle passion with trust.

You are wasting your time. It came and it went like a flicked finger. You have to forget it. Now you are into this story as deep as you are, you have a job to do, facts to find, words to write and a life to lead when it's all over.

Easier said than done. In any case, Elena is still relevant to that story. Which is why it's so hard to keep going.

It always is. You must surely know that by now, you unreconstructed day-dreamer.

We crossed the great river Tagus and arrived in a small town.

"Trujillo," Carlito informed me. "Like our priest in Castillo. It wouldn't surprise me if he came from here. The birthplace of one of the cruellest men in history. And, some say, one of the smartest. Francisco Pizarro. Conqueror of Peru. As he slaughtered the Incas in the name of Christ and his Catholic Church, he said, 'God is on our side'. And the Spanish believed him. He procured wealth and an empire. Gold, silver and land. If we had time I would show you how Pizarro brought Peru to Trujillo. The houses bear Inca statues and gargoyles. Look at it. Even in the first light of day you can see that it's a place too grand for the reputation of a wayward son. It's the illusion that's bedevilled Spain for five centuries or more."

One café had opened early. We drank more coffee and toyed at omelettes and newly baked bread.

"Do you want me to drive, Carlito?"

"No. It would take too long to dismantle the attachments to the footbrake and accelerator. And besides I know the way. Not far, Charlie. Up into the hills from now on."

He said little else, wiped his mouth with the napkin and stood up, ready to make a move. And, as ever, I followed suit.

'Up into the hills' meant extra skilful driving. Steep climbs, hairpin bends and breathtaking vistas as dawn crept slowly across arid slopes and sparse pastures grazed by a few sheep and goats. The clouds kept low and it began to rain again until torrents of the stuff hit the windscreen and made the wipers useless.

Then we were slipping into a valley made verdant by the downpour.

"It won't last," said Carlito. "The greenery will vanish when the water subsides. The streams will rush through gaps in the hills for an hour maybe. The ground will shine with moisture until even the winter sun will make it dry again. That's what it's like up here."

He smiled not at me but at the spectacle in front of us. I could tell he was glad to be coming home. He let the car coast downhill, took his hands off the wheel and threw his arms in the air with delight.

"There!" he shouted. "There. Look at that!"

As we freewheeled into the village, I saw a collection of small houses with whitewashed walls festooned with desiccated vines and terracotta roofs topped with the stubs of chimney pots. In among them, a modest church, its bell tower almost without ornamentation apart from an iron cross at the summit of its spire.

We trundled into the main square.

It was too early for a winter sun to start warming things up. But there was some bustle as 'abnormally small people' headed for the bakery.

"So, this is your beloved *Fortaleza*?"

"Your height will embarrass you for a while, Charlie. Don't worry. They'll get used to you."

He led me to yet another café.

"Mind your head!"

I ducked under the lintel. There were five men imbibing coffee and rolls. They stopped eating and drinking and rushed up to Carlito. The greetings were loud and rapid and joyful to a fault.

"Where have you been, you old rogue?" one asked.

He wasn't given a chance to answer. More questions came thick and fast. More embracing and shouts to the proprietor to open a bottle of *costa* which I learned later was the name for any locally produced wine in Spain.

Carlito calmed them down and did his duty, introducing me in turn to all and sundry and especially to the owner.

"Manuel. You are to take care of my friend, Charlie. He will probably be spending a lot of time in here in the next few days. So, your best ham and cheese, please, and, for lunch, one of those *Fortaleza* concoctions of omelette with *patatas,* onions, garlic, peppers and what the hell mixed in."

I sat in the biggest chair they could find for me and watched the bonhomie swirl round the bar, a wraith of goodwill and happiness to dispel the dullness of a cloudy morning in the *sierra.* It took a good ten minutes for the merriment to subside. Then they started to leave, singly or in jolly pairs, presumably heading for what work was available. But one man stayed put at a table in the far corner. Carlito led me over to him. He didn't get up to shake hands. He simply stared hard at Carlito and frowned.

"Let me introduce you to my big brother, Charlie. This is Felipe."

Felipe shifted his gaze towards me. His expression never changed. To say the silence between us was embarrassing would almost have been a joke.

Then he spoke. "Six months, Carlito. Six months. Your kids have stopped missing you."

"Thanks, Felipe. I wasn't expecting jabs to the solar plexus so soon."

I could sense that my face was that of one dumbfounded but I tried very strenuously not to show it.

"There's no point in avoiding an explanation, Charlie."

Carlito told me he had married six years previously. His wife, Julia Teresa, had born him a daughter, Maria. They had lived happily at *Fortaleza* while he used his lawyer's skills to help the dwarves reorganise their town after the chaos generated by the end of Franco's regime. Three years later, Julia Teresa was pregnant again. She died giving birth to a son, Tomasino. The children now lived with Felipe and his wife, Consuelo. Carlito had made a bargain with the couple that if they would let him find work away from *Fortaleza*, in a sizeable town or even a big city, he would make sure they had enough money for the children and themselves.

"He bought us a house," said Felipe, almost losing his peevishness as he finally caught my eye. "I'll say that for him. It's a nice house. We like it." He stopped. And exploded again. "Damn you! Damn you! Damn you!"

"That's enough, big brother. Enough."

"Stop calling me 'big brother'. It's not enough. You don't write. You don't send messages. We have the internet here now. Email and all that stuff. You don't phone." He took deep breaths in a desperate effort to stay in control.

"I send presents," said Carlito. "Books, CDs. And what about that enormous Lego set?"

This wasn't like Carlito. It was the first time I had heard him making excuses for his behaviour. It didn't suit him. He wasn't exactly losing the contest, but he wasn't his usual confident self.

I rose and went to the bar and ordered two glasses of local *tinto*, one for me and another for Felipe. I knew Carlito wouldn't want alcohol. For him a juice, a *zumo de naranja*.

The two brothers sat with their heads down finding interesting patterns in the plastic table tops. Then Felipe stood up. His chair clattered against the wall. Carlito did the same.

"It's time we went to the house," said Felipe. "You follow me. We've got a new one-way system but they haven't put the signs up yet."

He was driving a small pick-up. We tucked in behind. The streets off the *plaza* were just wide enough for the Polo. I had time to take in the character of the dwarf houses. The Scots would have called each one a 'but and ben', a ground floor of two or three rooms, the walls thick enough to keep the heat out in summer and, at this time of year, ward off the cold wind coming off the mountains. Some householders had clearly had a bit more money or ambition than others. Their cottages sported small dormer windows poking from the roofs, suggesting the addition of another room in the loft. Where there was some shelter from the draught and the bonus of light to let in a spot of sunshine, pots of winter geraniums relieved the rigid lines of a wall. I marvelled at the low doors and the windows with sills only half a metre from the ground. Indeed, I marvelled at finding myself in such a place despite the questionable start to my visit.

The street led to a smaller square. I could tell immediately which house belonged to Felipe and Consuelo. It was, so to speak, a normal house, with two-metre-high doorways, wide sash windows with white wooden frames and at least three storeys. It was not in itself a house for dwarves. Over its front door the one word, *Ayuntamiento.* Carlito's investment in property was currently *Fortaleza*'s town hall.

The two brothers seemed determined to sustain their hostility and be as morose as possible. But the lady who ran from the house was altogether different. The first person she saw was Carlito. She hurtled towards him, arms outstretched and hugged and kissed him as though she would never let go. Then she saw Felipe and beckoned him to join them. To his great credit, he did. I watched from afar, leaning on the Polo, as this three-sided welcome continued, forcing me to utter a rare prayer to a God I didn't believe in but thought perhaps I should, given what I was witnessing.

Consuelo saw me and was confused. I nodded my head and with consummate courtesy she bowed towards me. And all this time, the good-natured smile never left her pink and homely face.

"*Señor!*" She bowed again. "You are Carlito's friend? Welcome to our home."

Felipe and Carlito had untied themselves from the great embrace and entered the house. Consuelo came towards me, arms and hands outstretched. I was meant to take them and hold on for the seconds that politeness allowed.

"What a handsome man!" she chirruped. "How lucky Carlito is to have found a friend like you."

"You don't know me yet," I responded. "I may harbour terrible portents. I may become the worst guest you have ever entertained."

"A man of wit and irony? How good to receive a man of irony – at last."

She drew me into the house towards the large main room combining kitchen, dining area and space for two armchairs and a sofa. Hams hung from strong steel hooks and appetising cheeses took up part of the working surface near the sink. A log fire burned in the grate. Carlito and Felipe had installed themselves at the big chestnut dining table. They muttered to one another as if they didn't want either me or Consuelo to hear.

I waited until spoken to. Consuelo brought food and wine and surveyed the scene with amused detachment.

"Leave them be," she declared, shooting disdain and exasperation in equal proportions. "Come with me."

Consuelo seemed less restricted by her dwarfism than either of the men. Her limbs were looser. She walked with some grace and apparently with no pain. We entered a small room at the back of the house. A little boy sat on a large rug in the corner. He was surrounded by toys and colourful books. He looked up and laughed softly.

"See what I've done," he said. He pointed to a pile of Lego bricks locked together in a shape I found it hard to put a name to.

Consuelo saw my puzzled expression and smiled. "And what have you done?"

"A house," he replied. "*Mi Casa.* My house."

Tomasino, at just over two years had inherited all the characteristics of his father. He had Carlito's foreshortened limbs and a face old before its time. But it was happy face, full of glee that he had achieved something.

"He can't move very easily," observed Consuelo confidentially. "He spends a lot of time in that corner with his toys. And the Legos have been a God-send."

"It was a present from Carlito, wasn't it?"

"Yes." She turned serious. "A present instead of a presence," she added, displaying the sad wisdom of approaching middle age. "Of course it was good of him to send it." She sighed and peered at me. "But it made Felipe angry."

"Angry or jealous?"

"Both, I suppose."

"Where's Tomasino's sister?"

"Maria's at the nursery school." I was to learn more about this all in good time. "It is one of the best community projects we have in *Fortaleza*. The teachers are all our own. Handicapped experts on how to overcome handicaps," she said with some vehemence.

I bent down slowly, hoping that Tomasino would show me his Lego. To my relief, he laughed again and held it up for my inspection.

"That's pretty good, Tomasino. It's a very fine house."

"*La Casa!*" he shouted lustily. He picked it up with some skill and handed it to me. I made a show of examining it, tentatively touching all the sides, surfaces and angles, and squinting in at the 'windows' he'd created.

"Windows," he said firmly as if I needed convincing. "I can see you!"

"Pick him up," Consuelo suggested. "He's given you the stamp of approval. He won't flinch. He's certainly not afraid of you."

I held out my hands, carefully placed them under his armpits and lifted him. He was no weight at all. He giggled. I hoisted him into my arms so that he could look over my shoulder. But first he winked at me and I winked back. He giggled again. Then he kissed me.

"Come on," I said. "Let's go and see Uncle and Papa."

"No," said Consuelo. "No. That can wait. Let's go into the garden and look at the animals."

I took my cue and we passed through a door at the back of the house into a sizeable pergola, its framework, even in winter, sheltering a variety of plants – more geraniums, purple daisies, a trailing vine, bougainvillea and pampas grass, all vying for space in the well-tended beds. There was no attempt at a lawn. We walked on gravel and stone.

The morning had grown warmer.

"I apologise for the flies," said Consuelo. "But thankfully, it is too cold for wasps and hornets."

She explained how Felipe had spent months building the pergola. He'd asked her to choose flowers and shrubs and throughout the late summer and autumn these had grown to form the beginnings of a garden where they could shelter from the beating sun in summer and the misty rains of winter. Beyond the pergola I saw a field with sections laid out for chickens and guinea fowl and after that a wider area fenced at the sides. About twenty healthy sheep stopped grazing and looked at me suspiciously.

Consuelo laughed. "They are monumentally stupid," she said, then checked herself. "But perhaps not that stupid when it comes to finding the best plants to eat. They keep the grass down but they also like to wander where they can find rosemary, broom and thyme."

"This must take some looking-after," I suggested.

"The biggest problems are predators and pests – foxes, wild cats, snakes and rats. And the insects."

She paused and looked at the landscape outside their property, the foothills of the *sierra* made very green by the recent rain. To the left a stream ran fast and vanished beyond a stone wall.

"It feeds our *acequias* –our irrigation channels. It's full of life right now. But when it's down to a trickle in summer – if we're lucky – we depend on what's left in the channels for all our water."

A wind had blown up, shaking an expansive eucalyptus and the willows and pines further afield.

"I can't think of a nicer place to bring up children," I remarked.

"I love it here." She paused and put on her glum face again. "I'm not so sure about Felipe. He's proud to be a member of the *Fortaleza* community and does a great deal for it. He knows what will work. He knows just how much oil we can get out of our olives, how many trees to fell for the beams for new houses, how much wine we can press from the grapes we gather; and a thousand and one other things. Will we have enough vegetables for the winter? Can we afford to slaughter this or that number of sheep and goats and pigs?"

"So the people of *Fortaleza* look up to him?"

"Some of them are lazy. Some think that if they do as he says, all will be well."

"It's a heavy responsibility."

"And he's beginning to get fed up."

Throughout this exchange, Tomasino stayed in my arms, pointing to the sheep and the chickens and whatever else took his fancy.

"Let him down, *Señor.* He should have the exercise."

I eased the child gently to the ground. He took the simple option and sat.

"Up, Tomasino," ordered Consuelo. "Up! Try to walk."

He didn't cry or wail. He just looked abandoned and wasn't sure what to do next. Consuelo lifted him so that his tiny feet touched the ground. He got the idea, held her hand and did his utmost to walk. But it was beyond him. I stood back, not wishing to interfere. Consuelo scooped him up.

"We must find out what our two men are doing."

We walked back inside. There was no sign of Carlito and Felipe.

"They'll have gone up to the office," she said. "You should join them."

I looked at her wholesome face and honest eyes. I wanted to ask her more. Instead she flashed one last question at me.

"You were on television last night?"

I nodded. "I was filmed at a news conference in Madrid."

"And you made certain allegations."

"*Señora.* I tried to warn everybody that there were some nasty men and women in Spain who were probably plotting..."

"A coup?"

I understood now that despite all the chores she had to perform, Consuelo found time to keep herself informed.

"We watch the evening news and sometimes listen to the radio. But the newspapers come a day late up here."

We wandered into the house.

"It's a very serious allegation, *Señor*."

"I would not have made it if I hadn't been sure of all the things that persuade me it's true."

"I will give Tomasino some lunch," she said. "You carry on – up to the second floor."

She left me feeling bewildered, even ashamed. She was not the sort of person I wanted to frighten or disturb. But then I remembered that there had to be millions like her who felt the same way and were wondering, after all I'd said, if and when their world would collapse around them.

Chapter 2

As I climbed the stairs to Felipe's office, I noticed how thick the walls were. This house must have been built well before *Fortaleza* was created. The deep sills of landing windows hinted that it might once have been the residence of some well-to-do farmer or the member of a profession who wanted to escape the rigours of the city.

The door to the office was ajar. I knocked.

"Come in," they said in chorus.

I found them staring at a computer screen. It showed the latest TV news from Madrid. The item was all about the aftermath of yesterday's news conference. More swift shots of me and cutaways to reporters but a new element had been added to the mix of pictures. Here was the prime minister trying to reassure Spaniards that my allegations had been nothing more than the ramblings of a crazy British journalist. He was followed by the interior minister informing viewers that I had gone into hiding but the police and *Guardia* had mounted a nationwide search for me *"and his friend, one Carlito Jimenez, who works for the Association for the Recovery of Political Memory and is easily recognised as a dwarf"*.

"Which is why," declared Felipe, "I want reassurances from my brother that you are not about to bring down the wrath of the all powerful on *Fortaleza*."

"Were we followed, Charlie?" asked Carlito.

"I don't know. I slept a lot of the time in the car. But I don't think I remember any persistent headlights behind us after we'd cleared Madrid."

Carlito had been trying to explain to Felipe how we'd organised the journey from GC headquarters so as to look insignificant and anonymous. He gave an account of our uneventful stops at the filling station in the middle of nowhere and in Trujillo, even if he did miss out the moments when I might have been spotted by the assistant working the levers of his percolator.

"No helicopters over the mountains," said Carlito. "No spotlights. In any case, the bad weather would have put them off."

"I hope you're right," Felipe muttered.

Television news had moved on to something on unemployment. I looked round the room. It not only had Felipe's laptop but a separate and larger computer which I assumed was for official business. There were filing cabinets, shelves full of documents, a row of legal tomes and an electric typewriter protected by a plastic cover which seemed to have gathered a fairly thick coating of dust.

A thought struck me.

"You've got an election coming up on the 20th. I didn't see any posters or hoardings in town." In fact, the outer walls of most of the buildings were free of any advertising material, graffiti or handbills. The only notices I'd seen were pinned to official boards on the outside of the *Ayuntamiento* or the church. "Are the people of *Fortaleza* not interested in the democratic process?" I asked, rather more superciliously than I'd intended.

"Don't be flippant, *Señor*," growled Felipe. "They are as interested in it as any other community in Spain."

Carlito eyed me as if to say, 'Tread carefully with this one, Charlie'.

Felipe pressed on. "We had a visit from a group of PP people two weeks ago. They came to me and said they were plastering a few walls with some of their stuff. I said we didn't want it. They said I couldn't stop them."

"But you are the elected mayor here."

He sat back in his chair and gave me a withering look.

"It didn't make any difference," he sniffed. "But we have a couple of good *Guardia* lads here, one a sub-lieutenant. He's an outsider but a good man. The other's one of us. He's a corporal and very efficient. And before you ask, he was given a dispensation from the height requirement."

They'd told Felipe to leave well alone. Much as they were on his side, if he'd tried to pull the posters down, he'd have been breaking the law, mayor or no mayor. Then he laughed. At last.

"We've had a lot of rain just lately. It washed off most of the posters. We weren't bothered by any of the other parties."

Carlito had explained to me a while back that the folk of *Fortaleza* did their best these days to stay out of politics. He was sure most of them were no friends of the PP, but they didn't want any of their private allegiances known to anybody or any authority, not even Felipe.

"But are they going to vote?" I asked. "It's a secret ballot after all."

"Oh, they'll vote. Probably for the Socialists. Or they might take a look at this *Podemos* outfit," he replied looking pointedly at Carlito. Then he asked outright. "Are you a member, little brother?"

Carlito heaved himself up in his chair and took a deep breath. He knew it was time come clean.

"Yes, I joined six months ago. I went to a few meetings in Seville and Carmona and approached them. They knew all about my work with the Association. They said they fully supported our attempts to put names to the corpses in the exhumed graves. Since it was obvious they were now on a roll, I didn't have any doubts about what I had to do. I knew I would need more political support for our work and I'd need the backing of people who might just promise to lobby for some money out of state funds. We can't go on relying on irregular handouts from private sources."

Felipe turned over some papers on the desk in front of him. He switched off his laptop and stood up.

"Time for a drink," he said. He had shed some of his reserve. He even smiled.

Chapter 3

Manuel's bar was buzzing again. It was well before three o' clock, the usual time for a Spanish lunch, but the 'abnormally sized' populace of *Fortaleza* was already tucking in to meatballs, kidney beans, boiled potatoes with sausage and bacon, stews and tortillas. The local *tinto* was flowing with the occasional brandy as a chaser.

Of course it was Saturday, not a day of rest for everybody but one where the anticipation of a happy Sunday seemed already to have overcome a sizeable number of the inhabitants. And there was a big difference from the usual Spanish bar. There were as many women as men.

"You see," Carlito whispered mischievously in my ear. "*Fortaleza* is not just for dwarves. It's for Equality with a big 'E'."

"But I don't see Consuelo here."

"She's not one for places like this. She's more preoccupied with the children, especially Tomasino."

"She's doing a marvellous job there. You should be bloody grateful." I felt myself on the verge of aggression and outrage but trying to contain them.

"I am bloody grateful. And I'm doing my best to show it, Charlie."

Knowing that we had trawled over the subject in the company of Felipe, I kept my mouth shut. I decided a little quiet social survey of the clientele wouldn't come amiss. I had by now conquered the habit of looking on all dwarves as more or less identical. And this lot proved the point. There were smooth middle-aged characters in suits, with female companions in fashionable blouses and trousers, young ones in jeans and t-shirts or sharp leather jackets with the latest sporty footwear, and those of both sexes who'd clearly got outside jobs or perhaps laboured away in local workshops.

"But," I put it to Carlito, "some of these women must have children to care for."

"And some of the men."

"So?"

"Not everybody in *Fortaleza*'s married, Charlie. And most of those who are have the support of exceedingly generous grandparents." He laughed in my face, aware that I still considered the apparent neglect of children a reprehensible feature of life in his town.

"Tomorrow it's grandma's turn – and grandpa's – *abuelas y abuelos*. They'll be in here, whooping it up with a game of cards or a round of *cartón completo* –

236

bingo to you! Husbands and wives stay away for the day. And the unmarried ones go to help them, cooking big family meals that last forever. You see. Equality. Sharing. The Commune. We've learned over the years it's the best way, Charlie."

Felipe approached with a plastic bottle full of red wine. "Last year's vintage," he said jovially. "Not bad for a tiny place like this stuck up in the hills."

There'd been a lot of talk about showing me round in the afternoon, if we ever got out of Manuel's. Or perhaps in the next few days. I was about to say that I'd like to see the school where, as Consuelo had put it, "the handicapped taught the handicapped". But the merrymaking came to an abrupt halt when two local *Guardia* men walked in with troubled looks on their faces. They made straight for Carlito and me.

"What's up, boys?" Felipe asked.

"*Señor,* we've been told there are men in uniform driving up the valley from Trujillo in jeeps and trucks."

"Who told you?" I asked.

"The dwarf officer looked at me artfully. "Your *Teniente Coronel* in Madrid. Manresa. He said that as of now he didn't know who they were. We got a call on our special line about a quarter of an hour ago."

"Did he say anything else?"

"Yes. He said, 'tell them to get out of there – fast'."

237

****

However much dirt the media and others had thrown at the firm of Volkswagen for tampering with emission data, it remained the case that they made bloody good cars. Bloody good cars with bloody good suspensions. The Polo took to a narrow dirt road leading up into the *sierra* with unquestionable gusto. For obvious reasons, we hadn't had time to adjust the height of the brake pedal and the accelerator. So Carlito drove yet again. And showed another talent which I certainly couldn't have emulated.

He steered like a seasoned rally driver. What's more, he did it with an automatic transmission. The rough ground was made worse by loose scree, rainwater pools deeper than they looked and slimy patches of pasture where the car's tyres lost grip.

"The lieutenant spoke of a shepherd's hut about three kilos up this track," I said as I tried to avoid being bounced around like a sheep's carcass. "Let's hope they haven't spotted us leaving. Let's hope they don't see a speeding car in amongst this divine scenery. Let's hope..."

"...they're idiots," Carlito chipped in. "We don't know how far up the road their little convoy's progressed. If they've only just left Trujillo, they won't have a view of this bit of country until they breast the hill leading down into *Fortaleza*."

He kept on driving like Sebastian Loeb. I decided against interrupting his concentration. We were high above *Fortaleza* by now, oblivious to the scenery and on the look-out for the hut. We saw it about five hundred metres ahead of us. Carlito parked quickly round the back, calculating that this might just keep the car out of sight.

His head drooped and fell to his chest. "Well, it'll have to do for now," he said through a round of panting and some deep breaths.

"Manresa doesn't know who they are or who sent them. They might not even be looking for us."

"Pull the other one, Charlie. I can hazard a damn good guess to all of that."

"Martínez Ortiz?"

"Him and his Moroccan pals. If it is them, it shows they've got money to fund a fairly well-equipped outfit."

"I wonder why Manresa didn't get wind of this."

Carlito bit his lip. "I think I made it a bit too obvious that we would head to *Fortaleza*. Someone close to Manresa who doesn't like him very much has spilled the beans to our version of Moriarty."

"Mobiles!" I declared. "We're high enough for decent reception even in rural Spain. You phone Felipe – see if he can bring us up to date from his end. I'll try friend Manresa."

Felipe told us that the unmarked convoy had stopped at a passing point about three kilometres short of *Fortaleza*. He and some of his closest mates had stood at the crest of the hill that had given Carlito and me our very first view of the town. They'd seen parked vehicles and a group of men in black military fatigues but no weapons. They'd sit and wait for the convoy's next move.

I tapped in Manresa's private mobile number. To my relief, he answered within seconds. I told him where we were and what we knew.

"I'm afraid Carlito advertised his strategy for keeping you hidden with too many ears wagging. They'd put two and two together. He is what he is. And so is *Fortaleza.*"

"It's too late to worry about that now," I said. "And incidentally you sound as though you're in the next room."

He laughed. "I should have tweaked your plan with a decoy – a diversion to head off those within the ranks of the *Guardia* sympathetic to our friend Ortiz."

"But who are these guys?" Manresa's *mea culpa* had irritated me. Had he any clues as to the identity of the convoy or what they intended to do?

"Unmarked vehicles are kept in a compound close to the Royal Palace."

"*Palacio Real* or *Zarzuela*?" I knew the royal family had chosen to live in the second, a more modest residence than the palace itself.

"*Zarzuela,*" said Manresa.

"Ah. So the king's men then? With barracks next to his bedroom, so to speak?"

"Don't jump to conclusions, Charlie. Whoever organised this lot may have access to the compound but on whose authority, I don't know."

"Come on, *Teniente Coronel.* It's obvious. Links in the chain as follows – Ortiz, friends in the party, more friends in government, prime minister's office, defence ministry, chaps in the army with ambitions to repeat February '81 and 'let's get rid of that bloody dwarf and that *cabron* of an English reporter'."

"If you say so, Charlie Barrow." He said no more.

This was getting us nowhere. And it was raining again, egged on by a vicious wind with evil intent.

But of course, you should have given Manresa more credit.

Please. Don't you get in on the act. I have enough trouble sorting this out in my head, as it is.

Carlito asked if he could speak to Manresa. I handed him the mobile and ducked into the hut out of the weather.

The conversation was short and clearly to the point. Two minutes later and Carlito was trying to explain. "Patience, Charlie. Just listen."

He handed back the mobile and I folded my arms.

"The two GCs in *Fortaleza* have been told to work with Felipe and his group. They've also been told to curb their enthusiasm for a confrontation and avoid anything crazy. If the guys in the convoy *are* armed, and there's no reason to think otherwise, they're unlikely to restrain themselves if they're provoked. They've got guns. We haven't. Simple as that."

"What else?"

Carlito said Manresa was sending up a helicopter with three trusted GCs in tow. They should be over *Fortaleza* in half an hour. They knew our position. As for our Polo, we were to keep it parked on the side of the shelter facing the higher ground and as close to the building as possible.

"At least it's black and covered in mud," I muttered.

Manresa was following in a separate chopper with more chaps with guns.

"I let him say, 'keep your heads down'," said Carlito, "even it was trite and superfluous."

"We could do worse than Manresa."

I knew the signs. All these bad jokes and statements of the obvious showed our frayed nerves. We looked round at the inside of the hut. It had two windows, each

242

about a square metre with no frames and no glass. There was a primitive stove and fireplace and a pile of wood.

"No fires," declared Carlito. "Chimney smoke. A give-away."

"Wood's too damp, anyway," I said.

The wind moaned and the rain swirled across the sparse grasses of the *sierra* out of the darkest of clouds. It must have been about half three in the afternoon. It felt like the middle of the night. And it got colder. We were reasonably well clad, but Carlito said he could have done with another layer. He huddled in a corner by the pile of useless wood. I sat on the other side of the stove. We should have been as miserable as sin.

"A touch of the Laurel and Hardys, Charlie. Another fine mess you've got me into." He flashed a smile and rubbed his hands. I shifted my right leg to get rid of a spurt of cramp.

"Good copy for a good story though," I replied. "And as luck would have it, I have a modest amount of Irish whiskey in this hip flask."

I was known as a man fond of his drink. I never denied it. Hence the habit of carrying this small vessel topped up with Jameson whenever I could get it. I handed it over. Carlito took a swig and coughed.

"*Madre de Dios*!" he yelled. "It's rocket fuel." He gave it back with a trembling hand.

"Don't insult the fruit of the grain," I countered.

"No insult intended. It certainly warms you up."

"We'll have some decent *tinto* when we get out of here."

In this half-farcical state, we withdrew into ourselves. I brushed aside a sudden memory of Elena and tried to work out what to do next. When the time came, I might be able to contribute some sparkling prose to Fred's foreign pages, but I had to admit that we had spectacularly failed in our mission to corral Ortiz and prevent the collapse of Spanish democracy. Our fate depended on a senior officer in the *Guardia Civil* with decidedly unorthodox anti-establishment tendencies and a group of the blessed 'abnormally small' villagers keeping an eye on a suspicious military convoy.

The wind dropped and the rain was reduced to an unconvincing drizzle. Weak sunlight pushed its way through thinning cloud.

Carlito woke with a start from his semi-slumber.

"Charlie, listen."

I staggered to one of the windows. There was a dun four-by-four whining its way up the track towards us. It was about a hundred metres away. It stopped. Four men jumped out, every one of them brandishing an automatic rifle.

"Christ! Stay down, Carlito. Stay down. For God's sake."

I stood by the window trying to work out what our visitors were up to. I caught a moment's glimpse of one of them unhooking what I thought must be a grenade.

"This is it," I thought. "This time I don't escape the inevitable."

I waited for the grenade to clatter against the wall of the shelter before it exploded. Nothing happened. I risked another glance through a gap in the wall. The four men stood still, weapons at half cock. One of them walked slowly towards the hut.

"Come out with your hands up," he called.

Carlito and I looked at one another.

"Don't think we have much choice, Charlie. But, as I've said before, you're the soldier. You should know."

"Follow me, Carlito. Keep your hands up and tight at the back of your head."

We shuffled through the door of the hut. The leader of the quartet raised his automatic, signalling that we should move out into open ground, well away from the shelter.

He was clearly nervous, kept his distance and covered us by continually waving his firearm.

"We have orders to take you into the town," he said. "We do not intend to harm you. But if you make any false moves, we will shoot."

He moved round behind us and shouted at us to follow his three colleagues down the slope to his vehicle. The wind had died and it had stopped raining.

"Towards that APC," he said. "And walk slowly."

I was praying that Carlito would resist the urge to indulge in his usual brisk walk. Instead he affected a limp, hobbling as if in pain, which in any other circumstances would have creased me up with hysterical laughter. I marched alongside him, trying furtively to keep one eye on our captors.

And then we heard it. The unmistakable sound of helicopter blades beating the mountain air like the sharpening of knives in a butchery.

One of the villains opened fire with a burst aimed at the chopper. He was wide of the mark. The four men had seen enough. They rushed back to their vehicle. Carlito and I dropped to the ground. The slope of the *sierra* seemed to prevent the chopper from landing but the pilot manoeuvred it to within thirty metres of the hut and stayed put at about sixty metres. There was a second helicopter hovering about five hundred metres to the left of where we were. We raised our heads and heard the sudden rush of a missile. The personnel carrier blew up in a blaze of orange. We felt the shock and stayed prone on the wet mountain grass. My mobile trilled.

"Your favourite *Teniente Coronel* here again. I'm not in the one who's become your friendly neighbour, but the captain inside says you look okay. Not too weather beaten?"

"Just bloody cold and scared to death," I shouted.

The chopper's chuntering rose and fell and rose again. A sudden gust of wind almost brought silence. I looked up and saw the pilot giving me a thumbs-up. Somewhat self-consciously I did the same.

"Have they hit the car?" Manresa yelled down the phone.

"I don't know,"

"Get in it and start it up."

I fumbled for the ignition key in a remote pocket of my jacket, crawled back to where the Polo was still parked behind the hut and squirmed into the driver's seat. Desperately holding my mobile to my right ear, I turned the key. It started as if life were as normal as it could be. The Polo was of a piece.

"Pilot says you're doing fine." Manresa sounded as if he was enjoying this. "Now, here's what you do," he said. I was struggling to hear his voice this time round and thought of handing over to Carlito. But he was already taking a call from Felipe.

"Get back in the car and drive into *Fortaleza*. Take it easy. The road's awash and the gravel and stone are too loose for a good grip. So don't get into a skid or you'll slide too easily and you could overturn. Just to be sure, the first chopper will follow you downhill. He says your tyres are intact."

I turned to Carlito and insisted I remove the dwarf attachments from brake and accelerator. He wasn't about

247

to object. He looked thoroughly wretched and drawn and resigned to what might follow.

"I'll say it again, Charlie. You're the soldier," he said. "You'll do this better than me."

"Was once a soldier," I replied. "Keep your fingers crossed."

The GC mechanics in Madrid had left a collection of tools including some smart adjustable spanners in a pocket behind the driver's seat. It didn't take me long to detach the special equipment. All the time I was acutely aware of the smouldering APC just a few metres away.

"Get in, Carlito."

With immense dignity, despite his aches and pains, he opened the door and sat as regally as he could in the passenger seat.

"You were saying something, Charlie?" he smirked.

We set off at a snail's pace keeping well away from the burning vehicle. I saw four bodies spread eagled around it. I had it in the back of my mind to ask Manresa why his helicopter had taken such drastic action. It would have to wait.

"Let's go," I declared, "and find out if we're still fundamentally safe and sound or the victims of another dirty great hoax."

Chapter 4

We sat in deep armchairs in the large main room of the *ayuntamiento*, each wrapped in thick woollen blankets and sipping mugs of hot black coffee. Consuelo drifted in and out with rolls and butter and plates of ham and cheese. She didn't fuss us. She threw Carlito some pained looks but smiled sweetly at me, finally wishing us both well and explaining that Carlito's daughter, Maria, was home from school and Tomasino needed some unspecified attention.

"I should like to see them a little later," said Carlito. "When it's convenient."

"So you shall," she replied and left it at that. He sighed.

From the vantage point of formal office chairs, Felipe and Manresa scrutinised us as if we were specimens in a cage of dead butterflies. The *Teniente Coronel* had arrived in his helicopter soon after the Polo had slithered down the long slope from the scene of battle. The car seemed to be of a piece despite the battering it had received.

"Okay, my friends." Manresa was taking charge again. "You look a little less punch-drunk than you were when you got back from your fracas. Can I assume that your brains are working well enough to take in some information?"

We drank our coffee and munched the food. And waited.

"A summary of what has happened today goes as follows. The suspicious little convoy turns out to have had no connection with the royal guard. Their unmarked APCs and trucks did not come out of the palace compound in Madrid. Instead they were a bunch of disaffected morons attached to the Engineers at Salamanca – well to the north of here but not so far away as to give them a long and troublesome journey. Four of them are dead, as you know. I make no excuses for that. The rest have given themselves up to the GCs I brought up in the helicopters from Madrid. We're questioning them."

"And if you find a link to Ortiz, you'll let us know?"

"You're doing it again, Charlie Barrow. Getting ahead of yourself. What I want to know now is how a group of disgruntled young men stationed at a provincial army base, which up to now has shown no signs of being a centre of rebellion – how were they persuaded to do what they did? *Who* persuaded them? Were they paid or bribed? I don't know the answers yet."

We were distracted by shouting and a general commotion outside the front door of the building. Felipe went to find out what was going on. Manresa continued by disclosing that he had quietly questioned two officials of the *Partido Popular* in Madrid who he knew were close to Ortiz.

"They might have been clever actors, but they convinced me that they knew nothing of his whereabouts."

Will we ever get behind that great wall of silence? It's driving me mad.

You might if you have the patience to listen to your friend, Manresa. He's as frustrated as you are, but he also has the best instincts of an intelligence officer. He doesn't let his disappointment show.

Thanks for that. It doesn't make me feel better.

"Your coup allegations are still making the newscasts, Charlie. You have been pilloried by the government, *Partido Popular* big wigs and the PSOE. But *Podemos* has called for a full enquiry into everything you said at the news conference."

"Well, since one of their number was on the platform, I suppose they have a vested interest in an enquiry." I wasn't feeling too charitable towards *Podemos* right now. They'd attached themselves to our cause but offered damn all in return. At least that was how I saw it.

"Ever the cynic, Charlie?"

"I'm not a cynic," I said. "Just plain bloody suspicious."

It was early evening by now. Felipe returned to announce that there was a crowd of angry citizens at his front door demanding that Carlito and I get out of town as fast as possible. Carlito swept aside his blanket and marched out of the room.

"Carlito!" shouted Felipe. "Carlito! No! Please, no!"

But he was too late. Manresa and I followed suit.

Carlito had found a wooden stool with steps attached. He clambered up and spread his arms. The angry noises subsided. They looked up and waited.

He didn't do a 'Friends, Romans, Countrymen' act. He just surveyed the crowd. By now there were about fifty of them.

"So," he declared. "You want me and my English friend to leave *Fortaleza*?"

"*Si, será cierto.*" In other words, "Too right, we do."

"*Tú lo has dicho.*" "You said it."

"Right now? This minute?"

"*Ahora...enseguida.*"

"Well, there's hospitality and friendship for you," Carlito almost sneered.

There were more boos and catcalls. But others called for peace and quiet.

"Some of us want to hear what you've got to say," said one of the women.

"I am a citizen of *Fortaleza*. I was born and brought up here. Some of you will remember my parents. I went to school here. I passed my exams and became a lawyer."

More boos mixed with sarcastic laughter.

"So you don't like lawyers. I don't blame you. But you – or most of you – wanted to live in a town with all the property held communally – which is what you've got now. If I hadn't stayed here for a while after I qualified, many of you would have been in a big mess with your finances, your rights to that property, to your houses, fields, animals, your vineyard and your olive presses. All that went to pieces in the Franco era. It took some hard work to get it right again. So, I am not apologising when I remind you that I and another lawyer, Adolfo Bescansa, God rest his soul, sorted it out for you and for *Fortaleza*."

He paused.

"Si, Carlito. Tienes razon."

"He may be right," came a voice from the back. "But why did you leave, Carlito? You left us when we most needed you."

"And now you want to kick me out again."

This time the laughter was sympathetic.

"But, since you ask, a man in Madrid, a good man, asked me to help out with a very important task."

"Yes, we know all about your Association for the Recovery of Historical Memory," said the same voice. "We know all about your part in the digging up of corpses who are supposed to have been the victims of Franco's oppression..."

"Supposed?" shouted Carlito in fury. "Supposed? Pablo Zamora, listen to me." He had identified the speaker. "Pablo! They *were* the victims of Franco's brutality, victims of his vicious troops who shot women and children in the back of the head, just because they belonged to Republican families."

"How do you know? How do you know they weren't shot by the Reds?"

"If you think that, then I invite you to come with me to a village called Castillo not far from Seville and I'll show you the mass grave and the bones and skeletons and the spent bullets and shell cartridges identified as ammunition from guns used by the Nationalists in '36."

Half the crowd turn to look at Pablo who was vehemently shaking his head in disbelief.

Another man asked, "What's all that got to do with why you're here now with your Englishman?"

"My Englishman, as you call him, learned about the story of the mass graves. He's a journalist. And like me, he witnessed how a man called Martínez Ortiz tried to stop the exhumations in Castillo and the work of my Association by playing ducks and drakes with the law. Then he made a big mistake. He decided to get rid of one of his PP henchmen who'd said too much. A detective in

254

Castillo had him in jail for a while, but some clever lawyers from Madrid got him released. We've been after him ever since. It's very simple. He's wanted for murder."

Carlito took a breath.

"But why are we involved?" asked someone from deep inside the crowd. "What has *Fortaleza* got to do with it?"

There were murmurs of support for this. Carlito pushed on with his explanation as quickly as he could. He told them how I had been targeted at least twice by somebody who having understood that I was on to a big story wanted me out of the way.

"And then your friend came up with these stories about a military coup to be staged before the 20th December elections?"

Carlito admitted that was true. So he had concocted a plan that he and I should hide away in *Fortaleza*.

"Until the coup plot had been rumbled and *Señor* Ortiz was nicely in jail – and you were therefore free as birds?" This Pablo was no fool. He had spotted the flaws in our argument and was aiming his guns at our self-centred strategy to exploit the relative isolation of *Fortaleza*.

"Meanwhile," he went on, "you put us in the line of fire. You expose this quiet community of dwarves to real danger. Carlito Jimenez," he pronounced stabbing the air with his forefinger, "and you should be ashamed of yourself."

Manuel from the bar, being something of a local spokesman, was determined to add his two pennyworth. "Pablo is right, Carlito. You've got to admit it's been a hell of a day. There we were having a happy time. Everyone glad to see you back. Then in burst our two *Guardia* lads and the next thing we know is you're making for the hills like frightened rabbits. A truckload of soldiers arrives, crashes through the town as if they were in *Star Wars* and takes the same route as you. Then we hear a bloody great bang. We see helicopters overhead. More troops arrive."

He took a swig from a bottle of *tinto*.

"Are you surprised that we have had enough. I'm sorry. But I agree. Bugger off out of here. Before we attract the wrath of God and the curses of St Pelagius."

"Don't take the saint's name in vain, Manuel." A new figure had joined the crowd. Father Eusebius, a dwarf like the rest of them and, according to Felipe, a hard-working priest who ran his church more as a social centre than a place of worship. He strode to the front and addressed Carlito directly.

"I know you have little time for the Church, Carlito. But you must know that the clergy here have, over many years, tried to protect the people from outside interference and even persecution. In doing so they defied their bishops, which was a dangerous thing to do in the days of the dictatorship. Thankfully this community of dwarves was probably considered too insignificant to pose problems. No rebels here. No Republicans to cart away and execute. Just a bit of an oddity in the remote *sierra*."

I was reminded of what Carlito had told me about Franco's apparent belief that the dwarves of Spain were somehow special, creatures of tradition who had served the country's monarchs as servants and jesters and must be respected. Though they were physically deformed, they were not to be put in the same category as the mentally backward. They were not to be persecuted. The dwarves of Spain had survived and *Fortaleza* had flourished.

"So I am asking you to help me, Carlito. I too do not want *Fortaleza* to be caught in the crossfire of disputes between renegade troops and gunmen with scores to settle. Nor do I want it turned into a media attraction with reporters and television cameras invading our privacy. I know you do good work in your Association. I am very sympathetic to its cause."

Carlito indicated that he wanted to answer. Eusebius gave way.

"But since there are, as far as we know, no mass graves in *Fortaleza*, Father, you would prefer that we do our work elsewhere. I think I have got your message, and Pablo's, and Manuel's."

The priest nodded his acknowledgement. There was a buzz of approval among the crowd.

"But they will not leave until morning." Consuelo had emerged from the house and stood below Carlito facing the crowd. "They will spend the night here as my guests," she announced in no uncertain terms. "Like all of you, they need their sleep. And a breakfast in the morning. Then they will be on their way. I give you *my* word on that."

Father Eusebius made the sign of the cross and began to applaud. The rest followed. Even Pablo and Manuel joined in.

Manuel in particular had been converted to a show of charity.

"They will eat supper in the bar with me and whoever wants to join us."

The crowd dispersed and we turned to go back into the *ayuntamiento*. Carlito gestured to the priest and Manuel to join us.

We gathered rather awkwardly in the big front room. Felipe had opened a bottle of *tinto*. Consuelo offered us small *pasteles*, sweet cakes tinged with honey.

"To your good health," said the priest. "And to your good work."

Carlito might have been tempted to say, "But not here!" But he held back with good grace. "And to yours," he replied. "My thanks for diffusing the tension, Father. And my thanks to you, Manuel, for your kindness even though we disagree."

I kept silent, merely raising my glass when it was appropriate.

Manuel was about to say something when Consuelo came back, leading the girl Maria by the hand and carrying Tomasino on her left arm.

"And now," she said decisively as ever, "I think it is time for Carlito to be with his children. This way, please." She led all three of them to the back of the house. Within minutes we heard the sound of his guitar and the voices of children singing their hearts out.

"That must be hard for you, Felipe," said Eusebius.

"No, Father. He must do as Consuelo says. Carlito knows I shall continue to look after them. And I know it too."

Chapter 5

Manresa was keeping a strict eye on us. He assigned one of the helicopter crews to make the best of it by spending the night in the shepherd's hut.

"They've got all the gear they need," he said. "They'll do some early morning forensic work on what's left of that truck and arrange for the corpses to be moved to Salamanca."

Manresa and the second crew bedded down at the *Fortaleza Guardia Civil* post. After a few hours of disturbed sleep and a pot of coffee from Consuelo, Carlito and I were on the road back to Madrid. Manresa's helicopter kept track overhead.

Manuel's farewell party had been a sombre affair, lightened only by more guitar music from Carlito and a general if surprising agreement that he and I should return to *Fortaleza* at some unspecified time in the future. This tied in with a promise from Carlito to Maria and Tomasino that he would 'come back soon' and take them on a holiday 'to the seaside'. Consuelo oversaw all this with her usual calm, quietly pleading to Felipe to accept what was happening without demur. He complied. It was very obvious that he worshipped the ground she walked on and would do nothing in public to upset her.

I stayed out of this, at long last spending some time consulting the notes I'd penned on recent events.

It was all a bloody waste of time.

No, it wasn't. It gave you the best possible insight into what drives Carlito.

I knew that already.

You didn't know enough. Apart from his family problems, you've had a chance to understand what he meant about Fortaleza's special place in the scheme of things.

And I nearly got killed again.

At the rate you're going, it's quite likely to happen to you again. You'd better file Fred some copy while you're still in one piece.

As we headed east, Manresa called my mobile. Since talking while driving was illegal in Spain, I handed it to Carlito. I heard his side of the conversation without understanding a word. Tyre and engine noise didn't help. After ten minutes or so, Carlito gave the phone back to me with sign language telling me to listen to what Manresa had to say.

"Carlito will explain more," he shouted into my right ear. "But I want you to make a detour – partly to keep the villains off your back. You may also like to spend a little time as a tourist admiring the scenery." I heard him laughing.

"I think you had better say *Adios*, before the traffic police pull me over."

"They're nowhere near you, Charlie."

It was too late to argue.

"So, where are we going?" I asked Carlito.

"We take the motorway to a place called Maqueda. Then we turn north up to Ávila where I have things to show you."

"Why will all this shake 'em off?"

"Because Manresa's chopper is still overhead and they won't want him to see them. And they don't expect us to leave the A5."

"Are you sure we're still being followed?"

"The *Teniente Coronel* is. I haven't seen any one on our tail so far, but he has a much better view than we have."

We pushed on. Carlito found some *flamenco* on the radio, closed his eyes and let a childlike smirk widen his lips. Even though I was driving, the daylight and a hazy sun gave me a better chance to take in more of the landscape. It was magnificent. Rolling hills, distant mountains covered in snow, river valleys, small villages with churches in a variety of styles, dry stone walls and thin grass struggling with stone and rock, pines, oaks, gorse and broom and the enormous reservoir at

Burguillo created by damning the Alberche river, its grey waters disturbed by a winter wind, a place for leisure in summer especially for those who loved their sailing.

"Some nasty things were done up here in '36," said Carlito. "Beautiful it may be, but there are mass graves in many of the villages which would keep me and the Association in work for the rest of our lives."

I was being asked to imagine how these fields and streams had witnessed one of the most brutal wars of the twentieth century.

"Franco had hardly got going after bringing his troops over from Morocco. But the nasty General Mola was already in charge in this part of the world. His lot had swept up from the south in the hope of taking Madrid. They had to wait another three years for that. So they spent July and August '36 purging this area of anyone suspected of Republican sympathies. They arrested them, tortured them, and killed them. Then they dumped the bodies. No burial. Just left them to rot. Just like Castillo."

We were approaching Ávila. You could hardly miss it, set on a hill, its crenulated walls and towers surrounding the old town. We drove right round them until we reached the Plaza Santa Teresa. Where else?

"Before the fascists murdered him, the great Federico García Lorca wrote a book called *Sketches of Spain* in which he said Ávila was the most Castilian, the most august city of the *meseta,* the high tableland of central Spain. Was he right?"

"Carlito, with great respect, I don't care. I don't want to visit the cathedral. I don't want icons, relics and symbols. I've heard enough about Teresa to know she had glorious visions and fell in love with Jesus. What I do want is a coffee."

He sighed. "I will add insult to injury, by telling you that Franco kept Teresa's mummified hand on his bedside table. How about that for devotion?"

Godless as I may have been, I couldn't avoid some juicy blasphemy.

We found a good bar and took advantage of the local *tapas.*

"What the hell are we doing here?" I asked. "We should be in Madrid looking for Ortiz. Though heaven knows how we start that caper all over again."

Carlito tried to explain the value of diversions. He also told me how Manresa had fixed up for us to stay in an out-of-town hotel once we got back and how he had arranged a rather important appointment with a rather important person.

"Who?"

"The minister."

"Which minister?"

"Interior."

"Good Grief. What's all that about?"

"Well, you did make public accusations against certain people that they were intending to stage a coup just before the elections. I'm not surprised he wants to hear from you."

I had to pull myself together. I had to get organised. I had to put my thoughts and my evidence, such as they were, into some sort of order. Manresa was springing this on me because he had put himself on a line and needed quick action before his enemies called time on his career.

"How's all that been playing in the media today?"

Carlito said they were still running stories about my disappearance and an official search for me. The chopper attack on the anonymous military truck at *Fortaleza* had had its fair share of coverage but everything Spanish was, in any case, overshadowed by events in Paris. The French were traumatised. The government said it was war. The jihadists had fled to Belgium. As for Spain's forthcoming election, the media seemed to have forgotten all about it.

I got up and poked my head outside the bar. For the first time I noticed posters, placards and hoardings urging the people to support a wide selection of candidates.

"How will they vote in this neck of the woods?"

Carlito had secured a couple of newspapers. "Judging by the local press, there'll be a turnout of about seventy-five percent and the PP will come out on top. They'll probably get about forty percent of the vote."

He pointed out that this was a very conservative part of Spain. "Like most of Castile and Leon. There won't be too many upsets."

"And *Podemos*?"

"Hard to say. They're newcomers here and everywhere else. It depends on how much of an impact they've made with the poor and the unemployed, how much they've been able to help people who've been chucked out of their flats and houses because they can't pay the mortgage or the rent. They might make fifteen percent or so."

If this was such a conservative place, how would it react to a right wing coup?

Carlito said it would probably sit back and watch. It was, incidentally, home to the Spanish army's military museum. Various governments had found the cash for this patriotic enterprise, despite heated arguments over what should be put in it and how it would deal with the Civil War. "A microcosm of the country. It bears out what I've already told you."

We strolled round the town. I was made angry by the way some of the locals stared at Carlito. I heard laughing behind our backs.

"Forget it, Charlie."

****

The two *Guardia Civil* were leaning against the bonnet of the Polo.

"*Señores!*" said the taller of the two as we approached. "This is your car?" He pointed downwards.

"All four tyres slashed," he announced. "In broad daylight in the middle of town."

He looked at us pityingly at first and then turned serious. "I shall need some particulars, please!"

"Hold on," I said. "Any further damage to the car?"

He stepped aside and opened the driver's door. "They didn't need to pick the lock. Your rear window was enough for them, I'm afraid. They smashed it to smithereens, probably with a brick. You may have a look inside, but don't touch anything yet."

We had been careful to put what we thought was important stuff in the boot and to draw a cover over the lot, Carlito's guitar, both laptops and a couple of holdalls filled with clothes.

"Did they get inside the trunk?" asked Carlito looking worried.

"No. You were lucky. They must have lost their nerve after trashing the interior. I'm still puzzled why nobody saw or heard them and raised the alarm."

"General apathy," said Carlito bitterly. "They don't want to get involved."

The GC took the car key from me and twisted it into the catch on the tailgate. Everything was still there, intact.

"St Teresa must have been watching over us," I quipped.

"Don't be flippant, Charlie. We've just been lucky."

The second GC was pulling his 'rugged tablet' out of a case.

"Names?"

We did as we were bid, adding several addresses, type of work, employers, my nationality and more trivia.

The GC's jaw dropped.

"*Carajo!*" he swore. "Fuck me. You're the two who are in the news all the time?"

His tall colleague was taking a look over his shoulder at the computer screen. They scrolled down carefully, looked hard at us, swore again, did more scrolling and tapping and stared at us awestruck. The tall one stood up like a ram rod and saluted.

"The computer says," he drawled, evidently only half-believing what he'd seen, "that you are under the special protection of *Teniente Coronel* Manresa at *Guardia Civil* headquarters in Madrid. I have to ask you – have you got proof of identity on you?"

We fished out my passport and Carlito's ID from the Association.

"We must get you back on the road as soon as possible."

"Wait a minute," said Carlito. "Let's have another close look at this car." He peered inside again. There was a sheet of A4 paper lying on the front passenger seat. Carlito asked the GC for some plastic gloves, picked it up and read it out.

'Señores. *We greatly apologise for damaging your car and interrupting your journey to Madrid. But this is a warning from people to whom you have continued to give a significant and unacceptable amount of trouble. You may have contact with certain persons in high places, but they will not be able to help you if you persist in continuing with your useless mission. We therefore advise you to bring this to an end and return to Carmona in Andalucía at the earliest opportunity. Please do not take this lightly. We know where you are and we have the means to watch you all the time. We also have the means to make life rather uncomfortable for you if you ignore what we are saying.'*

Carlito showed the paper to me and then the two GCs. Nobody spoke. The officers did more tapping into their tablet. The watery sun tried hard to warm us up. A small crowd had gathered, to be waved away by a couple of local police who'd obviously been told to help out.

"Jesus, that's quick!" said the tall one. "Manresa says, can you call him on your mobile, *Señor*." His colleague was busy entering the text of a reply into his computer.

"Charlie, listen carefully." Manresa's voice had an edge to it. Had he slipped up? Had he failed to spot the villains who were threatening us anew? "No cars this time. Better to travel back to Madrid by rail. Do it openly, in broad daylight, so to speak. The boys there will look after you. They'll get you to the local station and fix your tickets. Phone me when your train's just outside the city. I'll pick you up at Chamartín."

A thought occurred. "Do you think they can monitor these calls, *Teniente Coronel*?"

"We'll have to take a risk on that. If you make the next call to me on Carlito's, it might throw them off."

****

The train from Ávila to Madrid ran as smoothly as any train I have travelled in, even smoother than the ICE's in Germany. Carlito and I were ensconced in a first class compartment with a central aisle. After half an hour, a very pleasant young man in a smart uniform entered with a trolley of drinks and *bocadillos* but offered us more sophisticated fare if we were happy to move to the dining car. We stayed put.

As time passed, the call of nature became more insistent. I edged my way down the aisle through an automatic door to a toilet in the next carriage.

As I emerged, two swarthy young men seized my arms and clamped a gag over my mouth. The train slowed down and stopped. One of my captors produced an all-singing, all-dancing mobile and pressed a series of buttons. The carriage exit slid open.

"*Ya eben al sharmoota!*" he whispered into my ear. "Son of a bitch!"

He ripped at my trousers, pressed a needle into my buttock and pushed me outside. I hit the track ballast hard then rolled into a patch of rough grass and down an embankment. I came to rest against what seemed to be the trunk of a bush. I recall the bouncing of my body against various obstacles, but the injection had stunned me into semi-oblivion. I was very conscious of that bush though. Its spikes tore at my face and seemed to shred the sleeve of my jacket. I lay still and became aware of a noise I recognised as a disappearing train. It was very quiet.

We had left Ávila in the late afternoon. So it was dusk by now. It took a while for the swarthy man's injection to wear off. An hour maybe. Perhaps longer. And then I had the monster of a headache. And a thirst. There was cold wind and I remembered it was almost mid-winter.

But still no noises. No animals. No night birds. No rain, thank God. I swivelled my head on my neck and looked up. I saw a moon, possibly a full moon, and stars, and an occasional white cloud passing swiftly across a silver sky.

"I have to move," I said rather fruitlessly to no one in particular. But moving was hard work. The injection was passing its sell-by date. Every bone and joint began to protest.

Mobile phone, Charlie. Where is it?

For once, you're right. Where the hell is it?

You could have lost it as you rolled down the bank.

I could have indeed. And I could have lost my wallet. Cash and credit cards and all that stuff.

Then you're fucked.

But I wasn't. I took deep breaths and pushed myself up so that I sat instead of simply lying helpless. I saw the blinking blue light and the buzzing of a call sign. Just three metres away in the scrub. I scrambled towards it.

"Charlie? Where are you?" Manresa's voice was both insistent and comforting.

"For your information," I croaked, "I am taking this call sitting in coarse grass at the bottom of a railway embankment which, thankfully, is as dry as a bone, after being unceremoniously pushed out of a mercifully stationary train somewhere between Ávila and Madrid. My body aches like fury but as far as I can tell there are no broken bones. So, oh Wise One, tell me what I do next."

There was silence with '*atmos*' in my ear. I thought I heard a lot of background chatter. Then Manresa said,

272

"Do you see, or do you hear, a road near to where you are?"

I hadn't thought about this. I'd believed I was permanently stranded, fated never to go anywhere. I could have killed a bottle of water.

"You want me to search for a road?"

"I want you to get up, pull yourself together and flag down some kind, motorist. I want you to offer him some euros and asked him nicely to take you to the Chamartín station in Madrid. It should take about an hour."

I told him to hang on. My torn jacket was essentially intact. I remembered the zipped pocket and the wallet inside it. I fished it out and in the moonlight saw that I was all of a piece financially. I still had a Visa card and sixty euros in cash.

"*Teniente Coronel*, I shall follow your orders to the letter. Always assuming I can get up and walk."

"Has Carlito tried to phone you?"

"Well, if he has, he hasn't succeeded. Probably no signal from the train, which is still merrily making its way to Madrid. I'd be grateful if you would at least tell him what's happened to me. Maybe we'll see each other one day."

Manresa cut the call. He hadn't seemed too sympathetic to my condition. Perhaps his conscience *had* got the better of him. After all, here was I stranded in the Spanish countryside unsure of where I was and what to do about it. I'd become another problem for him.

You're feeling sorry for yourself again.

No, I'm not. I'm feeling damned confident that I can cope with this.

Go on then. Get moving.

I stood up very slowly and put one tentative foot in front of the other. I manoeuvred myself down the embankment until I met a low stone wall and a lot of thorns and brambles. I found a gap in the undergrowth and climbed over the wall. He'd been right. There was a road. A silent road heading west into the hills and east into a darkened avenue of tall trees. The moonlight persisted. Obviously I had to walk in an easterly direction, hoping at the back of my mind that Manresa had worked one of his miracles so that a car would appear, pick me up and take me to Madrid while I slept soundly curled up on the back seat.

A car did appear. It had a big illuminated 'Taxi' sign above the windscreen. I thumbed it down.

"And where the hell are you going at this time of night?" asked the driver winding down the window. She wore her fair hair short, a mocking smile, and sported a multi-coloured windcheater.

"You wouldn't believe me if I told you," I said in the best Spanish I could muster.

"Drop the Spanish, mister," she said. "You're as English as I am."

Well, there were some surprises in life that could never be matched again and this was one of them.

I took relief in explaining what had happened to me and put in a request for a ride to Madrid as ordered by Manresa.

"In any case," I asked. "Where the hell am I?"

"I think we should observe the courtesies," she said. "I am Rosie Roberts. And you are...?"

"I am Charlie Barrow. And you are not English. With a name like Rosie Roberts, you've got to be Welsh."

"What a clever man you are!"

My aches and pains had numbed my powers of enquiry as to why she had turned up out of the blue.

"We are very near the Escorial," she explained. "The bloody great royal palace to which I ferry English-speaking tourists with more money than sense. But it's a living. I was on my way to do a night shift because a lot of the clowns stay around to get plastered in the local bars and end up needing a cab to get them back to Madrid."

"Rosie Roberts. I have cash and credit cards despite my close encounter with death. So, can we cut the conversation and get on with it?"

She got out of the driver's side and steadied me into the back seat. We drove off into the night again and I drifted into a doze.

"If you're sick on my back seat, it'll cost you," she said.

The doze didn't last. There was too much going on in my head.

"You don't happen to have a bottle of water on you?"

"Two minutes and we'll pull up at a bar I know. You need more than water."

"But I need to get to Madrid as fast as possible."

"You will. But you can afford to spend a few minutes sorting yourself out with a stiff brandy."

Rosie was right. We passed through somewhere called Galapagar where she found what was needed. She sat me down at a table near the entrance and within seconds had produced a double *cafe solo* and a *copa* of something called *Mascaró*

"Those'll bring you back into the land of the living," she said.

And so I was wide awake enough to take in her story.

She wasn't loquacious. She didn't indulge in aimless chatter. In the broad accent of the valleys of South Wales, she just gave me a simple and seemingly honest explanation of why she was doing what she was doing.

She'd been an accountant in the UK. But she'd fiddled the books for a small company and got found out.

"I escaped with a bloody big fine and was struck off the list. So I came out here looking for sunshine and a bit of work as a financial adviser." She chuckled at the absurdity of it. "I've a Spanish partner and we've adopted two kids. Marvellous, they are – all three of them. No one wanted my financial advice, surprisingly. So I rented this cab and then made enough money to buy it."

We were nearing the lights of the capital.

"I've got a proposition for you," I said.

"Oh yes! What's that then?"

Take it easy. Don't get carried away.

Credit me with knowing a good thing when I see it.

I shall do no such thing.

I explained that I needed a car and driver for at least a month. "Here in Spain." I gave her the background and watched her face as she mulled it over.

"Got it!" she shouted. "You are..."

"Oh shit! Not you as well?"

"But you've been all over the television."

"Haven't I just."

"Okay. You're on, Charlie Barrow. God knows what I'm letting myself in for."

"That could apply to both of us."

We negotiated a daily rate which I was hoping I could wheedle out of Fred as a legitimate expense. I warned Rosie it would mean driving down to the south which would take her away from her family.

"Oh, my mate won't mind a bit of peace and quiet for once," she said. "And the kids are at school until Christmas."

Chapter 6

We had arrived at the drop-off zone outside Chamartín station.

"Helluva circus, Charlie!" said Rosie. "Look at that lot."

There were at least three GC vehicles with flashing lights and an ambulance on stand-by.

"Don't move, Rosie. Stay right there."

"I'm all yours unless the cops move me on."

"They won't," I tried to assure her.

As I crawled out of the cab, my body still protesting, I saw Manresa and Carlito heading towards me.

"Get in!" Manresa ordered. "Now!"

"No!" I bellowed. I held up my hands to make them listen.

"Charlie, we've got to get you out of sight."

I explained the presence of Rosie and the taxi. "They're both better camouflage than one of your limos," I pointed out. "And I don't need an ambulance. I'm sick of bloody hospitals."

We finally agreed that Manresa's car would lead us to the hotel he'd found for us. Rosie and I would keep it in sight but stay well back. Rosie, as it turned out, was an expert at all this.

"God knows what he's found you," she said. "We're well up north somewhere."

"He said he wanted Carlito and me to stay in something out of town."

"Well, it's not out of town exactly, but it's pretty anonymous."

We drove up to the front door of an old building finished in colonial style with a discreet and not too well-lit front entrance.

"Where will you stay the night?" I asked her.

"Don't worry about me. I have a mate lives out near the airport in Barajas. He'll put me up for now. Might even get another fare before I knock off."

We exchanged mobile numbers. I said I would phone in the morning when something had been sorted with Manresa.

"He's a bossy sod, isn't he?"

My laugh turned into a hacking cough.

"Go on, Charlie. Get some rest. See you tomorrow."

I wanted to make sure. "And our deal stands?"

"Solid as a rock, boyo. And yes, we do say 'boyo' if we're Welsh – sometimes!"

****

I walked unsteadily into the small lobby and stood there like a lost soul. The receptionist looked at me as if she'd seen Old Father Time himself.

"Grief!" said Carlito. "You are in a mess. Have you seen yourself in a mirror?"

I snapped that this was perhaps the silliest question he could have asked of me.

I was shepherded by Manresa to a room on the first floor, small but with warm lighting and a bed that looked temptingly comfortable. He told me to remove my tattered clothes and have a long, hot, shower. I slunk off as ordered. The *Teniente Coronel* was as ever nothing if not a minor miracle-worker. Even if he still couldn't stop the villains from following us or thwart their efforts to kill me again, he had managed to conjure up some very acceptable necessities clearly designed to cheer me up and refurbish my image. When I emerged from the shower, I found a clean shirt, clean underwear, clean socks, new slacks with a knife-edge crease in them, a new linen jacket and a handsome pair of slip-on suede shoes all laid out for immediate wear. The final touch was a silver tray on which sat a couple of miniatures of malt. A written message said, "Meet downstairs at 2230".

The hotel had a small, intimate dining room. Manresa had persisted with his efforts to improve our welfare by ordering omelettes and a salad with all the tasty bits in it.

"Nothing heavy before you two have a good night's rest," he said with a fatherly smile on his normally serious countenance.

We ate in silence. Carlito screwed up his face. He was perplexed and confused. He was bursting to ask questions but restrained himself until the plates were cleared away.

"They were Arabs," I insisted. "No doubt about it. Apart from their looks, they *spoke* Arabic. I may not understand it, but I sure as hell can recognise it. The one who pushed me off the train said something to me which I took to be a curse or an insult. What I want to know is, why wait until they stopped the train before dumping me? Why not do a proper job – get rid of me while it's travelling at speed. I'd have been a hell of a mess if you'd ever found me."

"Sloppy," said Manresa. It wasn't designed to comfort me, but he was convinced it was the right explanation. He asked me for more detailed descriptions and a blow-by-blow account of what had actually happened. But I hadn't finished asking questions.

"Why did they leave *you* alone, Carlito? I mean, I'm glad they did, but they must have known you were somewhere on the train."

"I think that through all of this, Charlie, you're the one Martínez Ortiz wants dead. He wants you out of the way before you say any more about plots and coups *and* before you file any more copy to your editors and the story gets splashed over the front pages of a few newspapers and the screens of Europe's TV networks. Think about how much you now know, how much you've been through. They've tried to kill *you* three times. Not me. I can be got rid of much later when they've started to discredit the work of the Association, when they know what the political scene's like after the election."

I suppose that if I'd stopped to think about it, I must have known this all along. I looked at Carlito with renewed respect for his nous and perspicacity.

"As it happens, they did pass through our compartment on that train," he said. "They stood over me and threatened me. I hadn't a clue what they were saying, but they weren't wishing me a long life. I was trapped in the seat. I thought I was done for. But after two or three minutes, they backed off. And I had no idea what had happened to you."

Manresa said it was time to move on. We were expected.

"Expected? Where?" I asked.

"The office of the minister of the interior at ten o'clock tomorrow morning," he announced.

My jaw gave way and I must have sat there looking like a raving idiot for a full minute.

"You aren't serious?"

"I am very serious. And there is nothing you can do to get out of this. If the minister summons you, you go. We go."

I was exhausted. But I resorted to all the arguments I could think of as I contemplated what Manresa was saying.

"Just a minute, *Teniente Coronel.* You are telling me that after all we have been through, this minister wishes to question us and ask for our opinion. How many times do I have to say it? We have been shot at and nearly killed by villains clearly driven by a wish to silence us. Sorry to flog a dead horse, but we still haven't tracked down the instigator of this attempt to stage a coup, who is incidentally wanted on a charge of murder in Castillo. We still don't know who gave the orders for a bunch of gunmen to open fire on us from a warehouse outside Madrid. And we still don't know who persuaded another bunch of young army engineers to take to the hills and attempt to butcher us in a remote shepherd's hut not far from a town where Carlito's countrymen and women normally live in peace and harmony. I note in passing that you were happy to wipe them off the face of the earth with a powerful missile. No holds barred there, were there? We also seem to have been stalked by young

284

men with swarthy faces who speak Arabic. We have no answers to any of this. And we stuck our noses out at an official news conference and motored over half of Spain – *to no fucking purpose whatsoever.* And now you tell us that the sodding minister, sitting in his well-furnished office here in Madrid, *thinks it is his God-given right to pick our brains."*

I paused for breath and they didn't move a muscle.

"I've done you some favours, *Teniente Coronel.* But if I go along with this, I want to be left alone thereafter – to do my job as a journalist without interference and file everything I know to my editors."

Manresa picked up a fork and drew patterns on the table cloth. Carlito looked at me with the broadest grin that had ever creased his cheeks.

"But if you get into trouble again, you'll still want my help?" Manresa said very pointedly. He had readopted his serious face.

"Touché," I said.

He stood up and offered his hand. I shook it and shook it warmly.

"Rosie will pick us up in her cab at half past nine. No GC car, marked or unmarked. We will be on time at the ministry." There was half a bottle of *tinto* in front of us. We still had our glasses. Manresa filled them, carefully. We leaned in, took the *copas,* raised them and clinked them together.

"Thank you, Charlie Barrow. Thank you very much for that." Manresa knocked his wine back in one. "You have done the Spanish state a great service."

"Too right I have."

He rose. Saluted me. And left. I was looking forward to that comfortable bed and the whisky miniatures.

Chapter 7

When Rosie came for us at nine o'clock, she had some news of her own.

"I was followed," she said. "When I pulled away from here last night, a black Merc tucked itself in behind and stayed with me most of the way to Barajas."

"Hell, Rosie. I didn't think they'd got their eye on you. I'm sorry."

"Ah, you didn't think they'd see me as a valuable link in the chain?" She had a twinkle in her eye.

"Don't worry. I shook 'em off."

"You want to call off the deal?" I asked.

"No way, Charlie Barrow. You represent a nice living wage for me – for a while at least. And a bit of excitement."

"I don't want it to get too exciting. I don't want you duffed up in some car park. Or worse."

"It won't happen," she said. And I believed her. I didn't know a lot about Rosie but she had an air about her which said, 'I've dealt with unsavoury customers before now. And I know how to look after myself.'

"Did you get a look at who was driving the Merc?" Carlito asked.

"You'll be interested to learn that they were Arabs of some sort. Moroccans probably. They were stupid enough to get out of their car at one point and show themselves. Smart shirts and slacks and expensive haircuts."

"They're not giving up, are they?" I said.

"I'll keep my eyes open while you're in that building. Phone me when you get out of there."

I had done this in other places, climbed vast, marble staircases at some cost to my lungs and heartbeat, sat in chairs covered in expensive fabric and been told to wait. Carlito, for all his small stature, ran up the steps as nimbly as a foal in spring. He was enjoying it all. I wanted to share his optimism, but my antennae told me to be circumspect.

We sat on the expensive chairs and took in our surroundings. We were in a lofty corridor where officials of both sexes emerged from enormous doors and strode up and down with armfuls of files, their footsteps echoing back from the vaulted ceiling. I was conscious that my new gear, smart as the individual items were, was perhaps little too informal for the occasion. But I looked a damn sight more civilised than when Rosie had picked me up in the countryside.

So stop worrying and be grateful. It doesn't matter what you're wearing.

Manresa and two of his boys arrived in full regalia, uniforms as smart as uniforms could be and covered with medals and braid. Other than giving one another the most cursory of greetings, we said nothing. We sat like naughty schoolboys waiting to be called into the headmaster's study.

After ten minutes or so, a flunkey in a smart suit and highly polished shoes poked his head out of one of the doors and beckoned us to follow him. We walked into a capacious room, with oak-panelled walls, portraits of past office-holders, long windows covered by startlingly white gauze curtains and a huge desk behind which, inevitably, sat our minister.

Why would it have been any different?

For once, you're spot on. It couldn't have been.

Carlito had filled me in on the great man. He was obviously a key member of the PP government. He'd been born in Valladolid, in the dead centre of the Castilian *meseta,* the son of a soldier in Franco's army. He'd moved to Barcelona to study engineering and then worked his way up through the bureaucracy and the party. He was in effect its man in Catalonia. And he was a member of *Opus Dei,* the Catholic fraternity that claimed to educate its members in how to practise spirituality in their working lives but which its critics regarded as nothing more or less than a Catholic mirror image of freemasonry.

"He's a hardliner," said Carlito. "Anti-gay for a start which he says puts the survival of the human species in great danger. And he's none too keen on women's rights. In short, a diehard with the mentality of a *Franquista.*"

I watched the minister rise from his desk and move over to a collection of armchairs and sofas at the side of the room. He beckoned us to occupy them. He was in his sixties, bald, with a wine-drinker's nose which might also have seen the boxing ring, and a double chin. He wore the standard dark-grey business suit and a very boring blue tie.

"*Señores.* Welcome. You know who I am. And I know the officers from the *Guardia Civil.* So, please introduce yourselves." He threw Manresa a disapproving look and frowned at Carlito and me.

"I do not speak much English, *Señor* Barrow."

"No matter, Your Excellency. I can manage with a little help from my friends here and as long as you do not speak too quickly."

He did not smile. But when I did hear him speak, I understood that his command of his own language was immaculate. Intonation, tone, grammar, all of them were perfect. I secretly thanked him for it.

He shifted his bulk into a comfortable position and looked me straight in the eye. "So, you think there is going to be a *coup d'état.* You think someone is plotting against both state and government. At least that what I heard you say at the ill-advised news conference

290

which, *Teniente Coronel*, I understand you organised on the basis of what you say is good intelligence."

I did my best to repeat the thrust of my allegations and speculation with references to arms shipments and certain events which had nearly led to my early demise.

He listened carefully, his gaze never leaving me. He brought his hands together in a steeple of fingers and sighed.

"Unfortunately, you are right, *Señor* Barrow. Everything you have said is perfectly true. There are some extremely misguided people, violent, brutal and with access to money, arms and drugs, who would wish to destroy all that our politicians, – not to mention His Majesty the former King Juan Carlos – all that they have carefully and painstakingly achieved since *la Transición.* They tried it once in 1981 and, thank God, the king told them what to do with their madcap ideas."

He paused. Manresa was straining very hard not to look too pleased with himself. Carlito, I could see, was judging that the time wasn't ripe for him to make a contribution. I must have looked as if I couldn't get out of the room fast enough to file some quick copy. We waited for the minister to move on. But he had driven the ball back into our court.

"May I ask," I pitched in, "whether the name Jaime Martínez Ortiz means anything in this context? Is he among those you describe as 'misguided'? And may I be bold enough to ask where he might be found?"

The minister started to say something, but I threw him another question.

"And if you know his whereabouts, what are you going to do with him? He is, after all, wanted on a charge of murder in Andalucía."

"We travel too fast, *Señor*," he replied. "I will at least tell you that the *Teniente Coronel's* department is very active in this area. And I am well aware that if we connect Ortiz's name to other actions which seem to have been the responsibility of the 'misguided', then he and his gang will face more than one murder charge and several of attempted murder, not to mention possible treason."

"You mean the brutal slaughter of the archaeologist, Elena Silva and the various attempts that were made to kill me?"

"Among other things, yes."

The minister said there were numerous enquiries and operations being conducted throughout Spain, notably by the *Guardia Civil*, trying to track down the would-be conspirators before they could do any more damage.

"As for Ortiz, he is small beer. He is no more capable of leading a coup than flying to the moon."

"But he has some troublesome assistants, Your Excellency. Young Moroccan men who, for a start, don't mind throwing people off trains in the middle of nowhere."

He called for coffee, wandered over to his massive desk and retrieved a bundle of papers.

"Ah, *Señor*, you think he has the help of jihadists? You think he has thrown in his lot with those groups of Islamic extremists who really would like to destroy Christian Spain and restore their old caliphate?"

"It's a fanciful notion, minister. But it might have a grain of truth in it."

He scratched his lower jaw. The coffee arrived. We sat silent while the flunkeys poured it out.

"We have another problem," he said.

"The election?" I ventured.

"You are suddenly very astute, *Señor* Barrow."

I shrugged. Carlito decided to intervene.

"Your Excellency!" he declared. I knew it stuck in his craw to utter these courtesies, but he recognised when they might come in useful. "You know of my work with the Association for the Recovery of Historical Memory."

"I do. I do not approve of your attempts to rake up the past. But go on."

I was asking myself yet again why this senior member of the government was seemingly so keen as to invite us to his office for a conversation.

"And you also know," Carlito continued, "that that work involves not only exhuming the mangled bodies of

293

the victims of the Civil War, and giving them a decent burial, but," and Carlito was plainly determined to put the emphasis on this, "that I am trying very hard to sift through hundreds of documents hoping to discover just who those victims were. It's a case of trying to match remains to the names we have, or perhaps the other way round." The minister merely nodded.

"Would it surprise you to learn that forensic tests have shown that two of the corpses we unearthed in the little village of Castillo in Andalucía share DNA with our friend, Jaime Martínez Ortiz?"

I had sensed that Carlito had a small bombshell in his armoury. I watched him search for a flicker of surprise in the minister's demeanour. There wasn't one. Instead the man fired back with both barrels.

"And would it surprise you, *Señor* Jimenez, to learn that your Association has received funds from some highly dubious and morally suspect sources who are no friends of the Spanish state, who would wish to cause it considerable embarrassment, and who in the end are no friends of the poor dead souls whose origins you have been trying to establish?"

We had reached deuce in a game of mental tennis.

"Which dubious and morally suspect sources are you referring to?" Carlito asked.

"You have close links with the new political party known as *Podemos*, links which involve the transfer of funds from that party to the Association."

"That's because your government took a decision to cut off state funding for our work."

"We will not enter into an argument about the merits of your work. But it is enough for me to tell you that *Podemos* has itself been receiving funds from outside this country, and if your Association has been a beneficiary, you have been indulging in some highly illegal activity."

Carlito looked straight at Manresa, who looked straight back without twitching an eyelid.

"Let's get this in perspective," said Carlito. "This has to do with *Podemos's* links to a certain political research organisation whose people have been advising a foreign government not of your liking. Namely, Venezuela under presidents Chavez and Maduro. It also has to do with a film transmitted by a private television channel with connections to the PP showing *Podemos* representatives boarding a Venezuelan military aircraft at Barajas airport bound for Caracas." He paused. "Am I right...Your Excellency?"

"Let me put it this way, Jimenez." The gloves of courtesy were coming off. "Those people want to break this country into pieces. If your friends in *Podemos* get into government after the election, they'll fix it so that Catalonia becomes the first region to leave Spain followed by the Basques and the *Gallegos*. While I am still a minister in an elected government, and interior minister to boot, I will do everything in my power to stop that. And if that means dismantling and banning your Association, that's what I will do."

"So, it's a trade-off," I said. "Carlito abandons his work and you produce Martínez Ortiz in court and put him on trial for being nothing more than a naughty boy?"

"We would if we could find him."

I threw my hands in the air. "We are going round in circles, minister."

It was Manresa's turn to speak. "Let me clarify from the GC's point of view. We haven't arrested Ortiz but we now know where he is. That is to say we have pinpointed a village in the Sierra de Gredos where we think he's hiding."

"Boy, you've kept that one quiet," muttered Carlito.

"And you are going to tell us?" I asked quizzically.

"No, he isn't," interrupted the minister. "The *Guardia Civil* are in the throes of an operation that will lead to the man's detention and that of some of his companions."

"His jihadist friends?"

"No comment."

Manresa looked distinctly uncomfortable. His glance said, "I'll fill you in on this later."

But I wasn't finished with this minister just yet. I wasn't going to be turfed out of this encounter prematurely. I wanted him on the defensive.

Cloud cuckoo land again?

We'll see. I think I can take this a little further.

Go on then. You've nothing to lose except a lot of face if it goes wrong. But that won't bother you, will it?

No.

"Your Excellency," I intoned as suavely and confidently as my blunderbuss manner would allow. He looked directly at me as if expecting some question he would be able swat away.

"As long ago as 1980, a man called Emilio Hellín, who belonged to a political movement called New Force, killed a left-wing activist, a woman by the name of Yolande Gonzalez. He shot her with two bullets to the head. It took thirty-three years for a journalist like me to write an article in one of your national newspapers disclosing that this Hellín had taught at the University Institute of Police Science Research, which depends for its very existence on the security secretariat of your ministry."

The minister sat like stone. Manresa had shifted further forward in his seat. I hadn't told Carlito of the time I'd stolen to do a little more homework, and I wanted to surprise even him.

"It was also revealed that Hellín was the director of a consultancy which advised the security forces. And he

297

had a brother in the GC. To add icing to the cake, he was arrested at the home of a police officer after one of his collaborators confessed to his own and Hellín's involvement in the murder. He was sentenced to forty-three years in jail. But he broke out of the prison at Alcalá de Henares. Am I not right, *Teniente Coronel*?"

Manresa nodded his agreement. Carlito was looking up at the distant ceiling as if expecting me to trip up at any moment.

"Hellín was recaptured and held in what is supposed to be the most secure jail in Spain at *Herrera de la Mancha*. Even there he managed to get permission for a home visit and promptly fled to South America – to Paraguay where he used his talents to help General Stroessner reorganise his own security forces. But he was unearthed, again by journalists – you see, we do have our uses. He was extradited to Spain in 1990. All well and good. But he still obtained early release from jail and in 1996 changed his name."

The minister made no attempt to stop me. He sustained his penetrating gaze and waited for me to carry on.

"Now, at the time of Miss Gonzalez's murder, prominent politicians here in Spain denounced Hellín's links with the security services. And there were allegations that the killing might have been ordered by the head of special operations, the late Manuel Ballesteros, a good old *Franquista* with one hell of a reputation for not sparing his opponents and victims, who'd been brought back into service as an anti-terrorist expert by, of all governments, a Socialist government."

The minister allowed himself a smile.

"Does it not say a lot about the *Transición* and the arrangement your party has with the Socialists – an arrangement which in effect allows the parties to swap power every now and again for the sake of political stability in Spain – that men like Ballesteros and Hellín could happily work for the security forces?"

He still didn't interrupt.

"My point being, Your Excellency, – and I apologise for labouring it – am I to expect that something similar to the Hellín case will rear its ugly head and let Jaime Martínez Ortiz off the hook? Oh, he'll spend a little time in prison, and then he'll be regurgitated into society as if nothing had happened. Along with his friends and relations of course."

His brow furrowed.

You can't expect the man to pick up on an allusion to Winnie-the-Pooh.

I didn't but I thought I might try.

You're getting too cocky again.

"My only other observation," I went on, "is that by allowing Ortiz to recruit a bunch of jihadists to his cause, your party and your government as his mentors might just be playing with a fire they cannot control."

I left it at that. He wasn't slow in coming back to me.

"Fanciful and outrageous," he said. "You could not have fabricated a more outlandish scenario, Barrow, if you had tried."

He strode back behind his desk.

"Ortiz," he went on, "has done nothing worse than persuade a lot of foolish people in the party and the army to stir things up..."

"...at your government's instigation, I suggest, and as a warning to the Spanish people that if they don't watch out at the next election, they'll get something they didn't bargain for. Either a left-wing government with a very radical agenda or a return to strong-man rule heavily disguised as parliament democracy? And I wonder who that strong man will be?"

I wasn't going to give him the pleasure of chucking us out unceremoniously. I got up and Carlito did the same. I didn't care what Manresa and his acolytes did.

"Thank you, Your Excellency. It has been very interesting. We journalists have work to do. You will excuse us."

"No, Barrow. I will not excuse you. I will dismiss you."

And he had one card up his sleeve.

"If you are thinking of filing material to your various outlets on the basis of what has been spoken about here today, I should forget it. This was a confidential briefing."

"No, it wasn't, minister," I broke in. "It was a summons. And on that basis, I obeyed you. Now you and the Spanish government will have to take the consequences."

He didn't rant and rave. He didn't lose his cool. He simply sat at his desk, a symbol of power and waved us away.

Chapter 8

This time it was my turn to run ahead, tripping down the marble staircase with distinct disregard for my sense of balance and safety. Carlito followed more sedately. Manresa and his officers joined us in the lobby.

"Well, you've really done it this time," he said.

"Precisely what have I done?"

"Charlie, that was very naughty. But very brave. You bated him like a toreador and, believe me, he'll react like an Andalusian bull. You've made a real enemy and you've put me in a rather difficult position. He's my boss, for God's sake!"

I squared up to him. "Your position is no more difficult now than it was before we went in there. What I did was lay down some necessary markers. He says, and you say, that you know where Ortiz is. But you're not sharing that information with us. You are under orders to keep us out of the loop. Now, I ask myself, I wonder why?"

Manresa allowed himself a deep sigh. "Because," he said wearily, "I don't want you and Carlito haring off on your own again. And I don't want to spend valuable time and money trying to dig you out of another hole. If you do, I'll bill you for those nice new clothes."

I recognised this as an oblique way of telling me that he was still on side. He was a high-flyer in the GC's intelligence arm and he had a lot of flexibility. But his body language during the meeting with the minister had been pretty clear. It said that however much he kept many of his intentions under wraps, he would always have our interests at heart. And the minister had reciprocated with grimaces and gestures of outright disapproval.

"Oh and by the way, *Señor* Jimenez," Manresa turned to Carlito. "Your little tit bit about the DNA match with Ortiz. Where did you get that from?"

"You will recall a nice young detective called Juan Codina in Castillo? He phoned me yesterday. He's been very hard-working. He's sifted through the DNA records from the exhumations – to which I gave him access before we left Andalucía – and made the discovery. He's now trawling through all the information he's gathered on Ortiz's past. The signs are that the man has denied his ancestry and has become what he has become."

"But we still haven't found the bastard," I muttered as darkly as I could manage.

Two security men had opened the main door of the ministry building. We walked out to face a media scrum, TV cameras, stills photographers, audio recorders in a fist of reporters' hands – the lot. Manresa waved his arms. "Nothing doing!" he called out. "No comment!"

I grabbed at his immaculate uniform. "We've got to give them something," I said. "Leave it to me."

"Charlie Barrow. I marvel at the way your Spanish has become so fluent in double quick time."

"I second that," said Carlito with a smirk.

I took it as permission to proceed.

Yes, we had met the minister of the interior, I told them. Yes, we had had a useful exchange of views on the how, why, where and when of *Señor* Ortiz's activities. Yes, he had reprimanded me for suggesting there was a plot to stage a coup, but he had admitted there were a few hotheads who were behind one. He'd criticised the work being done by Carlito Jimenez in the Association for the Recovery of Historical Memory and threatened to close it down. No, he had given us no information about what might happen to Ortiz if he were captured.

There was the usual flurry of indecision among the hacks. Some wanted to rush off straightaway to report my revelations. Others decided to stay behind hoping for more.

I spotted Rosie leaning on a newly washed taxi on the other side of the road, with a broad grin on her sunburned face.

"You will excuse us, ladies and gentlemen," I shouted hopefully. Manresa and his men created a gangway through the swaying crowd and we pushed through a babel of questions, suggestions and one or two comments of a less than friendly nature.

"That reporter with the agenda again," said Carlito.

Rosie held the rear door open. Carlito and I scrambled on to the back seat. She gave the media an intimidating scowl, got in and gunned the accelerator.

"Where are we going?"

"We shake 'em off first. Then I'll tell you."

She used what was clearly an encyclopaedic knowledge of Madrid's rat runs to find a quiet tree-lined square. She drove round it three times before niftily parking between two large white vans.

"This'll do," she pronounced proudly.

Carlito and I looked at one another, then at Rosie.

"What now?"

"I know where they are," she said. "I know exactly where your Moroccan friends are at this very moment, drinking coffee and smoking more cigarettes than are good for them."

"I'm hungry," I said.

Before I could suggest a civilised lunch somewhere, she had produced *bocadillos*, sausage, cheese and a bottle of *tinto*. "'Tis served, *Señores*. But you will have to consume it all in the back of this cab. Apologies for the lack of room but such is life."

We weren't complaining. The tensions of the morning had given me an appetite for the basic fare of a Spaniard on the move.

"Now," she pronounced. "I've worked it out that we stay here while you consume that little lot. Then we motor to where our friends are holed up which is just round the corner. We wait again – until they get bored. At which point they will head for their Mercedes. And we will follow them."

I couldn't see a flaw in this plan. "Okay. Let's do it. Agreed, Carlito?"

He was munching on a piece of chorizo with an enquiring look on his face.

"Rosie," he said. "This isn't the cab you were using when you rescued Charlie after he got pushed off the train, is it?"

She assumed an air of injured innocence. "True, *Señor*. It isn't. My dear old taxi is a yellow Passat. Our Arabs spotted it a mile off last night which is why they know where your supposedly secret hotel is. But I did a swap with my friend who lives near the airport. That's where I stayed overnight. He said I could use this Seat if I'd let him have the Passat for a day. Our Moroccans don't know this cab. It's just another car as far as they're concerned."

We finished the *al fresco* meal. Rosie climbed out to recce the square.

"Nothing to bother us," she said. She drove to a junction about fifty metres from where we had been parked, turned left and pulled up on the opposite side of the street, outside a café with flashing signs over the front door in Spanish and Arabic.

"Keep your heads down," she warned. I had already insisted that she must not put herself in danger on our account. It was not part of the bargain. She was adamant that she knew what he was doing and I was gradually coming to the conclusion that this Welsh woman abroad was more streetwise and generally savvier than either Carlito or me, especially when it came to negotiating the labyrinth of the capital.

We waited again. We were too anxious to be bored. And then they moved. They did exactly what Rosie said they would do. There were four of them, smartly dressed as always and well coiffured. As they came out of their eatery, they jostled one another like playful schoolboys. They laughed and joked and strutted towards their car. They climbed in. And didn't move.

"Patience," said Rosie. "Go with the flow. They'll move in a minute." And they did as she'd predicted. They behaved immaculately. They gave way to other road users. They never jumped a light. They stayed in the inner lane and kept well within the speed limit. Rosie drove roughly fifty metres behind. She was never in any danger of losing them. They led us out of the city on to an urban motorway which I vaguely started to recognise.

"I know exactly where we're going," I said.

"Yes, so do I," Carlito echoed. "To that bloody warehouse where we had the shootout."

And there it was in all its grey ugliness, with its non-descript entrance comprising a large version of a folding garage door and two poky windows. The main gates had been replaced by heavy steel contraptions, doubtless designed to discourage visitors after what had happened a few weeks ago. The chain link fencing had been topped with extra razor wire. There was a municipal police car parked just up the road.

We watched the Arabs swing their vehicle up to the gates. An arm came out on the driver's side. We were close enough to see the attached hand tap something into a keyboard with a metal facia. The gates opened slowly and the Merc slid into the compound and up to the garage doors.

"Slowly," I said fishing out my mobile. "Drive by as gently as you can. I want to take a picture, not least of that fancy contraption on the gate post."

"Not too slowly," mumbled Carlito. "We don't want a repeat of what happened last time we were here."

I snapped my photo, hoping the zoom lens would give me a close up of the keyboard, even if it wouldn't reveal the number they'd dialled. We motored on, pulling into a handy lay-by after about five hundred metres.

"We're stuffed," said Carlito.

"Methinks you're right."

"Well I'm glad you have no notion of trying to get inside again."

"I've no intention of subjecting either you or Rosie – or myself for that matter – to unnecessary risks," I said pompously.

Rosie asked if she could get out and have a smoke. Carlito and I looked at one another and tried to decipher our mutual silent thoughts.

"Sierra de Gredos, my arse!" I spluttered. "How the hell did Manresa think we would buy that one? Ortiz is in *there*. He always has been. His bloody Excellency knew it." I went on trying to inject some irony into my voice. "And Manresa knows it too."

"So, what do you think they're doing with him?"

"Keeping him on ice until just before the election. Then they'll produce him in court, rap his knuckles, give him a short stretch in chokey until *after* the vote and then, *listo,* Roberto's your uncle! Off he goes into the blue and the nation has been saved from infamy."

"And there's nothing we can do about it," Carlito declared.

"Not a sodding thing."

Rosie had finished her cigarette. "Where to now?" she asked.

****

After shuffling back into town with our tails between or legs, we went our separate ways. But we were determined to treat ourselves to one hell of a slap up meal in the evening. Rosie deserved recognition for some hard work and Carlito and I were out to reward her. She said she would drive to her home near the Escorial to see her partner and the children and return around about eight o'clock, guiding us to an obscure restaurant, well away from the centre but serving top notch Spanish cuisine.

Carlito and I would spend what was left of the day catching up on work. I needed to write and file, Carlito said he wanted to alert his colleagues in the Association to the ministerial threat to close them down. He would also be passing on this morsel of news to his friends in *Podemos.* It might well have some impact on the election campaign.

"It'll make the papers, Carlito. And I want their reaction."

"Don't worry about that. They'll be only too keen to respond."

"Tomorrow, we must get back down south," I said. "And I'd sooner go by road than take the train."

Rosie said she would be more than willing to take time out from her usual work. She would square it with her family, "not least because there's a promise of good money in it." I was banking on Fred sanctioning the

310

expenses, or some of them. Rosie said she would use yet a third car that our Moroccans wouldn't recognise.

I took to my hotel room and got down to the provision of copy for London. I had taken a lot of notes over the last few days, but what I wanted to file was all in the head. I knew I wouldn't get it all done in an afternoon. But I despatched the first piece to Fred in double quick time. The messages soon started winging their way back from London.

Fred was happy but imparted a few caveats.

"Pse confirm we safe using quotes attributed to minister and GC officers by name. Happy to confront Spanish government but think it wise to let lawyers take a look.

"Be aware international TV and radio still running backgrounders pegged to upcoming Spanish election. Full of politics I don't quite understand. Some running features linking Paris attacks to widespread nerves re terrorism all over Europe incl. Spain."

Why should I have been so amazed that my mobile was buzzing?

"Charlie! Can you talk?"

Fred sounded enthusiastic for once, his tobacco-stained voice tempered with traces of goodwill.

"Have you got the stuff I sent?"

"Have indeed. Congratulations. My editor is well pleased." There was a pause during which I again thought I heard the buzz of a busy newsroom. "These are exclusives, I presume?"

"In so far as you have them before anyone else. But if I get follow-up calls from radio and TV, I think I have the right to say 'yes' to two-ways and such."

"Only after the first edition is out. Agreed?"

I couldn't refuse. "And thereafter online?"

"Yes. Print first. Online follows straightaway. You should know that the time is coming when there won't be a print edition. It'll be all online and only online. One London newspaper's already gone down that road."

Fred continued to complain that his life was getting far too complicated. He had copy in front of him linking the Paris attacks to jihadists who'd acquired their weapons in Belgium and had connections with drugs and arms traffickers all over Europe "including Spain of course". They in turn were operating hand in glove with syndicates in Ireland who, incidentally, had threatened to do some nasty things to local journalists if they didn't lay off the story.

"Would you credit it, I now have a reporter in a place called Salford, next door to Manchester, telling me the gangs there are bosom pals of the Irish lot."

"And the Spanish police have just raided premises in Malaga owned by your Salford mafia. They found a nice little arms cache. Isn't the world wonderful, Fred?"

All I got was a grunt. "And I have an election to cover," I said pointedly.

"Don't tell me that ties in as well?"

I tried to explain that the Spanish poll was heavily overshadowed by the rapid rise of *Podemos* and *Ciudadanos*. The latest I'd had on all this was newspaper coverage of a raid by the *Guardia Civil* on the headquarters of the *Partido Popular* Madrid branch 'in search of incriminating evidence of illegal party funding', as the sub-editors had worded the story. The branch had its offices in the same building in Calle de Genova as the national party where I had once called for information on Martínez Ortiz. That seemed a long time ago, in an age when Elena was still alive and we had been in love.

Put that out of your mind right now.

But it was only a matter of days ago.

Which is why you have to forget it.

"I'm looking at something on Reuters," said Fred. "Looks like the PP boss in Madrid has resigned. She says it's a personal and political decision and has nothing to do with allegations of corruption." I heard his throaty laugh and bout of coughing. I promised to chase it up.

"Happy landings, Charlie. You are going to be a busy boy."

I wanted to step outside for a breath of fresh air. I sauntered out of the hotel looking right and left. I thought I would stroll a block or two and perhaps take a cab for a short tour of the town. I walked about fifty metres. The street was well-lit but some lofty plane trees cast their occasional shadows. There was no wind and it was pleasantly warm for December. Two men I recognised from Rosie's earlier pursuit of our group of Moroccans ambled past me, one of them nudging my shoulder and throwing me off balance. For once, old habits born of time in Northern Ireland reasserted themselves.

"My turn, this time, sunshine," I murmured as his ear brushed my face. He was on the ground with my knee in his groin before he could recite a prayer to his god. And in fluent Spanish, I told him he would suffer more pain if he didn't stop following me. His companion had legged it and we were all alone. I knew that if I relaxed a single muscle he would strike back. So I kicked him hard in the groin again and followed it up with one in the mid-drift. I stood over him, alert and ready for the riposte. He groaned and slowly held up his hands as if to surrender.

"I don't believe you," I said and kicked him again. "If you're the wazzock who threw me out of the train or fired a gun at me somewhere along a way, I hope you're feeling very sorry for yourself. I won't insult your mother or your manhood but I could summon up a few curses if you have the time to listen."

He held up his arms again.

"Get up!" I waited for him to move. He rolled over. "Now push off. Fast. Before I administer some more unarmed combat as bequeathed to me by the British army."

I never took my eye off him. He hoisted himself up on to his wrists and knees, looked at me in total confusion and staggered off into the night.

"Well done, Charlie," said a voice behind me. It was Manresa, now out of uniform and looking like the private detective he wasn't. "I told you not to go off on your own. But perhaps I underestimated you."

"Is it time for dinner?" I asked. "All that exercise has made me hungry – and thirsty."

"Rosie is waiting to take us to her favourite restaurant."

And so we ate. Carlito, Rosie, Manresa and me, making light work of roast lamb with honey and rosemary, garlic prawns in white wine and chilli, beetroot and potato salad with mint and onion, chicken stuffed with sage and cream cheese and several bottles of both red and white.

"I congratulate you, Rosie," said Manresa. "It takes an English woman to introduce me to spectacular Spanish cuisine."

Rosie grinned. "First off, I'm Welsh and proud of it. Secondly, to be honest, *Teniente Coronel*, it's more Mediterranean than simply Spanish. That chicken is probably Turkish."

"It doesn't really matter, does it?" Carlito pronounced through a mouthful of salad.

"Well, it's better than fish and chips," said Rosie.

"I have a proposal," said Manresa. "I think it's about time you all stopped addressing me by my rank and used my first name."

"Carlos, as I recall?" I offered.

He smiled and sipped some wine.

I wanted to steer the conversation round to what was becoming an obsession. "I've accused you of being secretive. I think I've sussed why you have to be and it's not just to stop Carlito and me going off on wild goose chases. But what I really want to know is why you do this job. If you have to work for a reactionary scoundrel like that minister, how do you get anything done to your satisfaction?"

Manresa rested his elbows on the table and clasped his hands into a tight ball.

"Let me ask Carlito as the one true Spaniard here," he said. "What is your take on the *Guardia Civil*?"

Carlito looked hard at Manresa, twitched his nose and was obviously considering a careful response.

"It has a bad reputation," he ventured, "even forty years after Franco's death. The people loathed it, feared it and did their best to avoid it. Many still do. I know it's changed for the better to some extent. It needed to during the *Transición*. Otherwise we would have had more violence in Spain than we have had. And I concede that it certainly suffered in the fight against ETA."

"But?" Manresa lifted an eyebrow and waited.

"You know and I know that there are older GC officers who are still dyed in the wool *Franquistas*. They love wearing that three-cornered hat at parades and your coat of arms is still a sword and *fasces*. It may be only a bundle of sticks but, given our recent past, it hardly persuades people that you guys are okay, the kind they might have a friendly drink with at the end of a tiring day."

Manresa waited to see if Carlito had any more to say.

"How old am I, Carlito?"

"A good guess would put you at forty-five."

"It is a good guess. Spot on, as a matter of fact." He separated his hands and took another sip of wine. "Let me tell you something I think you should hear from me. If I am forty-five, that means I was born four years before Franco died. I joined the *Guardia* in 1992 after getting a law degree from Complutense University. I rose through the ranks because I am competent and efficient. But I wasn't popular. Not with the older officers. A policeman with a university background was suspect. Too clever by half for the Franco generation.

"And then I started to meet the younger guys, born in the eighties, some who'd done more or less as I had, some less well educated but all of them wondering what all the fuss about the old days amounted to. I can tell you now that like me, they have become sick and tired of having to prop up a tired system, of which our minister is a typical relic. Even if we try not to let it show, we are angry that a wholesale cleanout of all our security forces

317

hasn't happened. Every year in February we baulk at having to listen to tributes from the *Franquistas* to the idiots who tried to stage a coup in 1981. They drive us crazy. And when we make an effort to expose officers who are determined to protect some of the nastiest remnants of the dictatorship, known torturers and killers for instance, we're blocked. And the villains carry on living in comfortable retirement."

He snorted his indignation, coughed and poured himself another large glass of wine.

"Now you know where I'm coming from. The light at the end of the tunnel is that that minister won't be there for much longer. The election will give me a new boss. And I don't think he, or she, will behave in quite the same way."

As justification for all his actions, including the unconditional backing he'd given us, it took some beating. Nor was he going to apologise for resorting to armed violence when it was needed, "like ferrying my men up to *Fortaleza* and smashing the living daylights out of the bunch that tried to finish you off at the shepherd's hut." He fixed his gaze on me. "If I hadn't, you'd be dead."

We hadn't had time to tell Rosie about this. Her face was a glorious mixture of surprise and expectation. So I picked this moment to fill her in on everything, without exception, and warned her again that she might be getting herself into scrapes she hadn't bargained for.

"I'm sticking with it," she said. "You want me to drive you south and I want to go south. I'm suddenly understanding things about this country I never knew before."

"There you are, Charlie. The lady is better informed. All thanks to you."

Rosie growled. "I'm no lady."

At last we had something to laugh about. After a barrage of noisy requests, Carlito surrendered, fetched his guitar and serenaded us to bed.

Chapter 9

After our splendid dinner, which lasted until one in the morning, I found it impossible to sleep. It had nothing to do with indigestion or inebriation. I was simply too excited. So I filed. Reams and reams of the stuff until my eyes ached and my head spun. I couldn't forbear to furnish a piece using Manresa's *apologia*, putting it into the context of the election and the increasing support for *Podemos* and *Ciudadanos*, even among officers and ranks in the GC. I fished out a cutting I'd taken from one of the newspapers, telling me about a retired senior GC general, two judges and a group of army officers who were standing as *Podemos* candidates. And they weren't of the younger generation.

I got to bed at three thirty and was deep down when the alarm call came at eight.

Life changes from now on.

How so?

You are showing Madrid a clean pair of heels. You will forget Elena.

Never.

Oh yes you will. And you will wash away bad memories of violent encounters with a string of villains.

But I still haven't found Jaime Martínez Ortiz. That's what rankles.

You will.

Your confidence amazes me.

It's meant to. Now get going.

Rosie had the new car ready. A Seat Alhambra. A truly Spanish vehicle. Black and shining and non-descript. Carlito looked at it with approval, lifted his bag into the back and lovingly and carefully added his guitar to the pile of luggage. My wardrobe had been somewhat reduced by being thrown off a train into inhospitable vegetation. I wanted time to add to the replacements generously donated by Manresa. But shopping for clothes would have to wait.

The *Teniente Coronel* was not there to see us off.

"He didn't want his uniform drawing attention to our little party," said Rosie. She'd scoured the street for Moroccan goons. "I think you frightened them off, Charlie."

The back seat gave us plenty of room for paraphernalia like laptops, notebooks, maps and newspapers. For now, though, I wanted to dwell on the mass of work I'd done overnight and stare at what we were passing, cafés, shops, crowds, not least the pretty girls, and the multiplicity of political posters. It was clear that Rosie wasn't taking the obvious route out of town.

But it wasn't long before she had us heading into bright winter sunshine.

"I know you want to get south as quickly as possible," said Carlito. "But I think we have to take it easy on this trip. It's not worth rushing back to Castillo. We've left a few dishes simmering in Madrid. Let's see what happens. And let Rosie show you a bit more of Spain."

His plan was to damp down the flow of adrenalin and get me to relax.

"Time to be a bit of the tourist, Charlie. We'll aim for Córdoba and stay the night there."

I didn't protest. Carlito was being his wise self, full of the common sense which had only deserted him when we'd been in *Fortaleza* and he'd had to confront his two children in the care of Felipe and Consuelo. But I did need to delve a little deeper before switching off.

"What luck have you had with the Association?" I asked. "Did you tell them that they're under threat?"

"The people in Madrid knew already. They're mounting a campaign to publicise the threat and *Podemos* has promised to help. They're going to insert an undertaking to keep us in business in their election manifesto. In any case, everything's up in the air while the election is on. If the PP lose or get a hammering, the dark clouds will probably go away. We shall still have to find ways of raising cash, but we might just get a donation or two from a new government."

Rosie drove on. She asked if she could switch on the radio.

"Music," she said. "Like the guitar you played last night, Carlito." She found the *Radio Clásica* channel with a programme called *Nuestro Flamenco*. Carlito listened intently. I detected he was picking up ideas for future use. The seraphic smile said it all.

I drifted off until I realised we were stopping.

"Coffee anyone?" Rosie asked. We'd pulled into a service area.

"Here we go again," I grumbled. "Someone else can get them this time. I don't want some clever sod in charge of an espresso machine recognising me from the telly."

Carlito was looking back and frowning. "That estate over there by the cash machine," he said. "Has it been following us?"

Rosie got out, blatantly walked up to the car and had a close look. "Don't think so," she said, brandishing the coffees. "Looks like a family. Mum. Dad. Two kids. And a dog."

Carlito subsided and shut his eyes.

We followed the scenic route to Córdoba, turning off the *autopista* at Manzanares, heading west to Ciudad Real. Thereafter, mountains and river valleys and the beginnings of the Sierra Morena, peaks, cliffs, outcrops of rock, scrub. Winding roads and hairpin bends brought us down to the great city by late afternoon, as a scarlet sun glowed somewhere over distant Seville and the Mediterranean beyond.

So efficient were my fellow travellers at organising this jaunt that we had no problems finding the right hostelry where Carlito eventually brought out his guitar and beguiled the locals with his hypnotising technique. Food arrived as ever dish after dish and wine flowed by the bottle. This far south it was warm enough to dine outside which was one of the reasons Carlito's music attracted ever more custom.

The temptations are too much. You are close to surrendering.

Not quite. But I'm getting there.

I slept well, making up for what I'd lost in Madrid. Carlito was determined that the next day should be spent visiting the sights. We went first to the *Mesquita*, Córdoba's original mosque, the serried ranks of its pink and white arches leading the eye to some mysterious secret chamber beyond its ancient walls. I was appalled that the Catholic Church, wallowing in past conquests and the expulsion of Islam from southern Spain, had inserted a monstrosity of a gilded cathedral into the interior of the mosque, showing off a debased taste for superstitious kitsch and elaborate ornament.

Then later to Madinat al-Zahra, the ruins of a palace complex built by one of the caliphs of Andalucía in the tenth century, before corruption and internecine strife had started to drain the blood out of Muslim rule, a sad monument to greed and hubris and eventual decline.

All this was told to me by a Carlito, enthused with the history of his country and imbibed by Rosie with a thirst for knowledge I hadn't expected in an expat taxi driver. It wasn't that it didn't interest me, but it was overshadowed by a suspicion that this was not how I ought to be spending my time. What would I do when we returned to Castillo, with our mission very much unaccomplished? Would I just pay a last visit to the exhumation site and quietly sidle out of Spain to my retreat in Portugal? And that would be that?

But I did learn one important historical lesson from Carlito, that there had been a time in the ninth and tenth centuries before Madinat al-Zahra had been sacked by Berber armies from North Africa, when Muslims, Christians and Jews had lived in relative harmony, tolerating one another's customs, languages and worship as the way to stability and prosperity.

"It was one of the tragedies of Europe that the golden age didn't last," said Carlito. "We could learn from it today now that we have Islamic State saying it wants to conquer Europe and demolish the Vatican while some in NATO would like to wipe Muslim fundamentalists from the face of the earth. Add to that the Israeli government's treatment of Palestinians and those in Iran who call for the state of Israel to be tossed into the sea. What a crazy world!"

"And now we have jihadists linking up with fascist goons in Spain," I added in a weak attempt to relate all he had told us to the search for Jaime Martínez Ortiz.

Carlito shrugged, placed his guitar on his left thigh and sang a sad song about a palm tree. "A caliph who had fled from Syria and crossed North Africa to build his Muslim kingdom in Andalucía wrote these words to sooth his pain in old age," he explained.

A palm tree grows in the middle of the courtyard.

Born in the West, far from the land of palms.

I say to it, How like me you are, far away and in exile.

Long separated from family and friends.

You sprang from earth where you are a stranger.

And I, like you, am far from home.

"That was very beautiful," said a deep voice from the depths of the restaurant.

And there he was. All the clichés came into my head at once; 'smooth as silk' and 'as large as life'. Jaime Martínez Ortiz had left his table and was ambling towards us. I pushed back my chair, ready to confront him. Two heavies appeared at his shoulders.

"Moroccans again," Rosie observed, rising quickly to her feet and flexing her fingers.

"This is an unexpected pleasure," purred Ortiz.

"I don't think Mr Charlie Barrow would agree," Carlito observed. He stayed seated, holding his guitar as if his life depended on it. He caressed the finger board and strummed a couple of chords.

"Perhaps not," Ortiz replied.

There was only one way to deal with this encounter and move it on from the stalemate it had already reached.

"Sit down, *Señor*. Please!" I took great care to rearrange the chairs and create a space at our table. I beckoned him to take it. He accepted with oily courtesy.

"Your friends?" I asked.

Ortiz gave a scarcely visible wave. The Arabs melted away to their own table. Rosie had taken a silent cue from me and sat down.

"A glass of wine, *Señor* Ortiz?" I poured some *tinto* and placed the glass in front of him. He looked at it with disdain. No one spoke for at least a minute. The restaurant chatter had abated, with most eyes fixed on our encounter.

"Aren't you supposed to be under arrest?" I ventured.

He took a deep breath and smoothed back his well-oiled hair. "The charges against me were dropped," he said. "It was hardly surprising given the clumsy way that oaf of a detective in Castillo handled the case. I was never guilty of any crime."

"Pepe?" I enquired.

"Whoever killed him goes free." Which begged a few questions.

I wanted to ask him about the evidence Juan Codina had found in the cell at the police station – the expensive pen with his embossed signature on it and the DNA tests. I intended to question him about his friends who'd tied me to a bed in Madrid; who'd shot at me from the warehouse and put me in hospital for two weeks; who'd killed Elena and tried to kill Carlito; who'd been out to machine gun us to oblivion in the hills above *Fortaleza*; who'd pushed me out of a train and left me battered and bruised in the cold night air. But I changed tack.

"Why do we find you in Córdoba?" I asked.

"It should come as no surprise," he drawled, "that I have had you and your companions in my sights for some time. Given what you have been saying about me in public. In any case you are far too easy to follow."

Rosie made a move to intervene, but Carlito raised his hand. "Not your fault," he said. "These gentlemen have their *red de contactos*. Friends and relations up and down the country. Some of them are Arabs who, as we know, Rosie, keep popping up all over the place just to annoy us and ready to do mischief at this man's bidding."

"Ridiculous!" countered Ortiz. "I have many friends, yes. I have contacts. They have nothing to do with my attempts to keep tabs on you."

He had unwittingly contradicted himself. Did I detect that he was suddenly rattled? Everything that had happened since I'd first met him in the *parador* at Carmona suggested that Carlito and I had at last disturbed his sophistication, his urbanity and his ambition.

"So you are not planning a *coup d'etat*?" I asked point blank.

"That does not deserve an answer. I am a loyal member of the *Partido Popular* campaigning in a Córdoba constituency for a seat in the next parliament. It's all perfectly straightforward and above board."

He preened himself.

"And when I am elected, I will make damn sure your so-called Association for the Recovery of Historical Memory, *Señor* Jimenez, packs its bags and leaves our graveyards alone."

Carlito was unmoved. But I was livid enough to scratch at what I thought was an open wound.

"So the documents I saw bearing your name and linking you to the seizure of arms in Galicia are bogus? Like those showing how much cash you received from party slush funds?"

Ortiz blinked, stroked his glossy hair again and sighed.

"Mr Barrow. You have defamed me time and again."

"I have spoken the truth," I replied. "And I've taken a few knocks in the process. If you and your people had had their way, I'd be dead by now. And so would my friend, Carlito Jimenez. Who, for example, fired into the restaurant in Castillo while he was entertaining us with some fabulous music?"

He lost his cool, thumped the table and bent towards me, eyes wide with undisguised hatred. The clientele became ever quieter.

"I warn you for the very last time. If you persist in spreading your lies, you will indeed suffer again."

"Be specific."

He ignored this. "I demand that you stop your investigations into my affairs and spike all the copy you have written for newspapers and other media."

"I see you know the jargon of the trade, *Señor*." It was my turn to sit back and grin. Rosie and Carlito did likewise.

"Too late," I declared. "Far too late."

"Meaning?"

"I have produced thousands of words on the subject of your nefarious doings which have appeared in print, online, and on TV and radio. Everybody who's anybody knows all about you. Even the story that your DNA matches that of one, perhaps two, of the corpses in the mass graves at Castillo."

I watched his face twitch and his desperate attempt to keep still.

"Even the attacks in Paris have failed to push you out of the headlines. I'm amazed you haven't understood this. Don't you read the papers or watch television?"

He sprang to his feet. "And now I see you're consorting with lesbians," he hissed.

I was about to punch him on the nose when I felt a hand on my arm.

"Forget it, Charlie," whispered Rosie. "Not worth it."

Ortiz stood up, to be joined by his heavies and flounced out of the restaurant.

"I think that calls for another song, Carlito, or some frenetic *flamenco*."

"I think it calls for some more food and drink," said Rosie.

****

We saw no sign of Ortiz in Córdoba after that. His escort had vanished as well. Rosie was thankful to be free of the job of watching our backs. She took off to do some shopping. But I wasn't wasting the opportunity to file copy on our confrontation. I sent a short, sharp piece to Fred who was quick to phone me back.

"It gets better," he croaked.

"It seems to," I replied with a smile in my voice.

"What are you going to do now?"

I said I would do as Carlito was suggesting. "Play the tourist for a few days, swim in a pool and enjoy some more meals. And do some reading. Apart from anything else, I want to take a closer look at the election campaign. This is Andalucía, stronghold of the Socialists. But there could be an upset. *Podemos* are doing very well in the polls. They could make inroads into the Socialist vote. Which may or may not be a good thing if it benefits the PP."

There was another bout of rasping and coughing at Fred's end of the line. "Careful, Charlie. Don't let your skirts show."

"I beg your pardon?"

"Your prejudices."

"Hard not to," I countered. "The more I learn about political corruption in this country, the more I wish for *Podemos* to do well. Will file as and when."

"Accepted. And you can charge us for your driver too. Satisfied?"

"That's very generous," I muttered cautiously.

"I know." The croaking became a chortle.

Fred was happy. And so was I, at least as far as the journalism was concerned. I wasn't so relaxed about our security. But Rosie was as vigilant as ever but less anxious than of late. And we had to let Carlito have his head.

The owner of our hotel and restaurant, far from regarding us as a bloody nuisance and a threat to his profits, treated us as star attractions. The hungry and thirsty flocked to sample his menus. They also came to listen to Carlito. Some were *voyeurs* curious to see a dwarf musician with or without a dazzling technique and a temperament reflecting the soul of Andalucía. But most came with a genuine wish to listen and appreciate. The applause at one of his performances was spectacular and infectious. And he was getting better all the time.

"I'm writing a piece about you," I told him.

"Complimentary I hope."

"You know I can't judge your musicianship, but I can judge my own reaction to it."

And I wasn't leaving out the touchy subjects. I told him I wanted to include references to his children and *Fortaleza*.

"I trust you to do an honest job," he said.

Guard him with your life. He's tough but he's vulnerable.

He's a polished gem.

And you're a rough diamond, I suppose.

Chapter 10

The time had come to move on. We set off for Castillo on a morning of bright sun, up into the *sierra* again where the warmth gave way to a breeze across the hills and mountains from the north. It was still winter and the ground stayed firm, parched and light brown. We dropped into the town at about three in the afternoon and found our hotel of old where the staff had laid on a welcoming ceremony. We walked into the lobby to be greeted with cheers and applause and a feast of small dishes of tapas and sparkling cava.

"You are celebrities," said the manager whose name, to my shame, I still didn't know. Carlito made a short speech of thanks and introduced Rosie who was immediately offered a room at a reduced tariff. She winked at me well aware that I was grateful for a chance to save a little money on expenses.

We were about to inspect our rooms and dump our bags when three visitors walked in, with broad smiles and open arms. Juan Codina, *La Celestina* and the boy Juan José. There was more embracing and back-slapping and cross-fire conversation.

Carlito dived into one of his bags and brought forth a parcel which he presented to Juan José. It was essentially a large box measuring about thirty cubic centimetres.

"Can I open it now?"

"Be my guest," said Carlito.

The boy didn't tear at the wrapping paper. He took great care to keep it intact and undo the knotted string that had held it together. The rest of us watched patiently while he unveiled the contents.

It was a globe, but not of the world. Its surface was deep blue. Juan José was confused at first. Carlito told him to carry it over to a table close to a power point. He took the lead dangling from beneath the globe and plugged it in. Picked out on its surface were spots of light showing the stars and constellations just as Juan José had seen in the illustrated book his father had bought him. The boy's face was a picture of rapture. He turned to Carlito and hugged him as if both their lives depended on it.

"I shall show it to Father Trujillo," said Juan José.

"I should wait awhile," I warned. He understood all too well and grinned at me.

Carlito looked into his bag again. He took out a second package which he handed to *La Celestina*. She was another who unwrapped parcels with exaggerated care almost as a gesture of courtesy to the donor. As she peeled off the paper, she revealed a glazed plate, broad

335

but shallow, painted with a peacock motif surrounded by bright flowers.

"A present from Córdoba," said Carlito.

She was struck dumb. And then for one as old as she was, squealed with delight.

We could not escape a party there and then. Carlito had to play his guitar again. The hotel lobby was filled with an assortment of revellers, dancing, chatting and imbibing more tapas and cava. Rosie was certainly enjoying herself.

Watching all this with a beneficent smile, Juan Codina stood in a corner, a little aloof, until he caught my eye.

"I may still call you 'Charlie'?"

"Oh, come on, Juan. There's no need to be formal."

He guided me away from the merrymaking into the small courtyard beyond the lobby.

"We need somewhere quiet," he said.

We sat down on the stone benches that surrounded the hotel's pride and joy, its ornate fountain of indeterminate age.

Juan told me he had officially been taken off the enquiry into Pepe's death.

"In any case," he said, "it has been closed."

"Well, that doesn't surprise me." I tried to give him a reassuring glance, but he was clearly agitated. "But your bosses here must know of your summons to Madrid from *Teniente Coronel* Manresa and your appearance at the news conference. Your face was on national TV, for pity's sake. They can't rule you out altogether."

He threw me a sly glance as if to puncture my naivety.

"I haven't given up altogether," he said. "I am a threat. And they know it. So far they've kept their distance."

He lowered his voice. He told me he was in daily contact with Manresa. The message from Madrid was, 'Keep digging and keep looking'. Manresa had suggested he would if necessary pull rank over the police chief in Castillo. But he would have to pick his moment.

"It's not rocket science, Juan. You have two distinct jobs to do, related but separate."

He listened with what I took to be revived enthusiasm.

"First, you must do as Manresa says. Keep sniffing at the murder and, if you can, name names. Who here in Castillo called in the lawyers and officials who sprang Martínez Ortiz from jail? Who ordered you to stay off the case? Were they one and the same, or is there a kind of jolly mafia inside the local police and the GC which reckons it can push you around?"

He was looking more confident.

"Then there's this DNA link between Ortiz and a corpse unearthed in the cemetery. Any more on that?"

"The corpse is Ortiz's grandfather," he declared.

"What? Are you sure about that?"

"The documents prove it. He was a captain in the Republican army. He led a squad of about twenty soldiers who tried to resist Franco's troops when they attacked the town early in 1936. They didn't stand a chance. All the evidence says they were either shot as they fought or captured and executed with a bullet to the back of the neck. Among the remains of women and children are those of a dozen or more young men. Their bones are partly clothed in the rags of uniforms worn by the Republican army."

I said nothing for a full minute and Juan inspected his fingernails.

"You are telling me that Martínez Ortiz has Republican ancestry?"

He nodded.

"Christ Almighty! I knew there was a DNA link with one of the corpses and Ortiz knows that too. We faced him with it in Córdoba. But I didn't know the details. And I also don't know whether he's been told the full story."

I gave Juan an account of the row we'd had with Ortiz.

"I think he knows well enough," he said. "The records show his father was born in 1936, obviously grew up under Franco and managed to persuade the

338

regime that he was a supporter. He survived and fathered Ortiz. Which is why he is such a staunch PP man."

Juan's matter-of-fact remarks were showing me what a fine example of the good, taciturn policeman he was turning out to be.

"There's a second set of bones which may also be one of his relatives. The DNA also matches his."

"It gets better," I said.

"He's finished," he replied. "The PP will disown him. They'll hang him out to dry. And I'll have him back in court on a murder charge."

"*Levantará un revuelto.* A cat among pigeons."

"*Exacto!*"

We looked at one another as if we had rediscovered America.

"You must choose the right moment to let the world know, Charlie."

A thought struck me. "Does Carlito know?"

"Not yet. He let me wade through his documents, which is how I put two and two together. But, as far as I can tell, he missed the connection."

We wandered back into the lobby. The celebrations had died down. *La Celestina* and Juan José had left and Carlito was sitting with Rosie, quietly consuming a beer. Our bags had been taken to our rooms. It was six in the evening.

"You two have been in secret conclave?" observed Carlito.

"Secret and fruitful," I replied. "And you will taste the fruit ere long."

I suggested we convened at eight in our favourite eatery – Carlito, Rosie, Juan and myself.

"And tomorrow we go straight to the cemetery," I said in a voice that was brooking no argument.

Their faces told me I would get none.

Chapter 11

It had rained, not heavily but enough to make the red earth of the mass grave a little more than moist and, for now, impossible to excavate. We sheltered under the striped awning. Alex was there, accompanied by his team of six workers.

"I find it impossible to tell you how sad I am," he said after we had shaken hands. "Elena was more than my boss. She was a true friend. She knew that I am gay and I knew she wasn't. But that did not stop us from having something special. Why should it, of course. *Señor* Barrow, I loved her."

"And you know that I did too." I looked at him and suspected he knew much more about Elena, knowledge that I would never be party to. He linked his arm into mine and led me to a far corner of the exhumation site. The rain began to soak our shirts but I wasn't resisting.

"This is what you want to see, isn't it?" he said. Juan Codina stood a little way behind us, Carlito behind him. Rosie kept a distance she thought appropriate to the circumstances.

We bent down. I reckoned there were the remains of at least six corpses in a shallow grave, the bones longer and thicker than those I had seen before, the skulls a little larger. Next to them were the remnants of khaki uniforms, leather boots and Sam Browne belts, arranged as if they had been exhibits in a military museum. I beckoned to Juan and Carlito.

"Are these the remains you're talking about? The troops who tried to defend Castillo against the Nationalists?"

Alex knelt beside me and inspected the bones and clothing without touching them. And nodded.

"And which one do you identify as the grandfather of Jaime Martínez Ortiz?"

He had clearly worked with Juan on this. He pointed to a set of remains carefully separated from the others. There was a special marker showing the officer's name, rank and number.

"That's him," said Juan. "Or what's left of him. There was enough from which we were able to take the DNA sample. There's no doubt about it. If you look at the bits of uniform, you'll see his cap badge, a length of lanyard and the tin whistle he used during combat."

"I knew it," said Carlito coming forward. "I knew there was something I'd missed when I waded through those documents. I should have made the connection. But my eyes have wandered over so many pieces of paper, they've lost the ability to spot the clues." He turned to Juan. They shook hands vigorously and triumphantly. Carlito insisted that this set of remains had to be removed immediately and taken in some kind of sealed container, first to Juan's office and later perhaps to his own in Carmona. Juan agreed and Alex did not object.

We stood and stared at the bones. I thought of Elena and the day Ortiz had tried to thwart the exhumations with a fake court order. The rain had stopped and the clouds parted, allowing a hazy sun to brighten a sombre sky.

Then we heard it. A helicopter. Then another. Carlito and I had become uneasily accustomed to the clatter.

"And who the hell is this?" I bawled over the noise of the rotors.

The pilots showed no respect for the dead. They put their machines down on a patch of ground next to the exhumation site. Even though the earth was damp, the whirling blades raised enough of a dust storm to foul our vision and disturb some of the graves. We shielded our eyes against the flying detritus but saw enough to make out one group of men in black combat gear advancing towards us with automatics at the ready.

"Dear God," Carlito shouted. "Look at the man. He's donned camouflage and an officer's beret." Jaime Martínez Ortiz was leading his little army like a bad actor in *Apocalypse Now*.

"Put your hands up," he yelled. "Up! Up! Up! All of you."

343

We did as we were told, visitors and workforce alike. The dust began to settle. Ortiz walked up to Carlito, gave him what he thought was a withering look and pushed him to the ground. Cursing loudly, I moved in to stop him doing any more damage.

"Stay where you are, Barrow."

My body language told Juan, Alex and Rosie to keep still. Ortiz's men covered every one with a firearm. Another group from the second helicopter rounded up the exhumation team.

"The first thing we do," said Ortiz, "is put a stop to this little lot."

His men knew what to do. They waded into the mass graves and started to kick the skulls and bones aside. They ripped down the protective awning, swept excavation tools from the worktable, pulled up the grave markers and threw everything into black waste bags.

Alex was weeping. His co-workers looked on with a mix of fear and loathing. Ortiz joined in the general mayhem. He stamped on any object that caught his eye. He screamed at his men to finish the job as fast as possible. I watched him stalk up and down waving a gun. A Sig Sauer 9mm combat pistol. He was overtaken by a madness he couldn't control. Any trace of suave, civilised behaviour had long since deserted him.

He turned his attention to Carlito, still sprawled on the ground and plainly unconscious. His head had hit a sharp stone and blood was seeping into the soil. Waving his gun to hold me at bay, Ortiz knelt over Carlito, lowered the weapon and fired two shots into his skull at point-blank range. Carlito's small body twitched and lay still.

I didn't care anymore. I didn't care if I died there and then. I saw the red mist and flung myself at Ortiz. We fell together and rolled over in the dirt. He was stronger than I thought. But he'd lost his Sig Sauer. I saw it half buried a couple of metres to my right. I fought to push him off, stretched my arm and grabbed the gun. I forced it between our two writhing bodies and stabbed the barrel into his chest.

"Get up, you bastard! Get up now."

I expected him to struggle again. But he lay still. I pushed my left knee into his groin, got a foothold and stood up.

I took a chance and looked round. The armed posse had melted away. Juan Codina had drawn his own pistol and aimed it at Ortiz. Rosie had gone to help Alex and his bewildered colleagues. The two helicopters roared off into the sunlight. The pilots were clearly anxious to get well away from the cemetery. Juan never took his eyes off Ortiz.

"I said 'Get up!' Now!" I kicked him hard. He hauled himself to his knees and slowly got to his feet.

"At least that bloody dwarf's dead," he said.

I grabbed at his uniform and slapped his face. "Before we do anything else to you, we have something to show you. Over here."

Juan was with Carlito feeling for any signs of life. He looked at me in desperation and shook his head. I saw blood oozing from Carlito's skull. Ortiz had blown half his face away.

I grabbed at Ortiz and dragged him to the spot where his grandfather's skeleton still lay undamaged.

"Concentrate," I said. I shoved him forward, keeping the gun trained on his torso.

He challenged me. "I don't have to do this," he said.

"If you don't lower yourself into that grave and take a close look at those bones, so help me, I'll kill you."

Juan heard me, walked towards us and put a hand on my shoulder. "Step back, Charlie, before you regret it."

"That was your father's father," I yelled. "A loyal Republican officer who tried to defend this town against Franco's thugs. And paid for it with his very being. You should be proud of him. But you're not, because your mind has been twisted." I paused for breath. "Jaime Martínez Ortiz, you're mad."

There was a huge explosion. I was distracted and looked up. Juan was a master of concentration, his attention fixed on Ortiz.

"The choppers," he said. "They've collided. Just above the outcrop of rock on the other side of the main road."

Thick clouds of oily black smoke had started to drift our way. There were more explosions. We lay flat to avoid the flying debris.

"Fuel tanks," said Juan. He allowed himself a satisfied smile. "We just got rid of an extremely dangerous group of jihadists. And we didn't have to do a damned thing."

"Where did they get the choppers from?"

"They hired them, Charlie. They have money, as if we didn't know. And they bought their weapons through the usual channels. You described them at your news conference in Madrid. Remember? There are no mysteries, Charlie. It's all too obvious."

The noise had drowned out the arrival of two Nissan patrol cars now parked as close as possible to what was left of the exhumation site. Manresa strode forward, brandishing his own weapon. He saw Carlito's body, slowed his pace, knelt beside it and took off his GC cap. For one moment I thought he was about to make the sign of the cross. He caught my gaze.

"No, Charlie. I may have been brought up a good Catholic boy, but I have long since lost my faith. You should know that by now."

He stayed kneeling and called for a towel or a pillow or an item of clothing on which to rest Carlito's head. The blood from his wounds was still staining the ground. What was left of his face gave no sign that he had been in agony only a short while ago.

"Bring some water and a clean cloth," Manresa said to one of his men. As soon as they were handed to him, he set about bathing the head with infinite care and firmly closed Carlito's eyes. When he was satisfied that nothing more could be done to bring dignity to the body, he stood up, took a pair of handcuffs from his belt, walked up to a stunned Ortiz and shackled him to a short chain.

"I'd charge you with murder here and now. But there's little point, is there? Let's leave that to the magistrate."

Ortiz spat hard.

"Take him to that cell he was in before," ordered Manresa. "And Charlie, give me that gun."

I surrendered the weapon, walked away, sat down on a low wall, looked at the grey sky, sighed deeply and wept with my face buried in the jacket Manresa had bought me.

After ten minutes of grief and self-pity, I felt another hand on my shoulder. I looked up and saw Rosie fixing her gaze on mine. She was trembling and holding back her own tears.

"Time to leave, Charlie," she said. "Let's go back to town."

"What about those lovely people who've got to clear this mess up?"

"Leave them to it. They know best. At least, like us, they're still alive."

****

All I knew after that was deep sleep. Someone had given me a pill and I didn't wake until the following afternoon. When I opened my eyes, I was alone. My mouth was painfully dry and I cried out for water. But no one came. I stayed still until I'd gathered enough strength to push myself up, lean against the headboard and reach for the carafe and glass on the bedside table. I thought it strange that I had no headache. I looked at my hands and saw purple bruises. They had to be the results of my tussle with Ortiz. Then I laughed, mocking the empty room. I would need yet another set of new clothes after rolling over in the dirt with the bastard. Would Manresa come up with the goods again?

I decided to take advantage of the stillness of my surroundings. It was disturbed just enough by the usual murmurings of life beyond the walls; a car horn, a hint of conversation, someone humping a heavy suitcase along the corridor beyond the door. They brought a womblike comfort.

It didn't last long. I felt the surge in my throat and wept again. I wept for Carlito, for Elena and for all the victims whose desecrated remains littered the exhumation site. To fight the tears, I swallowed more water. I drank too fast and gave in to a bout of coughing.

There was a timid knock at the door. Its feebleness almost annoyed me, but I forced myself to call out a courteous, "Come in!"

Manresa, Juan Codina and Rosie filed in like overawed worshippers entering a cathedral. The room was small and the three of them only just managed to squeeze into the spaces round the bed.

I needed to puncture their solemnity. I smiled.

"What a depressing trio!" I muttered.

Now that they saw I was perhaps recovering from the shock of recent events, they smiled back, diffident and nervous.

"Well, you don't look that bad," observed Manresa. Then the collective solemnity reasserted itself.

"Carlito," I asked. "A funeral?"

"Tomorrow afternoon," he said. "A secular ceremony in a room at the *ayuntamiento*. You might be interested to learn that the mayor himself wishes to be there. But he won't preside. You will do that."

I was taken aback, as indeed I think I was expected to be. But I didn't hesitate.

"I'll be immensely honoured," I replied. "Who else will be present?"

"We're in touch with his brother in *Fortaleza*. I am sending transport early in the morning. Probably a chopper to save time. Felipe has said Consuelo would like to be there and they will bring Carlito's two children. Felipe reckons they are tough enough to understand what it's all about. And maybe they'll enjoy the chopper ride."

Delegates from the Association would come from Madrid and Seville. Two guys from *Podemos* had said they would like to be there.

"I told them they were welcome, but they must not turn the ceremony into any sort of political demonstration. They said they had no intention of doing anything of the kind. For which I am grateful. Carlito will be taken to *Fortaleza* and buried there. I will use the chopper again. He won't be interned. He'll be properly buried. Felipe says there is a plot of ground waiting for him. And the burial won't involve the priest."

"And Ortiz?"

He'd been banged up in the same cell as before. He was saying nothing. He didn't need to. If we never managed to get him for killing Pepe, surely we had evidence enough to have him convicted for murdering Carlito? Manresa had raised merry hell with senior police and GC officers in Castillo and Juan Codina had been reinstated as chief investigator.

"With the blessing of a chief prosecutor from Seville," said Juan. "It hurts to have to go through the necessary procedures. But we must have a formal enquiry and a trial. He'll stay in jail this time. He will have no chance of bail."

"And no clever lawyers from Madrid?"

Manresa pointed to the stars on his epaulettes. "Oh, they'll come and do their worst. But I don't wear these just to let people like that make a monkey out of me."

Chapter 12

"*Señores y Señoras*. You will forgive my Spanish, please. But I shall try my hardest."

I looked at what in church would have been called a congregation. Every face was turned to me. Expectant and forgiving. Apart from men in uniform and representatives of the organisations Carlito had worked for or dealt with, I saw Juan José, his parents and *La Celestina*. And lying at their feet, the dog Orlando, as aware as any of the humans of the importance of the occasion.

"I met Carlito Jimenez two months ago over an agreeable meal in a restaurant in Carmona. Only two months ago. Think about that. For in that short time he became one of the closest and most loyal friends I've ever had."

I paused and even now was fighting back the tears.

"Carlito should be known as one of the greatest Spaniards of the twenty-first century. But he would have ridiculed me for saying so. He was highly intelligent, honest to a fault, industrious, and devoted to his work for the Association for the Recovery of Historical Memory.

He was witty and kind and generous and guided me through many crises and adventures."

I looked at them again and this time the tears had been conquered.

"And he was a dwarf. He was not ashamed of the word. He took pride in it. And he was proud of his dwarf ancestry, of his family and his community in the *Fortaleza de los Enanos.*"

I caught Felipe's eye and saw that he was calm and collected. Consuelo too. And the children, who seemed to understand that from now on they would have to be proud of their father.

I more or less left it at that. Except for one final remark.

"Carlito was a fine musician. I am no expert. I know only the evidence of my ears. But if Carlito had not worked so hard for justice for the victims of the Civil War, I am sure he could have been one of the country's finest players of the guitar. And the sound of his instrument will linger with me for many years. He would have wanted to play for you all today."

Felipe stepped forward and said he would recite one of Carlito's favourite poems.

Inevitably it was from Federico García Lorca.

La Guitarra

Empieza el llanto

de la guitarra.

Se rompen las copas

de la madrugada.

Empieza el llanto

de la guitarra.

Es inútil callarla

Es imposible

callarla.

Llora monótona

como llora el agua,

como llora el viento

sobre la nevada.

Es imposible

callarla.

Llora por cosas

lejanas

Arena del Sur caliente

que pide camelias blancas.

Llora flecha sin blanco,

la tarde sin mañana,

y el primer pájaro muerto

sobre la rama.

¡Oh, guitarra!

Corazón malherido

Por cinco espadas.

The Guitar. 'The lament of the guitar begins. The wine cups of daybreak are broken. The lament of the guitar begins. It is useless to silence it. It is impossible to silence it. It weeps as monotonously as water weeps, as the wind weeps over the snowfall. It is impossible to silence it. It weeps for distant things like the sand of the warm South, which asks for white camellias. It weeps arrow without target, evening without morning, and the first dead bird on the branch. Oh, guitar! A heart grievously wounded by five swords.'

I looked up again and saw Father Trujillo standing at the very back of the mourners. He held his head high and fixed me with a penetrating stare. Then he nodded and gave the traditional sign of the cross presumably as a blessing. He turned and left.

****

"And what happened to the bodies of the men killed in the helicopters?"

I put the question to Carlos Manresa as we took our seats at the back of the courtroom. Ortiz would be appearing at a preliminary hearing on a charge of murder and several more of attempted murder.

356

"The crash and the explosions left us with body parts and not much else. We also have the remains of weapons and clothing. There were apparently seven in each chopper and all of them were killed."

"Any chance of identification?"

Manresa said it was obvious that some of Ortiz's gang were North Africans, Arab or Berber, but there'd been Spaniards as well.

"How did he put all this together? It must have cost him the earth."

"Slush funds," said Manresa. The prime minister and others at the top, including the minister who'd called us in, had naturally denied they'd ever existed. "But there's no doubt Ortiz got his hand on some of this money. He used it to finance his pathetic coup attempt and all the other shoot-outs we know about. And we also know there were enough young out-of-work Arab toughs ready to yield to temptation. I doubt they were genuine jihadists. They were probably *not* motivated by religious fervour. They were simply looking for a way to make some cash."

Even so, the courts were investigating at least three hundred cases where crimes had been linked to jihadism, terrorist activity, recruitment of fighters for the wars in Syria and Iraq, propaganda glorifying terrorism and general criminal association.

"Last year we arrested about ninety men and women with connections to Islamist terrorism. And there'll be more as long as Spain holds on to Ceuta and Melilla just across the water in North Africa."

"Now you tell me."

"Not much point in keeping anything from you, is there?"

Manresa was cut off by the entry of the examining magistrate and various lawyers. Ortiz was brought into court by two police officers. The magistrate didn't beat about the bush. He read out the charges and heard the lawyers' submissions in quick succession. As expected, Ortiz was represented by two smooth characters from out of town, but the magistrate was not impressed.

"The defendant may make a statement if he so wishes. But I have to tell him that even at this early stage there is enough evidence in this case of the possible existence of a criminal offence." Then he added slyly: "Personally I would have preferred to put that more bluntly. But I am obliged to abide by the rules."

No one laughed. Time seemed to stand still until Ortiz got to his feet. They'd reduced his wardrobe to shirt, pullover, slacks and his highly polished expensive shoes. But he was determined to put on a show.

"The court should know that there are always only bad people in this world," he declared. "And they will always stand on both sides of any argument. I am no exception. I do not claim to be a good man. But I was doing my duty for Spain. People will follow any leader and do as he asks them whatever the consequences. They will turn a blind eye to violence and brutality, murder and mayhem. They just have to proceed as normal. Such is life for these people. The daily round, the common task, as I believe a Protestant hymn has it."

He was annoyed that no one had understood this attempt at an erudite joke.

"Carlito Jimenez, the man I finally managed to silence, thought he was a good man. But he wasn't because he and those like him will never be able to make things work. He was a bad man because he opposed leadership. Only leaders make things work..."

The magistrate held up his hand. "If you are about to recite a paean of praise for a past political personality, or even one who is still alive, then don't."

Ortiz had lost control again. "You will all go mad," he shouted. "Your souls..."

"Take him to a cell," ordered the magistrate.

One of Ortiz's lawyers rose to his feet. The magistrate didn't even try to wave him down. He just stared at him. And he didn't blink. The lawyer resumed his seat. Ortiz was led away, still uttering words that none of us could hear.

He was to be kept locked up for many weeks until the case moved on, to be tried by three judges at the *Audencia Nacional* or High Court in Madrid. When I left Spain some days later, his fate remained unknown. Manresa said he was in for a long spell and it would not be comfortable. I never forgot our first meeting in

Carmona and cursed myself for failing to detect that he was bad news.

For all that you've been around a bit, Charlie Barrow, you're pleasantly naïve at times.

One of my good points?

That depends.

But you think Bad Luck has now given me up as a lost cause?

I refuse to answer that.

I paid one last visit to the exhumation site. Alex and his team had worked more miracles, reorganising the distribution of the skeletons and making absolutely sure in their own minds that the mass grave would at last be laid out as the victims and their relatives would have wished. They had negotiated an act of reconciliation between Carlito's Association and a group of sympathetic priests which ensured that all the corpses received their proper burial rites with dignity and compassion.

Alex drew me aside. "You may like to know that Elena's family have given us her ashes to scatter over the site, as she would have wished." He took me over to a niche in the wall occupied by a small urn.

"We shall do that next week."

"Who has paid for this?" I asked.

"Her two brothers. They live in Madrid but will come here for the ceremony."

I asked if I could make a contribution to the costs. Alex agreed to this.

"I do not think I can be here when it happens," I said. "I shall pay my respects now and leave her in peace."

"I understand."

Alex and his colleagues had even gone so far as to accept the remains of the villains who'd died in the helicopter crash. They too were to be given a formal burial but without the presence of priests or imams.

He left me alone. As if from nowhere, I recalled a joke Carlito had cracked over coffees in Ávila.

"Saint Teresa said that in the light of heaven, the worst suffering on earth will be seen to be no more serious than enduring one night in a cheap hotel."

I walked away.

Chapter 13

"Rosie? Will you run me to Seville airport?" I stood in the hotel lobby in Castillo with bags packed and an untidy sheaf of newspapers under my arm.

"Charlie Barrow. I will take you anywhere."

"But you have a partner. Someone who is close to you and lives in that house you own near the Escorial, not far from where you picked me up as a waif and stray. Don't you want to get back?"

She looked at me with a mixture of pity and something akin to ridicule.

"Where do you really want to go?"

"Back to my little apartment in Portugal."

"Then why don't I take you all the way?"

I was one big question mark.

"Rosie, you are as gay as gay can be."

She held the look.

"So what? It doesn't mean I can't love you, Charlie."

Carlos Manresa walked in with Juan Codina. The *Teniente Coronel* had thrust his hand into his departmental budget again and provided me with yet another set of clothes. Now he was urging me to write and write till my wrists ached.

"Let's get it all out in the open," he said.

Juan produced a case with a bulbous base and a long neck.

"One guitar," he said. "He would have wanted you to have it."

"But I play piano."

"Then you'll have to take lessons, won't you?"

I cancelled my flight. I was more than happy to avoid an airport where I had been an inept failure. Rosie drove me to the Portuguese seaside town where I kept most of my worldly goods, including my piano. Her partner, Maria, flew down from Madrid with the two children. Maria was as brisk as Rosie and the boy and girl boisterous but polite. There was hardly enough room for us all but we had some happy times on the beach.

Spain held its elections on December 20th 2015. As soon as I learned the results, I phoned my contacts in *Podemos*. The party had won a fifth of the votes cast. Their rivals in *Ciudadanos* had also done well. Between the two, they had garnered more than a third of the 350 seats in parliament. The *Partido Popular* was still the largest party but had lost its overall majority. And the

Socialists, even though they'd come second, had had their worst result since the start of *La Transición*.

"Congratulations!" I bellowed down the line to Madrid.

"It's not over yet," said Raul. "This is when the fun starts."

A thousand hacks churned out their copy. Most of them resorted to cliché. Spain's parliament was now more 'fragmented' than at any time in recent memory, they said. If that meant that some withered branches had fallen from the aged oak tree of the body politic, then, frankly, it wasn't a bad cliché.

There was 'a new political order'. And the immediate question was – who would form the next government? The PP and the Socialists had been so used to taking turn and turn about, washing one another's dirty linen – and not always in public – that neither could quite grasp the notion that the spoils of power were no longer theirs to share as they felt fit. King Felipe followed precedent, offering the job to the incumbent prime minister and PP leader, Mariano Rajoy. He refused. He said there was no point in trying. He couldn't form a grand coalition with the Socialists when they had no intention of supporting him. The King then turned to the Socialist leader, Pedro Sanchez. To produce a government, he needed the backing or tacit agreement of at least two other parties. Sanchez tried to do a deal with *Ciudadanos*. But that still left him short of a majority. And *Podemos* said it wouldn't back Sanchez if he pulled the deal off. *Ciudadanos* ruled out any arrangement with Sanchez which depended on support from *Podemos*.

And if you grasped all that, you were doing better than most of the pundits on TV and the columnists in the major newspapers.

"What a mess!" said Rosie.

"Frankly, I don't think most Spaniards are too worried," I replied over what had probably been my fifth cup of coffee that morning. Rosie and Maria were experts at housekeeping. I was being pampered. I had to brace myself for their departure.

"I know what they'll do," she said.

"Go on!"

"They'll have another election."

"If the stalemate lasts, they'll have to wait until June before they can do that."

"Can't stay here until then, Charlie. Got to get back to work."

So off they went, Rosie, Maria and the kids, a jolly family with, I suspected, a jolly future. I said I'd keep in touch. They insisted they'd hold me to that.

My mobile rang. It was Carlos Manresa.

"Thought you'd like to know that Ortiz will appear in court in Madrid tomorrow."

"Will the defence manage to string the thing out?"

"They'll try. But one of the effects of the election is that we have no effective government for the time being. And since *la casta* has been broken on the electoral wheel, so to speak..."

"That's very erudite," I quipped.

"Shut up and listen."

We both burst out laughing.

"There is no minister, Charlie, who can or wants to interfere in the legal process. The one you met couldn't give a monkey's about the fate of Ortiz. He's probably looking forward to retirement."

"So, the judges will have the courage of their convictions and apply the criminal law on the basis of some rather obvious evidence?"

"Let's hope so."

He had guessed right. Instead of a series of protracted hearings, the judiciary wanted this one out of the way. It didn't take long. After a rather pointless trial, Ortiz got the maximum forty years.

He served six months until he was found dead in his cell one morning. A heart attack.

"*Así es la vida,*" said Monresa later. "That's the way the cookie crumbles!"

"Or not, as the case may be," I replied.

Manresa had something else to tell me. "Would you like to hear some really good news?"

"Go on."

"Juan Codina is transferring to the *Guardia*. He's coming to Madrid to work under me. I hope I don't disappoint him."

"It's what you both deserve," I said.

The sad news was that *Podemos* was pulling itself apart. Rivalries at the top were devaluing its currency, diluting its prospects as a lasting political movement. Did it want to stay a party of protest, as some inside insisted it should? Or did it want to demonstrate that it could be a party of government in a viable coalition?

I wondered what Carlito would have made of it.

He'd have shrugged his shoulders.

Why so?

Carlito had no great expectations of politics or the Law.

But the verdict and sentence and the demise of Ortiz would have given him some satisfaction?

Perhaps.

You sound depressed.

Carlito would have been happier if the judges, or a new government, had valued the work of his Association and given it some money to get on with the exhumations. For him, that would have been the Law and politics really working for justice.

I left my apartment and strode to the nearest bar. This was Portugal. The people in my town weren't that interested in what happened in Spain. I always found the way the two countries held one another at arm's length strange and rather comical. Portugal itself had just gone through an inconclusive election. It had its own 'fragmented' parliament. But it produced a government of sorts. Now Spain would have to tread the same weary path.

It was the moment to switch off from my adventure. I would watch the sunsets and remember its tragedies and bitter failures, its successes and the fostering of new friendships. I would drink more red wine than was good for me and, being where I was, eat too much salted cod.

But there was the piano. Neglected and looking slightly sorry for itself. I lifted its lid, adjusted the stool and played my way back into a fair imitation of Oscar Emmanuel Peterson. I wished I could have played for Carlito. I brought the improvisation to a perfect cadence.

Leaning against my bookcase was Carlito's guitar. I hesitated. To disturb it seemed like sacrilege. But I couldn't resist. I unzipped the case and carefully extracted the instrument. As I pulled it free, the six strings brushed against my shirt sleeve. The sound lingered. I slid my thumb across the fingerboard. The sound was louder this time and lasted longer. Why should I not weep? Because Carlito would have mocked me. I took hold of the guitar's neck with my left hand, and sat on a dining chair. I wasn't sure if this was the correct posture for playing but I slung my left leg over my right and thumbed the strings again.

You will have to do more than that if you want to do it properly.

Nagging again?

No, just trying to be companionable and helpful.

The following morning, I asked my friends in the bar if the town had a music shop. I found it in a narrow passage a few blocks away. I'd never been there before. It was a treasure house of all things musical, instruments, CDs and scores, among which I found a guitar tutor.

Anyone who's taken up a musical instrument in middle age will tell you that the pain of trying to make a decent noise is heartbreaking. At least I could read the dots, but acquiring a measure of skill, with the fingers of one podgy hand on the frets while those of the other vainly sought to pluck the right string at the right time, was beyond me. I didn't give up altogether, but I found wonderful relief in returning to the piano. If I stopped for a moment, I could distinctly hear Carlito's cackle.

All of which prevented me from descending into melancholy. My landlord, Jorge, continued to promise that he would find me a good Portuguese wife. I continued to tell him to piss off. Fred phoned one day and asked if I was interested in an assignment to Belgium where more bombs had exploded and the innocent had been slaughtered.

"More jihadists?" I asked.

"Looks like it. A spin-off from Paris. The Belgian police arrested one of goons behind the November bombs. Seems he had mates ready to take revenge."

"Can I think about it?"

"Not for long, you can't."

The mobile rang again.

"Charlie?"

"Dagmar."

"Can I come and see you?"

"As long as you don't bring your lousy weather with you."

I wasn't going to Belgium.